She is Me

This is a work of fiction. Similarities to real people, places, or events are entirely coincidental.

SHE IS ME

First edition. September 9, 2022.

ISBN: 979-8986432144

Written by Jessica Terry.

I can never release a book without thanking God, my family, friends, church family, and especially, my readers. Love you all.

Jessica Terry

Chapter 1

It was all Tonette Andersen could do to keep her mind on what she was supposed to be doing. She was teaching her last class before her vacation to Barbados and she couldn't have been more excited.

"Watch those eyes, Amy," she warned to one of her students as she slowly paced through the rows between the desks where her sixth graders sat hunched over their papers. Tonette had to keep an extra eye on Amy because since she came from a privileged background, she seemed to think her good grades should be given and not earned. Tonette had caught her cheating multiple times throughout the year.

"Hmph," the blonde student grunted, tossing her long hair over her shoulder. Tonnette ignored her.

Trying to keep her mind on the social studies quiz she was administering and not on the sandy, sunny beaches she would be digging her toes into in forty-eight hours, Tonette continued to monitor her students, eventually taking a seat at her desk in the front of the classroom. Her eyes strayed yet again to the clock on the wall, counting down until three o'clock. In her ten years of teaching, she had never anticipated the ending of a class like she was today.

It was her friends Olarion and Blue that finally convinced her to take a vacation, and to actually go somewhere instead of just hanging out in her apartment with a stack of books and DVDs. Tonette had resisted at first, not really wanting to go anywhere by herself, but she let them talk her into it. Most people thought Tonette's life was pretty boring; all she did was go to work then go home and read or watch documentaries until bedtime. She only got out of the house to go to church and meet up with her friends once or twice a week. She loved to work out, but she usually even did that at home, unless she just felt like going to the gym. Tonette agreed that her life wasn't all that exciting but it was fine for her; she had never been a person that needed much excitement or variety.

Finally, it was time to take up the quizzes and dismiss class, and she couldn't do so fast enough. She loved her job, but she always looked forward to her time off from dealing with just-coming-into-their-hormones students and parents who wanted to place a little too much of the disciplining responsibilities for their children onto her. And even though she had been initially nervous about traveling by herself, the more she thought about it, the more she anticipated the adventure of it. If nothing else, she'd have a good story to tell her friends and her students when she got back.

After she finished up at school, Tonette headed to meet Olarion and Blue at Chili's for their weekly session of drinks and gossip. She loved hanging out with her friends, even though outside of their shared workout ethic and appreciation for men, they really didn't have much of anything in common. Blue was one of the top hairstylists in town, mostly with braids and extensions; it was amazing to see how fast he could braid someone's hair. He was always trying to get Tonette to let him work his magic on her head full of bushy, natural brown tresses. Olarion was business owner who was obsessed with all things marriage and weddings and just knew that she was going to be meeting her future husband any day. Tonette had never seen anyone have so many subscriptions to wedding magazines, memberships on wedding sites, and make regular trips to wedding trade shows and expos, all without even having a boyfriend.

"There's our Barbados-bound friend," Olarion greeted Tonette when she approached the table. She was already nursing a vodka and cranberry.

"Hey guys," Tonette greeted, giving them each a hug and kiss on the cheek before removing her jacket and taking her seat.

"How was work today, boo?" Blue asked her, taking a sip of his beer.

"Pretty much the same as usual, other than me constantly watching the clock waiting for it to be over."

"Uh-oh! Looks like somebody's anxious to get their vacation started so they can get their groove back!" Olarion hooted. "It's about time, girl...I almost wish I was going with you."

"I'm not going to try to get my *groove back* or anything else," Tonette protested with a smile as she flagged down the waiter. "I'm just going to relax and have a good time."

"That's it? Baby, relaxing is all good but you need to have some fun while you're over there, too," Blue said. "'Cause Lord knows you don't have any here."

"Yes, I do."

"No, you don't."

"It might not be *your* kind of fun, but it's still fun."

"Honey, you can slice it and serve it any which way you want to, but dull is still dull," Blue said with a flip of his hand. His huge biceps flexed in the fitted t-shirt he wore and a couple of women that were walking by eyed him in appreciation. Tonette wanted to let them know they were wasting their time; the only thing about a woman that Blue had any interest in was her hair.

"Yeah, well...I plan on enjoying myself, nonetheless," Tonette replied, after she gave the waiter her drink order. "Where are the wings we usually get?"

"They're coming," Olarion said. "Although I don't need to be eating any of that stuff."

"Please. A few wings won't hurt you."

"Plus, if anybody needs to be worried about what they're eating, it's Tonette," Blue said with a nod in her direction. "She's the one about to be on the beach showing off her tramp stamp in a bikini."

"Aww...hush, Blue." Tonette hated that she had ever gotten that tattoo...she had done it on a dare in college and had regretted it ever since. She tried to keep it covered as much as she could.

"But seriously, girl," Olarion said, turning to her, "I really do hope you enjoy yourself over there. Experience some new things, meet people, let your hair down a little bit. Don't just spend the whole ten days holed up in your hotel room watching Netflix and reading Terry McMillan novels."

"I promise, I won't do that," Tonette assured them.

Just then, their two orders of buffalo wings arrived and they all dug in. As Tonette enjoyed her food, she thought about Olarion's advice. Little did her friends know, she planned on doing exactly what they suggested, and more. While she was in Barbados, she was going to be a completely different person; nobody knew her there so nobody had to know how mundane her life really was. She planned on getting some sexy vacation clothes, getting her hair done...normally she would just have Blue do it but she didn't really want her friends to know about her plan yet.

If they wanted to think she would just be reading and watching movies there the same as she did at home, that was fine with her.

Chapter 2

The morning of her departure, Tonette woke up with the excitement of a kid on Christmas morning. She jumped out of bed an hour before her alarm went off, anxious to get her day going. Her flight was later on that evening, and she had already packed most of her things after going shopping the day before and buying several bikinis and outfits that she never dream of wearing here at home, but couldn't wait to debut in Barbados.

After a quick breakfast of grapefruit and oatmeal, Tonette took a lengthy shower then hurriedly got dressed and headed to her hair appointment. She wanted a style where she wouldn't have to really worry about it while she was on vacation; her head full of hair took enough of her time at home.

"What do you think?" the hairstylist, Naima, asked two hours after Tonette had sat down in her chair. She handed Tonette a hand mirror and fluffed the wavy hair that now cascaded across her shoulders.

"Wow," Tonette murmured, perusing her new hairstyle in the mirror. She had opted to get a sew-in weave instead of braids, not wanting to sit for hours getting them done. The hair she now had was three shades lighter than her own and fell around her face in loose, flowing waves that screamed *beach*. She couldn't wait to get to Barbados and flaunt it.

"I love it!" Tonette exclaimed, grinning up at the hairstylist. "It's exactly what I had in mind."

"Yeah, it'll be great for your vacation," Naima commented. "It's human hair so you don't have to worry about it getting all matted and stuff when you go in the water. It'll get even curlier when it gets wet and you can either leave it like that or blow it out. And your pretty brown natural hair is all safe and braided up underneath."

"I can't believe how natural it looks," Tonette commented, bringing the mirror closer to her head.

"Girl, we only do quality stuff in here," Naima boasted. "That's why I can charge so much."

Tonette couldn't disagree; she was spending more on this weave than she had probably spent on her hair in the past two years, but she figured it was worth it. She hadn't had a real vacation in forever and had saved her money for it, so she figured if she was going to do it, she might as well go all out.

After getting her eyebrows and makeup done, Tonette headed back to the house to get everything together so she could head to the airport. With every minute that passed she was getting more and more anxious to get to that island. She couldn't pass a mirror without looking at herself and smiling. Her students wouldn't even recognize her if they saw her like this.

While Tonette was gone, she planned on being someone completely different than herself; she would take on a whole new personality. While she was fine with her life and herself the way it was, it would be fun to pretend to be someone else for a little while. She figured there was no harm in that; she was going somewhere where no one knew her and whoever she met would be left on the island, never to be seen again. And since she was traveling alone, none of her friends would know anything more than what she told them.

"Yep, this is gonna be some trip," she said to herself.

Tonette had a good feeling when she hadn't been at the airport a good twenty minutes before getting hit on.

"Damn," a man hissed when she strutted by in her low-rise jeans and tank top. Her weave was piled on top of her head in a messy bun and silver hoop earrings hung from her ears. It was a casual enough outfit but still not something she would have normally worn. "Wherever it is you're going, take me with you."

Tonette just grinned and winked at him, but kept right on walking. She felt if this was any indication of how things were going to be over the next ten days, she was in for an awesome vacation.

After a pleasant-enough flight, Tonette arrived at Grantley Adams International airport and took a route taxi (which she heard someone refer to as a ZR) to her hotel. She excitedly put away her things and eyed the comfortable-looking queen-sized bed, but resisted the urge to dive onto it. Spending the rest of the evening curled up with her Kindle was something that the regular Tonette would do, but vacation Tonette was going to get out of the room and immediately get down to enjoying her time on this beautiful island.

It wasn't quite midnight yet, so Tonette took a quick shower, let down her new hair, and headed downstairs. She felt surprisingly invigorated, even after the long day she'd had, and couldn't wait to have some fun. She started to head towards the front desk for directions when someone else got her attention first.

"Excuse me, miss."

Tonette wasn't quite sure she was the one being addressed, but when she glanced over her shoulder, the bronze hunk with the closely-shaven head and dimple in his right cheek was definitely looking right at her. Internally telling herself to chill out because her nervousness was already starting to kick into overdrive, she smiled and made herself boldly look right back at him.

"Yes?"

He walked over to her, the smile still on his face. "You look like you're headed out."

Tonette loved his accent. And he smelled like heaven on a stick. "I am, actually. Just wanna see what I can get into."

"Can I go? I wouldn't mind getting into some things with you," he winked at her and took a sip from the bottle of water in his hand.

Tonette hoped to Mount Hillaby that he wouldn't be able to see her knees shaking. "You know what? I'm going to take that invitation and put it in the safe for later." *Oh my gosh, how corny was that??* she silently scolded herself.

"A raincheck, eh? I suppose I can grant you that, as long as you promise I can cash it in before you leave," the handsome gentleman flirted with another wink.

"I guess we'll see, won't we?" Tonette replied, winking back at him. She made her legs start moving towards the door, forgetting all about her earlier intentions to ask the front desk attendant for directions towards St. Lawrence

Gap, which she had read was the place to be for nightlife. This handsome stranger had thrown her all off kilter. She was definitely attracted to him, but she was wary of fooling around with someone who seemed to be staying in the same hotel as she was.

It wasn't until she was out in the breezy nighttime air that Tonette got her bearings back. Half expecting the man to follow her, she glanced over her shoulder to make sure before heading in the direction she saw some of the other guests going. From their conversation, she knew they were headed to St. Lawrence Gap, or The Gap, as it was apparently referred to. She took in the sights and sounds around her as she enjoyed the warm air kissing her bare shoulders; part of her still couldn't believe she was actually there. She had actually come to Barbados by herself; she hadn't chickened out as she knew her friends probably expected her to do. Something told her this was going to be a very memorable vacation.

Tonette strolled along until she felt herself being drawn into the intoxicating music coming from the reggae club. Even though she didn't go out much back home, she actually liked to dance and reggae was one of her favorite kinds of music to dance to. It was so lively and energetic, yet it could also be very sensual and magnetic. Her fingers were already snapping when she entered the club, intent on enjoying some good rum and some good music.

The place was pretty full, but for some reason Tonette could feel eyes on her. She didn't want to seem paranoid by looking around, but it didn't take long to see where the feeling was coming from. When she turned to look for the bar, she saw a man who was so cute that it was almost unfair heading towards her. His eyes never strayed from her, as if he didn't want to lose her in the crowd. Just like with the man at the hotel, Tonette quelled her quaking nerves and told herself not to look away.

"I had to come to you," were the first words he spoke to her. His dark eyes roamed her face, as if committing it to memory. "I knew I'd never forgive myself if I didn't."

Tonette didn't know if this was a good line, a cheesy line, or even a line at all, but she knew her panties were wet.

"It must be my lucky night, then," she heard herself say.

"Perhaps..." the man said, gently taking her hand and bringing it to his lips, "We *both* will be able to say that by the night's end."

He kissed her hands with soft, moist lips, and Tonette was surprised at just how much she wanted to feel them against her own. She had never experienced such a reaction to any man before and could only attribute it to the atmosphere.

Reminding herself to not be her usual, slightly-uptight self, she grinned and shook some hair out of her face. "I surely hope so."

"I am Troy, beautiful," the man introduced himself. His eyes were still boring into hers. "Troy Anton. And you are?"

"Toni." It just came out; Tonette hadn't planned on giving out a fake name. She had planned on taking on a new vacation persona but had fully planned on using her real name. She didn't know why *Toni* came out but she felt she would look ridiculous if she retracted it now. "Toni Andrews."

"It is my pleasure," Troy said with another kiss to her hand. He gently bit his bottom lip, causing an automatic arousing heave to Tonette's chest. "I want to dance with you."

"I'm all yours," Tonette said, becoming momentarily mesmerized by Troy's intensity. She internally told herself to snap out of it and to just go with the flow; there was no need in coming off as naïve as she was feeling right then.

Troy slid his arm around Tonette's waist and led her out to the middle of the dance floor. His body immediately started winding to the music, and Tonette made hers wind with his. She wasn't expecting to dance so seductively right off the bat, but it was totally in sync with the music, and most importantly, she didn't hate it; her body felt like liquid as she grinded her hips against this. He held her close to him, almost possessively, and Tonette couldn't help but love it. This was exactly what she had in mind; tossing out her inhibitions and enjoying herself, throwing caution to the wind. And she hadn't even had any rum yet.

Troy was about 6'2, with skin the color of brown sugar and bourbon-brown heavy-lashed eyes that looked like they could see right through her. He seemed to like to look into her eyes as they danced, and Tonette felt a strange sense of comfort with him...it was as if she had met him in another lifetime or something, as corny as that sounded. She wrapped her arms around his neck and threaded her fingers through his thick, soft curly hair that was low on the sides and full at the top. They didn't talk; they just danced. And they danced only with each other until the crowd started to thin out a little bit. Tonette had no idea what time it was or how long she had been there, but Troy didn't let her go, so she didn't let him go.

"I am not ready for you to leave me yet," Troy whispered in her ear as people milled around them. His arms tightened around her. "Come home with me?"

Tonette leaned back to look at him.

"No pressure to do anything you don't want to do," he quickly assured her. "I just don't want our time together to end. I promise to be the perfect gentleman."

Strangely enough, Tonette almost didn't *want* him to be the perfect gentleman...her mind and body were thinking things anything but ladylike and had been for the past couple of hours she had been dancing with Troy. Atlanta Tonette would have scoffed at such an invitation, but vacation Tonette, or Toni, as apparently was her alter ego now, was automatically intrigued.

Boldly taking his hand, Tonette smiled and told him to lead the way.

This is crazy, she thought to herself as she got into Troy's car and went with him to his place. *I am on an island by myself in a car with a man that I just met about to go to his house and do...what? What if he tries to rape or kill me or something?? I should jump out of this car right now...if I time it right, I can do a good tuck and roll...*

Despite her thoughts, though, Tonette kept the smile on her face and engaged in surprisingly comfortable conversation with Troy, not letting on at all about the internal battle that was going on as she did so. Maybe it *was* crazy, going to Troy's place with him so soon after meeting him, but that didn't mean she didn't want to do it. She felt a surprising and welcome sense of comfort and even safety with Troy, and something told her that he wouldn't do her any harm.

If you're going to do this, keep your eyes open, she silently warned herself when they arrived at Troy's place. *Don't get so relaxed that you don't pay attention to what's going on. He might be waiting for you to let your guard down before he springs something on you.*

Tonette gave Troy a tight smile as she followed him into his house, taking the hand he offered her once they were inside.

"Welcome," he said, sliding an arm around her waist. "Make yourself at home while you are here, please."

"Thank you," Tonette replied, appreciating the powder blue walls, dark wood furnishings with pale yellow accents, and light carpeting. She glanced down at her feet. "Do you want me to take my shoes off or something?"

"Only if you want to," Troy replied. "I don't have such a rule for my guests."

"Okay," Tonette simply replied, resisting the urge to persist and comment on how she didn't want to risk messing up his nice carpeting. That was a Tonette concern, not a Toni concern. She sauntered ahead of him slowly, continuing to take in her surroundings, mentally taking note of everything. *Just in case*, she thought. "I love your place. It's like a vacation home or something."

Troy chuckled. "I appreciate the compliment. It's small but cozy, just the way I like it."

"Small and cozy is good," Tonette said, turning to face him with a grin. She held out her hand. "Come give me the tour."

Taking her hand firmly in his, Troy obliged her and took her around the small house, showing her the kitchen, the two bedrooms, and the restroom. Every room was as colorful and welcoming as the next. It wasn't anything fancy but it was very well-kept, clean, and inviting. There was a small deck on the back of the house that Tonette could just imagine sitting on for hours with a good book.

"I love your house," she complimented sincerely. "It's exactly the kind of place I'd want to have if I lived here."

"Glad you like it," Troy replied as she led her by the hand back to the living room. "Are you enjoying your visit so far? To the island, I mean."

"So far, so good," Tonette answered as she joined him on the couch after slipping out of her sandals. For some reason, she didn't want to let him know she had just arrived on the island a few hours earlier. "Everything is so colorful and breezy; I immediately felt relaxed as soon as I got off the plane."

"It is a beautiful place to live," Troy concurred, resting his arm along the back of the couch. "So tell me, Toni...where are you from?"

"Oh, um..." Tonette stammered, slightly caught off guard by the question. She hadn't considered just how much about herself she would really divulge. "Atlanta."

"Atlanta, huh? I have always wanted to visit there."

"Really?"

"Yes. There seems to be a lot of interesting things and people there, from what I have heard."

"Well, yeah, I guess you could say that. I grew up there so I guess I don't appreciate it like someone else would; it's just home to me."

"That is the same way I feel about Barbados. Do you have any siblings? What do you do in Atlanta? Tell me about yourself, Toni."

"Oh, we can save all that boring yadda-yadda for another time," Tonette dodged with a wave of her hand. She didn't want to tell Troy her life story. She wanted to say in her Toni persona, and Toni was going to maintain a certain air of mystery. It was just easier that way.

Sliding a little closer to him on the couch, she swirled her finger along his smooth shoulder. Her eyes were flirtatious. "I'm glad you invited me over," she said sincerely.

"I'm glad you accepted the invitation," Troy replied, turning to face her. He placed a hand on her knee and Tonette immediately covered it with hers. His fingers began to stroke her skin. "You are the most beautiful thing that has been in my house since I moved in."

Oh, he's smooth, Tonette thought to herself as she grinned at the compliment. "Well, thank you," she blushed.

"Would you think I was strange if I said that it feels like I've known you longer than just these past few hours?" Troy asked. "I am so drawn to you..."

He was looking right into her eyes. Tonette found herself mesmerized again. "No...no, I don't think you're strange for that. I'm extremely flattered." She didn't want to admit that she felt the same way.

"Do you feel comfortable here?"

"Yes. Quite comfortable."

"Just let me know when you are ready to leave and I will take you back to wherever it is you're staying."

"I'll do that." She eyed him as she ran a hand up his arm. "Eventually."

He eyed her back, the rising arousal matching hers. "Forgive me, Toni."

She arched a brow. "For?"

He grabbed the side of her face with his hand. "This," he whispered as he brought her face to his.

He claimed her lips as possessively as he had claimed her body on the dance floor earlier. Tonette had already been attracted to this man, but she was extremely turned on with how he had just grabbed her face and taken the kiss like he had. There was something about it that just did something to her, and as they melted into each other, their sighs and moans mingling as they sank against the back of the couch, Tonette tried to resist the urge to start taking off articles of clothing. She had been with her share of men but she was hardly someone who slept with a man on the first date. Yet here she was, wanting to give her body to Troy. *Voluntarily*. His hands roamed and caressed her, but they didn't venture anywhere inappropriate, to Tonette's chagrin. He was being a little too much of a gentleman.

After several minutes of intense kissing, Tonette couldn't take it anymore and led his hand to her heaving, aching breasts. Troy could immediately feel the hardness of her nipples through the thin material of her dress, and when she threw her head back and moaned, he slid his tongue up her neck, his fingers teasing her to the point of madness. Tonette's back arched as a throaty groan escaped her lips.

"Yes," she whispered. "Oh god, yes..."

"You like that?" Troy asked in a low voice.

"I *love* that."

Troy dipped his head, replacing his hands with his lips on her breasts through her dress, and Tonette screamed in pleasure. She wanted to tell him to rip the dress from her body and have his way with her completely, but she didn't quite have the nerve, even as Toni. She doubted she would stop him if he tried to on his own, though. She wanted him just that much.

"Toni," Troy whispered, gathering her dress in his hands. He grazed a finger against her womanhood and Tonette shivered in pleasure. "May I?" he asked for permission as he licked his lips.

"I'll be so mad at you if you don't," Tonette replied breathlessly, lifting her hips so she could pull her dress up further for him.

"Well I certainly don't want you upset with me," Troy smirked, giving her a wink before taking his first taste of her.

Tonette felt like she was being air-lifted from Barbados right to heaven. Her head fell back, her mouth fell open, and her legs fell apart. Troy feasted on her slowly, diligently, and moaned in pleasure as he was doing so almost as much as she was while receiving it. She managed to sit up momentarily and get a glimpse of his head between her legs, but when he slid two fingers inside of her, she collapsed onto her back again, placing a hand on his head to make sure it stayed right where it was.

Troy spent a considerable amount of time pleasing Tonette that night, but that was as far as it went; they didn't remove any clothing, they didn't have sex, they didn't even leave the couch. Tonette's body might have wanted more, but she told herself to be satisfied with it. She wanted to enjoy her vacation but she didn't come to Barbados to be a slut.

True to his word, Troy took her back to her hotel when she gave him the word, without hesitation. She had been at his house for about three hours and while she had immensely enjoyed herself, she didn't want to spend the night with him, even though it was morning light outside that greeted them when they emerged from his house. He gave her his number before she got out of his car, and Tonette couldn't wipe the smile off her face as she headed up to her room, still tingling and exhilarated.

Now, she could collapse onto her bed. And she did.

Chapter 3

Troy was the first thing on her mind when Tonette finally woke up.

She could still feel his hands and lips on her when she finally rolled out of bed later on that afternoon, still fully dressed in her outfit from the previous night. She couldn't resist smiling to herself as her mind replayed the previous evening. Troy had brought her four orgasms on a silver platter, and everything in her wanted to tell him to take her to his bedroom. But she remembered Olarion's advice about always leaving a man wanting more, and she was glad she hadn't given in to that temptation, even though she knew she would have enjoyed it.

Eventually, Tonette made herself get up and get in the shower, her stomach starting to grumble slightly. She realized she hadn't eaten since the plane the day before; Troy had offered her something while she was at his place but she had declined. Now she wondered where she would get something to eat as she got into the shower, pinning her hair up before doing so. Her mind was still replaying snippets of the previous night, then the smile started to ease from her face when she wondered if Troy would think she was being a tease or pushing him away by insisting he take her home instead of just staying there. He seemed fine at the time; he had repeatedly assured her he would take her home whenever she was ready, and that's exactly what he did. Everything that transpired between them happened because she allowed it to; he always asked her permission before taking anything further. But who's to say that he wouldn't feel slighted or something in the light of day? Tonette chewed her lip as she considered the possibility.

But she made herself dismiss those thoughts. That wasn't something Toni would worry about; she'd just move on to somebody else. Tonette told herself to put Troy out of her mind as she went on about her day.

Realizing she hadn't let her friends know she had arrived safely, she turned her phone on and sent them a quick text. After asking someone at the front desk for a breakfast recommendation, she went and got something to eat, then went and changed into her workout clothes. Back home she always worked out in sweats, but in Barbados she wore a sports bra and short shorts. Part of her was a little self-conscious about it, but she told herself to chill out. She was always relatively conservative when it came to showing her toned body; this beautiful island was the perfect place to flaunt it a little bit.

She went for a long run on the beach, becoming so taken with the beauty of her surroundings that she ran for longer than intended. It was pretty warm out, and the beach was filling up with people wanting to take advantage of the beautiful weather and clear water. Tonette noted the families that were out there, looking happy and carefree together, and she couldn't help but smile longingly at them. She had grown used to being alone and was somewhat comfortable with it, being satisfied with her life as it was. But watching the couples and families around her, there was a small part of her that started to wonder if she would ever have that for herself.

Tonette shook her head, clearing those thoughts. No need in bringing herself down on her vacation.

After running just short of three miles, Tonette headed back up to the hotel. She spent a couple of hours in her room reading, then made herself get up and take a quick shower. She then slid into a light blue short romper, threw her hair in a ponytail and slid some earrings into her ears, then headed back out towards The Gap. She could already hear the music playing and the enticing aromas in the air. Part of her still couldn't fully believe she was there as she casually strolled along, her hands in her pockets. She couldn't remember when she had ever felt so at peace. Every now and then she pulled out her phone and snapped a picture or two. She was in her own little world and didn't even notice the man from her hotel that she had met the night before approaching her.

"We meet again," he greeted her with a smile.

It took a second for Tonette to remember him, but she smiled when she did. "Hello, there."

"I was hoping I got to see you again."

"Yeah?"

"Absolutely."

"Well, here I am." Tonette's smile widened.

"I never got the pleasure of learning your name last night," the man said, holding his hand out to her. "I'm Emmitt."

"Toni."

"Toni," Emmitt repeated as he brought her hand to his lips. "It's a pleasure."

It absolutely is, Tonette thought to herself, feeling a tingle at the feeling of Emmitt's soft lips on her hand. "Nice to meet you."

They engaged in small talk, but Tonette found herself not as at ease or as engaged as she had been the previous night with Troy. Emmitt was gorgeous, but he didn't cause the fireworks in her belly that Troy had.

Tonette was wondering how she could politely end the conversation when she got that feeling again that she was being watched. She glanced around her and felt her heart skip when she saw Troy over Emmitt's shoulder, watching them. And he looked *so* good. She didn't know why, but she found herself wanting to make him jealous a little bit. That must have been her Toni persona kicking in again, because that wasn't something Tonette would see the need in doing.

"How much longer is your stay?" Emmitt was asking her, unaware that her attention had been temporarily diverted.

"Oh, just a few more days," Tonette responded vaguely. "And you're from here, I take it?"

"Yes. But I've been to America several times. I dabbled in modeling for a while in New York before I decided to return home."

"You didn't like it?"

Emmitt shook his head. "I could not get used to the atmosphere. After a couple of years I had to come back. I was miserable."

"That's understandable."

They continued to talk, and Troy continued to watch them. Tonette made herself laugh a little harder at Emmitt's jokes than she normally would have, and even touched his arm flirtatiously once or twice. She didn't know why she was doing what she was doing; she didn't have any reason to make Troy jealous. He didn't even seem upset by the little show she was putting on; just intrigued.

Tonette also noticed that they were getting looks from more people besides Troy, namely women. She wondered the reasoning for this, and began to feel slightly uncomfortable that they were getting so much attention. To her relief, Emmitt got a call and said he had to leave, but he made her all but promise to let him see her soon.

Troy wasted no time coming over to her after Emmitt left. Tonette couldn't resist the smile that came across her face when he got close to her.

"I suppose I should have asked if you were in a relationship before now," he said without preamble. His eyes bore into hers with their usual intensity, more curious than accusatory. "Are you?"

"Absolutely not," Tonette insisted with a shake of her head.

Troy's relief was noticeable. "That is good to know," he said, smiling. "I was starting to feel guilty about what we did last night."

"You don't have to feel guilty about anything," Tonette assured him, lightly grabbing his wrist. "*I* certainly don't."

"More good news." He glanced towards the direction Emmitt walked off. "I could not help but notice he seemed as taken with you as I am, though."

With a coy smile, Tonette shrugged.

"I have no right to be jealous," Troy continued. "But I did not like seeing you flirting with another man."

"Flirting?" Tonette replied innocently.

"I know flirting when I see it, Toni," Troy replied amusingly, as if he knew exactly what she was doing. "But as I said, I have no right to feel this way."

"Hmm." Tonette felt that delicious swirling in her belly again. She figured she probably should be offended at Troy's possessiveness, but she couldn't help being flattered by it. Part of her even loved it. She wondered if that was just her relative inexperience coming into play or if it meant something else.

"You look beautiful," Troy commented, his eyes sweeping over her body before returning to hers.

Tonette blushed. "Thank you, Troy."

"I was hoping I saw you when I came over here."

"Really?"

"Of course. I frequent The Gap occasionally but I rarely come two consecutive nights. My one and only goal was to see you."

Aaaand...wet panties again. "I'm flattered...and glad you did."

The two of them stood there smiling and eyeing each other for several moments. Troy's eyes kept straying to her lips and Tonette actually ached with how badly she wanted him to kiss her, but figured he probably wouldn't do so with so many people milling around them. She found herself wanting to be alone with Troy, despite her initial plan to play it cool with him. Spending two nights in a row with him wasn't in the plans, but she convinced herself that Toni would do as she damn well pleased and not worry about protocol.

So it was with that in mind that she asked him, "Would you like to spend the evening with me?"

Her smile widened when Troy's did. "More than anything."

Boldly taking his hand, Tonette led him back towards her hotel.

Chapter 4

The following morning, Tonette woke up in bed alone and smiling. The sun beamed on her through the sheer curtains on the window, and she stretched languidly, releasing a satisfied moan.

Her evening with Troy the previous night had been wonderful, again. After they had come back to her room, she quickly stuck her phone into the bottom of her suitcase, changed clothes, then she and Troy went dancing. The entire time they had been in her room, he stood near the window with his hands in his pockets, talking to her as she went about her tasks. They had kissed a couple of times, but he remained the gentleman, not making any moves on her or trying to take advantage of the situation. Tonette appreciated this, but she wouldn't have minded at all if he had thrown her on the bed and had his way with her body like she had been fantasizing about.

They went dancing at another club on The Gap, drunk what was probably too much rum because Tonette found herself at the center of the dance floor, putting on a show she couldn't imagine having the nerve to put on otherwise. After she and Troy left there, they took a barefoot walk along the beach, hand-in-hand. Their rapport was effortless, and Tonette felt that familiar, comfortable, safe feeling envelope her again. She really felt as if she and Troy had known each other for years, or even a lifetime. There were times when she would look over at him as they walked and just gaze at him as if in awe, or lovestruck, and she had to quickly make herself turn her eyes away. She wasn't supposed to be feeling like this. More than a few times, she had to remind herself that Toni would not allow herself to become so enamored with this man, and especially not this quickly.

After a while, they sat on the beach, Tonette in between Troy's legs, his arms wrapped around her from behind. Tonette released a long sigh, silently telling herself to remember how she felt at that very moment, because she seriously doubted she would ever again feel so content.

"Can you tell me more about yourself now?" he asked softly. "Or are you going to try to divert my attention again?"

Tonette giggled, somewhat nervously. "You think that's what I did last night?"

"I know it was. But I certainly didn't mind the diversion," Troy said, squeezing her and kissing her neck. "But I really do want to know some more about you, Toni."

"Okay," Tonette acquiesced. "What would you like to know?"

"Everything you can tell me. Do you have any siblings?"

"No." *Truth.* "You?"

"Unfortunately not, though I have always wanted some. What is your occupation?"

"I'm a paleontologist." *Complete and total lie.*

"Really? That sounds pretty interesting."

"It can be. What about you? What do you do?" Tonette didn't want him to start asking him a bunch of questions about her supposed career.

"I am a teacher, actually, but my passion is writing."

Tonette turned to look at him, her attraction to him taking a major spike. "You're a teacher?"

"Yes. We are in our second term now."

"Second term?"

"Yes. There are three terms of the school year, beginning the second week of September and ending at the end of June. School holiday is the nine or ten weeks between."

"That's interesting," Tonette said sincerely. She almost told him how that differed from the school calendar in Atlanta, but remembered she had already lied to him about her career. "Do you enjoy teaching?"

"Very much."

"You said your passion is writing...what do you like to write?"

"Poetry, short stories..."

"I'd love to hear one of your poems sometime."

"It would be my pleasure."

"Tell me some more things about you."

"My parents are deceased...my mother passed when I was a child and my father, two years ago."

"I'm so sorry to hear that, Troy."

"Thank you. I don't have any family left here, really. My parents were in their forties when they had me so they were kind of up in age, and any siblings they had are deceased, as well."

"Wow...so you're here all alone?"

"No, I have friends. And having grown up here there are many people who are *like* family to me. I have no complaints."

"That's a great attitude," Tonette complimented, turning to look at him again. "A lot of people might use that as an excuse to be negative or bitter or something."

"I am certainly not the first person to lose their parents," Troy shrugged. "Though I do miss them very much. They always taught me to enjoy life while I have it and not have any regrets. So that is how I try to live."

"That's a wonderful lesson," Tonette said wistfully, turning her eyes back to the splashing ocean in front of them.

"And you? Are your parents still with us?"

"Oh, um, yeah...my parents are still alive. They live in Florida, though, so I only see them every few months or so." *Truth*.

There was a comfortable pause in the conversation as Troy's hands languidly stroked Tonette's arms. After several moments, he asked in a low voice, "Do you think they would like me?"

Gasping softly, Tonette's eyes widened at the question. She suddenly felt nervous as her eyes darted in zig-zagged directions in front of her. "Wh-why do you ask?"

"Because I am very enamored with their daughter."

Tonette's heart was beating at a rhythm she couldn't keep up with. "Oh, Troy..."

"Do you think they would?"

"Yes...I'm sure they would," Tonette replied softly. "You're wonderful."

"I think you are wonderful, as well. It might seem premature to say, but you are the kind of woman I could fall hard for, Toni." He began slowly kissing her neck as his arms tightened around her. "I mean that."

Tonette's eyes rolled into the back of her head. His lips felt amazing, but she was also trying to wrap her mind around what he had just told her. Part of her thought it was the rum and the atmosphere talking, but the other part wondered if he was being sincere.

We haven't even known each other two full days; this was crazy, right? She thought to herself. *I know I've been thinking that it feels like we've known each other longer, but we haven't! Is he just feeding me a line, here? Is he just caught up in the moment? Even if he is telling the truth, shouldn't I still run for the hills at how fast it is?? Is he desperate or something? Am I, because I actually believe him and feel the same way???*

Troy gently grabbed her face and turned it to his, giving her a deep, spine-melting kiss. Tonette sank into him as all of her internal thoughts paused on their own, and she wrapped her arms around his neck, fully giving in to the moment. She closed her eyes and allowed herself to imagine that Troy was hers and she was his, and they were as in love as the characters in the book she had read a few hours before. Something washed over her that caused her to shiver noticeably, but they just held on to each other tighter, their kiss never breaking.

They stayed out on the beach for a while longer before Troy walked her back to her room. She had invited him inside, and they spent several hours talking and kissing and rolling around on the bed, but still no sex. Tonette's body was disappointed, but her heart and mind appreciated him not expecting that from her. It only made her like him more, which she didn't think was possible.

Ever since Troy had left, Tonette wondered what it was about this man that had her all jumbled up like a destroyed jigsaw puzzle. It wasn't like he was the first attractive man to ever catch her attention, or to be taken with her. Whenever Tonette bothered to go out, she got her share of looks from the opposite sex; and she went on the occasional date, but she hadn't been in a relationship in years. Not necessarily because she couldn't be, but because it just hadn't been a priority to her...she wasn't like Olarion who was counting down the days until God sent her a husband, and planning the wedding of her dreams in the meantime. Tonette was fine with her life the way it was, but now she was imagining Troy in the mix, and it was kind of freaking her out. This wasn't what she had come to Barbados for...she didn't know how, but somehow she would have to snap out of this trance Troy seemed to have her under.

Really, Tonette wondered if Troy would even be interested in her as her bland, regular self like he was interested in stylish, carefree Toni. Tonette wasn't insecure, but she just couldn't imagine catching Troy's eye and keeping his attention as her real self. Her real personality wasn't as bold and flirtatious and wonton as Toni's. Troy wouldn't go for that; she was sure of it.

Despite these thoughts, though, Tonette allowed herself to again imagine her and Troy together. She could picture introducing him to Olarion and Blue, and them welcoming him into their little group. She could picture him coming home to her every day, or even them teaching at the same school together so they could see each other all day long. And of course, they would never get tired of each other. They would discuss their students, swap stories and trade advice as they shared dinner together, and occasionally go to an open mic night where Troy would recite some of his beautiful poetry (that she still had yet to hear any of, but she already knew it would be beautiful). Then they would come home and make passionate love before holding each other as they went to sleep, resting up so they could do it all over again the next day. And in all of these fantasies, they were both wearing wedding rings.

Tonette knew she had to get a grip. As much as she was enjoying these thoughts and fantasies about Troy, she had to remind herself that after she left Barbados, she would never see him again. So it would just be foolish to allow herself to get attached.

She ignored the voice in her head telling her it was too late for that.

Knowing she would do nothing but sit in her room thinking about Troy if she didn't get up and do something, Tonette made herself get out of bed so she could go work out. A long, invigorating run on the beach was just what she needed to clear her head.

She had just stepped onto the beach and was about to put her ear buds in when she heard someone calling her name. Or rather, her vacation name.

"Toni! Hey, Toni, wait a second!"

Tonette turned to see Emmitt trotting towards her, shirtless and smiling. She was glad she was wearing dark shades because she wasn't quite able to tear her eyes away from his chest the way she wanted to.

"Hey, Emmitt," Tonette greeted casually, doing some arm stretches so she wouldn't just be standing there drooling over him.

"You about to go on a run?" Emmitt asked her, adjusting his own shades over his eyes. Tonette could tell he was focused on her bare midsection, though.

"Yep."

"Do you mind if I join you? I was about to get a run in, myself...it could be fun to do it together."

Yeah, I bet, Tonette thought to herself. "Sure, that's cool."

"You are not going to tease me about not being able to keep up?" Emmitt asked her jokingly as he followed her further onto the beach.

"I'm sure you can hold your own," Tonette replied lightly as she glanced around her. Part of her wondered if Troy was going to show up again, but she didn't see him anywhere.

"That I can," Emmitt confirmed confidently as he adjusted the heart rate monitor strapped to his arm.

They made small talk as they went through a few stretches, then they began their run. Emmitt seemed to like to talk as he ran, and Tonette was as grateful for the distraction almost as much as she was regretful of agreeing to let him join her. She realized that while she was physically attracted to Emmitt, that's where it ended; she wasn't interested in him beyond that. He seemed like a nice-enough guy, but he didn't seem to have much more going for him than a gorgeous face and a set of ripped abs. He certainly drew his share of attention, though, because more than a few women had their eye on them as they ran up and down the beach. It was much like the previous day when they were talking on The Gap. Tonette wondered what was behind all that, but didn't care enough to ask.

Towards the end of their run, Emmitt invited her out to dinner for later that evening. Even though Tonette hadn't enjoyed her time with Emmitt nearly as much as she always enjoyed her time with Troy, she agreed to go, figuring it would do her some good to get her mind off Troy for a while. She had been thinking about that man entirely too much and she needed to shake things up.

After their run, Tonette and Emmitt parted ways, agreeing to meet in the lobby of her hotel later that evening. When she went to get some breakfast, a couple of women approached her, looking as if they were on a mission.

"We saw you with Emmitt earlier," one of them said in a hushed voice. She had black hair pulled back into a short ponytail and a nose ring.

"Yeah..." Tonette replied cautiously. "Is there a problem? Are you his girlfriend or something?"

The women laughed. "Oh, Emmitt doesn't believe in having a girlfriend. He is too much of a player to have just one woman."

"Yeah?" Tonette casually replied, going back to cutting up her fruit.

The women looked at each other, obviously surprised by her calm reaction. "Did you understand what we said?"

Tonette chuckled. "Yes, I understood you perfectly."

"Then why are you not angry?"

"Why would I get angry?"

"You are interested in Emmitt, are you not?"

"I hardly know the man. No, I'm not."

"The two of you seem awfully close, then."

Tonette tried to think of an at least somewhat-polite way to tell these women to mind their own damn business. "Like I said, I hardly know Emmitt. I'm not worried about how many women he hits on. So thanks for the warning and everything but if you don't mind, I'd like to enjoy my breakfast in peace."

They looked at each other again in shock before walking back in the direction they came from, whispering amongst themselves. Tonette just shook her head. Either Emmitt really was a major player as they said, or they were some jilted exes or cast-offs who thought Tonette was stepping on their toes, but either way, Tonette wasn't concerned. She didn't want a relationship with Emmitt so they were wasting their time worrying about her.

After going to her room to shower and take a short nap, Tonette decided to join some of the other hotel guests that she had met for a tour of the island. It took the majority of the remainder of the day, and she captured a lot of pictures on her phone. The beauty of her surroundings overwhelmed her, and she said a silent prayer of thanks that she was able to experience it; she couldn't wait to tell Olarion and Blue all about it when she got home.

Her mind was still reeling from her tour when she returned to her hotel. She was so caught up in her thoughts that she almost didn't notice Troy approaching her as she crossed through the lobby.

"Hello, Toni."

"Oh!" Tonette shrieked, almost dropping her phone. She looked at Troy in surprise. "Troy?"

"Did you forget about me or something?" Troy asked with a smile.

"No...I just wasn't expecting to see you, that's all."

"Yes, I know. I am sorry if you feel like I am bothering you."

"No, you're not bothering me..."

"I have never been this persistent with a woman but I cannot seem to help myself...I am drawn to you and do not want to miss an opportunity to see you before you go back home."

Tonette couldn't help blushing again. "That's really sweet, Troy."

"I missed you, Toni."

Feeling lightning surge through her, Tonette tried to keep her face from breaking out into the thrilled grin that it wanted to. "You hardly know me, Troy."

"I feel like I do. You do not feel like a stranger to me. Do I feel like a stranger to you?"

Hell no, Tonette thought to herself. "I wouldn't say that. But still—"

"Tell me I am coming on too strongly, and I will leave you in peace," Troy interjected, looking right into her eyes. "The last thing I want to do is make you uncomfortable."

Tonette knew peace would be the last thing she felt if he left her alone. "I'm not uncomfortable."

Troy's eyes were still boring into hers. "Are you sure?"

"I'm absolutely sure."

"Good." He smiled. "Do you have plans for the evening?"

Tonette started to say no, but then she remembered her dinner date with Emmitt in a couple of hours. Everything in her wanted to blow that off and spend the evening with Troy, but she reminded herself that she was supposed to be weaning herself off of him.

"I do, actually," she replied, almost shyly.

"Very well," Troy replied easily. "I hope you enjoy yourself. If you like, please give me a call later. I would love to spend more time with you, if I can."

Smiling, Tonette nodded. "I'll keep that in mind."

"I hope to hear from you, then," Troy replied, taking her hand and bringing it to his lips. He planted a lingering kiss to her skin before stepping around her and walking out of the lobby. Tonette couldn't resist turning to watch him as he did so, resisting the strong urge to call him back over to her.

Shaking what she hoped was some sense into herself, she turned to head up to her room to prepare for her dinner with Emmitt, which she was looking even less forward to now. She could already feel a weighing sense of sadness come down on her, but she told herself to snap out of it...she was not in a romance with Troy and she needed to stop acting like she was. Emmitt was just what she needed to detour her from this path she was going down entirely too fast. It was going to be a great evening.

She kept telling herself this over and over as she got showered and dressed. She tried her best to push Troy out of her head and concentrate on Emmitt, and when she went down to the lobby and saw him standing there in all white, she hoped it wouldn't be as difficult as she thought.

Emmitt smiled upon seeing her, walking over and taking her hands in his. "You're beautiful," he greeted, leaning down to kiss her cheek.

Tonette hoped he couldn't sense how nervous she was. She simply needed this evening to go well, and 'going well' meant keeping her mind off Troy. "Thank you, Emmitt. You look good, yourself."

"I appreciate it. And if I may be so bold," he leaned in and whispered close to her ear, "You're actually looking quite sexy."

"Sexy is good, right?"

Emmitt grinned. "Sexy is *preferred*."

Tonette smiled, but didn't respond. She just let him take her hand and lead her out of the lobby.

The entire time they were at dinner, Tonette had to resist the urge to check how long they had been sitting there. Emmitt was proving to be someone who wanted nothing more than to charm her panties off, and Tonette wasn't intrigued or offended as much as she was just bored.

"You are the most beautiful woman in the room, Toni," he said to her, eyeing her from across the table.

Taking a sip of her water, Tonette gave him a tight smile. "Thanks."

"I am glad that I get to spend some time with you before you leave. I've been hoping to."

"Yeah?"

"Absolutely. Ever since I first saw you, you have had my attention."

Tonette wasn't flattered by this. "Well, that's interesting."

"I think *you* are interesting."

"How so? You don't know that much about me."

"I know enough, I think. There has to be a reason I am so taken with you."

Yes, there's a reason. You want to get between my legs. "And you don't know what that reason is?"

Emmitt gazed at her as he stroked his chin. "I am still figuring that out."

"Hmm."

"And I think that we should stay in each other's company tonight until I do."

"What if you don't figure it out by the time the night is over?"

Emmitt gave her a slow grin. "The evening will not have been wasted. Trust me."

The lust in his eyes was blatant. He reached across the table and grazed her wrist with his long fingers, and Tonette had to resist the urge to retract her hand. Whatever minimal interest she did have in Emmitt was dwindling with each passing second. He didn't try to get to know her or anything about her; his conversation was full of one-liners and come-ons. Even though Tonette hadn't really been interested in Emmitt anyway, she still found this dinner they were on to be a complete waste of time and wished she was back in her room with the latest Eric Jerome Dickey novel. Either that, or with Troy.

She had tried her best to keep her attention on Emmitt and not on Troy, but the longer she endured Emmitt's single-minded train of thought, the more she slowly gave in to the urge to let her mind wander where it really wanted to go.

Troy.

Just about everything that Emmitt did and said was being subconsciously compared to Troy and what he might say or do, and regardless of how Tonette tried, she couldn't seem to resist that. And of course, Troy came out on the favorable end of every comparison. This evening was supposed to be about moving away from Troy, but that obviously wasn't working.

"Will you excuse me, Emmitt?" Tonette said, not caring that she was interrupting his latest come-on.

Slightly caught off guard, Emmitt blinked. He wasn't used to women not being putty in his hands already and Tonette clearly wasn't. He nodded graciously. "Certainly."

Tonette quickly stood from the table and headed for the ladies room. She didn't have to use it; she just needed a reprieve. Hunched over the sink, she looked at herself in the mirror. Every part of her wanted to be with Troy at that very moment and that realization was making her extremely uncomfortable. This whole evening with Emmitt was turning out to be a disappointment; because Emmitt just wasn't interesting company, and because she felt like she was wasting it by spending it with him and not with who she really wanted to spend it with.

She sighed and stood up straight, straightening her dress and fluffing out her hair. Despite her disapproval of how the evening was going, she couldn't help but smile at how she looked. Her skin was a toasty brown from all her time in the sun, and she was still loving her carefree weave. She was turning to check the view of her backless dress when two ladies walked in; Tonette recognized them as the same ones that had warned her about Emmitt after her run on the beach with him.

"So you are still seeing Emmitt, I see," the one with the nose ring said without preamble. She folded her arms.

"Did you not learn anything from our earlier warning?" the other one asked. She had light brown locs that hung down to her waist and a crop top that showed off her belly ring.

Tonette sighed. "Ladies, as I told you before, I am not interested in Emmitt."

"Yet you are out to dinner with him," Nose Ring countered.

"I've gotta eat."

"He is just going to mislead you," Belly Ring warned.

"He can't *mislead* me because I'm not trying to *follow* him anywhere," Tonette informed them.

"Hmph. That is what they all say."

"Did he jilt the two of you or something?"

Both women looked shocked. "Don't be silly," Nose Ring stated, averting her eyes.

"Then why are you so concerned with 'warning' me about his intentions?"

"We are just tired of watching him try to get his hooks into every beautiful woman he sees," Belly Ring replied. "He preys on beautiful foreigners, especially."

Tonette was more flattered that they considered her beautiful than she was concerned about their warnings about Emmitt. She smiled as she spread some more lip gloss onto her lips, then popped them with a final fluff to her hair.

"Well, again, this is not an issue for me," she said to them as she put her lip gloss back into her small purse. "I am fully aware of what Emmitt is trying to do and it's not going to work."

"We've heard *that* before," Nose Ring scoffed with a shake of her head. "Then the next thing you know, you're—"

"What? Part of the Rejected Lovers Club you two seem to be the president and vice president of? Or are you in the No-Attention-Getting Alliance since he doesn't want to get into *your* panties?"

Both women gasped. "How dare you!" Nose Ring exclaimed, her face turning red.

"We're trying to help you and you want to insult us??" Belly Ring admonished.

"He must be something else in bed if y'all are making such a fuss over him like this," Tonette teased. "Maybe I *will* see what all the hype is about."

Both women looked enraged. "Do *not* do that!" Belly Ring exclaimed.

"Why shouldn't I? I'm single, I'm on vacation, and I have a bag full of condoms. And Emmitt *is* fine. Don't worry, I can send him back to you when I'm done." She laughed as she headed for the door and pulled it open.

"Wait a minute!" Nose Ring called out.

Tonette ignored her. She headed back to the table with an amused smile on her face, not believing that these women were putting so much energy into worrying about what she, a complete stranger, was doing with who was apparently the local heartbreaker. As far as she was concerned, they could have him. It wasn't like she was having a good time, anyway.

"Is everything all right?" Emmitt asked.

She was just about to suggest they cut their evening short when the two women stormed from the bathroom right over to their table. Emmitt saw them before Tonette did and his eyes widened slightly before he groaned and rubbed his right temple. Tonette whirled around right as the women approached.

"I see you have gotten another one," Nose Ring spat at him angrily. "You just cannot help yourself, can you??"

"Now is not the time for this," Emmitt hissed at her.

"Well, when *is* the time?"

"I am on a date, Eva. Do not be rude."

"You weren't very polite to *us* when you slept with me in *her* bed," Belly Ring retorted, jerking her head towards Eva.

Tonette's jaw dropped.

"I *knew* you were going to fall for that trap," Nose Ring, aka Eva, accused Emmitt snidely. "You made all those claims that I was the only one, then as soon as I leave town, *or so you thought*, you sleep with my cousin. In *my* house!"

His face slightly flushed from embarrassment, Emmitt stood and reached for Tonette's hand. "I am so sorry about this; let's just leave."

"Oh, do not try to run now!" Eva swatted his hand away. "Everyone needs to know just what kind of man you are!"

"And it wasn't even all that good!" Belly Ring added loudly, clearly wanting everyone to hear. "Emmitt Steele is a two minute man!"

Tonette clamped a hand over her mouth. She couldn't believe these women were showing out over Emmitt like this!

Emmitt was clearly angry and embarrassed. "So you are lying on me now, Corina?" He towered over her short frame. "You and I *both* know better than that. Being malicious and petty does not make me want you any more than I did when you were calling me yesterday."

"You called him yesterday?" Eva asked, whipping her head around. She clearly hadn't been aware of that. "You didn't tell me that!"

"I...had some things to discuss with him," Belly Ring, aka Corina, replied somewhat sheepishly.

"Like *what*?"

"Don't worry about it right now, Eva!"

"Toni, please, let's just go," Emmitt pleaded. "Please accept my apology for these disruptions."

Corina blocked his path when he tried to step around her. "You and I have some things to discuss, Emmitt."

"*What* do you have to discuss?" Eva pressed.

"Eva!"

"We have nothing to talk about. And even if we did, I cannot do it now; you have already interrupted my evening with this lovely lady enough," Emmitt said to Corina, motioning towards Tonette.

"Well, if you would answer your damn phone, I would not *need* to interrupt your evening, would I?" Corina snapped.

"What is going on, Corina?" Eva demanded. She was no longer even worried about Emmitt.

"Not now, Eva, damn!"

"You've obviously been keeping something from me! You didn't say you had something special to tell him when we came here!" Eva exclaimed.

"Toni!" Emmitt called out.

"Emmitt!" Corina yelled.

Tonette was just looking back and forth between the three of them, as engaged as if she was watching a blockbuster film. This was by far the most interesting part of the evening for her.

"I *said* we need to talk, Emmitt!" Corina insisted.

Losing his patience, Emmitt pointed a finger at her. "Look, Corina—"

"Did you keep sleeping with him after we set him up??" Eva asked Corina, as if just coming to the realization. "Or were you *already* sleeping with him?"

Corina looked at her, then looked away.

"Answer me!" Eva screamed.

"Okay fine! Yes! Yes, we had sex a few times after the set-up! What can I say, the man is wonderful in bed!"

So that two-minute man stuff was *a lie*, Tonette mused, her eyes still transfixed on the little scene before her.

"I cannot believe you!" Eva yelled incredulously at Corina, her hands on her head.

"Eva, please. You know good and well if he hadn't dumped you, you would still be trying to ride him now," Corina spat.

Eva's face reddened. "He did not *dump* me; I caught him with you and dumped *him*, remember?"

Emmitt scoffed, then tried to play it off by coughing into his fist. Eva glared at him before hitting him in the chest with her fist.

"Don't start with the hitting, Eva!" Corina warned.

"Are you *defending* him now??" Eva asked, shocked.

"Emmitt," Corina said, ignoring her cousin, "I just need five minutes..."

"I'm gonna leave you all to your...*discussion*," Tonette announced, stepping back. She was over this whole scene and just wanted to get away from there.

"Toni, wait!" Emmitt exclaimed.

"Emmitt, listen!"

"I do not have time for you right now, Corina! Stop acting desperate just because I let you into my bed!" Emmitt said harshly.

Corina recoiled at the statement. "You mean like this morning?" she retorted, folding her arms.

"*This morning??*" Eva exclaimed.

The three of them continued to argue and Tonette was actually starting to feel embarrassed for them; they were airing their personal business and drama right in the middle of a restaurant.

Suddenly someone grabbed her hand and tried to pull her away. When Tonette whipped around to see who it was, she almost couldn't believe her eyes when she saw it was Troy.

"Come with me," he said.

The authority in his voice could have offended Tonette, but it didn't. If anything, she was enamored by it. Maybe it was because of the situation, or maybe it was because he was who she really wanted to be with in the first place, but she was grateful that he showed up seemingly out of thin air and rescued her from an escalating situation.

She let Troy lead her out of the restaurant, ignoring Emmitt calling out to her as Corina screamed that Emmitt had knocked her up.

"*Wow*," Tonette marveled once they were out of the restaurant. "That was *crazy*."

"Yes, I know."

"Where did you come from, Troy? Did you follow me here?"

"No, Toni. This happens to be one of my favorite restaurants and I had decided to come and get some takeout before going home. I had no idea you would be here."

"Oh. Sorry."

"No apologies necessary."

"Thank you for rescuing me from that. That was turning into a bigger and bigger mess."

"I could tell. I stood and listened for a few minutes before stepping in. That is the same gentleman you were talking to yesterday, yes?"

Tonette blushed slightly. "Yes. Though I would hardly call him a *gentleman*."

"You two must have hit it off."

"I don't know about all that." Tonette wasn't about to tell him that she only went out with Emmitt to get her mind off him.

Troy was eyeing her, his hands stuffed into his pockets. "I'm sorry your evening was ruined."

Tonette eyed him back, amazed at how adorable and sexy he was all at the same time. "Are you, really?"

Trying to suppress a smile, Troy glanced away briefly. Looking back at her, he shrugged casually. "Okay, I'm not. I admit it. Is that bad?"

Tonette grinned. She couldn't help it. He was just so cute to her. "No, it's not bad, if that's how you really feel."

"So now that your date has ended prematurely, what are you going to do?"

Spend the rest of the night up under you, she wanted to blurt out, but thankfully stopped herself. "I don't know," she hedged, shrugging a shoulder slightly. "Any suggestions?"

"I have many *suggestions*...not sure how many you would agree to, though," Troy flirted, a mischievous gleam in his eye.

Tonette's grin widened. "I'm listening."

"Come home with me...and I will share them all with you." Troy took her hand and looked right into her eyes. His eyes were almost pleading with her to say yes.

Biting her lip, Tonette looked away. Everything in her wanted to say yes. Her heart and body were already screaming it, while her head was still campaigning for aloofness. But the more Troy looked at her like he was, his thumb stroking the back of her hand, she knew there was no way she could refuse him. Sincerity radiated from him like a sunbeam. But more importantly, Tonette simply *wanted* to spend her evening with Troy; he was who she had wanted to be with all along. And hell, she was on vacation. She could do what she wanted.

Linking her fingers with his, she stepped closer to him. "Lead the way."

Grinning, Troy did just that.

Once they were back at Troy's house, they wasted no time kicking their shoes off and cuddling on his couch. Tonette snuggled up to Troy and sighed in contentment, again cementing the moment in her mind as one she knew she wouldn't be forgetting any time soon. She just felt so comfortable with Troy; it was an unexplainable thing. She had no way to rationalize it to herself. And for the time being, she didn't want to; she just wanted to revel in it and enjoy it.

"I am so glad you're here," Troy murmured into her hair before kissing her temple. He held her close to him.

"You and me both," Tonette purred, her arms tightening around his waist.

They sat in a satisfied, comfortable silence before Troy lifted her chin with his hand and lowered his lips to hers. The kiss started out soft but in no time at all, the mood intensified and the kiss displayed all the desire and even desperation that they were each feeling for each other. Tonette absolutely loved how Troy held her and caressed her and grabbed her; his hand had the side of her face in a grip that let her know she wasn't going anywhere, and she loved it.

"This is not what I invited you over here for," he murmured between kisses.

"You hear me complaining?" Tonette replied breathlessly, biting her lip as his kisses traveled down her neck.

"Tell me when you want me to stop," Troy instructed as he brought her even closer to him.

"You're gonna be waiting a long time for that...I'm close to begging you *not* to."

"You don't have to beg, baby..." Troy grabbed her under her arms and lifted her slightly, placing wet kisses between her breasts. "I am all yours for as long as you desire."

Tonette's body turned to fire at Troy's statement. She felt something overtake her that she couldn't explain, and it temporarily jarred her. But when Troy slid the top of her dress aside with his teeth and ran a tongue over her bare breasts, she forgot all about anything else. Throwing her head back, she hissed and shuddered with pleasure, and if it wasn't for Troy's grip on her she would have collapsed backwards onto the sofa. Troy was making her melt.

"Can we go to your bedroom?" she panted, repeatedly sliding her fingers through Troy's hair as he continued to slowly and tortuously savor her breasts. "Please?"

Troy looked up at her and bit his lip, moaning as he stood up, taking her with him. His eyes never left hers. He had Tonette transfixed as she wrapped her arms around his neck, caressing the back of his head, everything in her hoping that he would end up inside of her by the end of the night.

As soon as Troy laid Tonette on his bed, she boldly pulled her dress over her head, sending the signal that she wanted more than just kissing and petting this time. Troy eyed her body that was now in nothing more than a white thong, his brown eyes darkening with desire by the second, and whispered to her how beautiful she was. He removed his own shirt and Tonette's thighs rubbed together at the sight of his chest. She loved that he wasn't overly muscular but was far from skinny; it was clear that he worked out and took care of himself. Her eyes tightened as they traveled down to his flat stomach, and before she knew it, she was on her knees, crawling over to him. Troy groaned.

"Do you have *any* idea how sexy you look right now?" he grunted.

Tonette grabbed his waistband and started unbuckling his belt. "Well...what are you gonna do about that?"

"You are driving me *crazy*..." Troy closed his eyes and leaned his head back as Tonette leaned in and started licking his chest.

"Good," Tonette whispered, pushing his pants and underwear down over his hips. She gripped his behind before sliding her hands up his back, lightly grazing his skin with her nails. She sucked his neck, pressing her body as close to his as she could get it.

"Toni," Troy whispered, gripping her face with both hands, giving her a searing look before laying a hard, deep kiss on her. His hand came down and ripped the thin panties from her waist, eliciting a gasp from Tonette, before pushing her back onto the bed with his body. He nestled himself between her legs, his hardness pulsating against her, and Tonette immediately started winding her hips into him.

"Troy, please," Tonette begged, wrapping her legs around him. "Don't make me keep waiting..."

"Believe me, Toni, I want you as badly as you seem to want me," Troy assured her, matching her hip thrusts with his own.

"Put it in me, then," Tonette whispered.

"Let me get a condom," Troy kissed her before reaching over to his nightstand. Tonette kept her hold on him around his neck, not wanting to break contact with him for even a second. She kissed his neck and face as he rummaged in the drawer for a few moments, then pulled back when he cursed under his breath.

"What's wrong?" she asked.

Troy dropped his head, frustrated. "I'm out," he growled, looking away.

"Out of condoms?" Tonette clarified.

"Yes."

"*Damn it!*" Tonette screamed, collapsing back onto the bed. She threw an arm over her eyes and flopped onto her stomach, not believing it.

Troy fell down onto his side next to her, running a hand over his face. "I am *so* sorry, Toni." His voice was anguished.

Sighing, Tonette looked over at him. She was frustrated at the situation but she wasn't frustrated with him. It wasn't like they had planned this. Her body still ached for him, but she knew she had to be responsible, despite the part of her that wanted to just hop onto his still-erect penis, condom or not.

"It's okay," she said, reaching over to caress his face as she turned onto her side, facing him. "These things happen, you know?"

"I suppose."

"Do you want me to leave?"

Troy's head snapped up. "Why would I want you to leave?"

"Well...since we can't..."

"Toni, come on, of course not," Troy assured her, taking her hand in his. "Like I said before, I did not invite you over here to get you into bed. Of course I would love to be making love to you right now but as long as I still get to spend time with you, I am happy with that."

Tonette couldn't help blushing at that. A lot of men wouldn't have wanted to continue the evening if they had been that close to sex and ended up not being able to have it.

Not being able to resist, she leaned over and placed a tender kiss on his lips. "Then I'd love to stay."

"Good." Troy smiled at her.

They got underneath the covers and just talked as they held and languidly caressed each other. Troy told her more about his background and his upbringing, and Tonette answered any questions he had for her. Some of the answers were either embellished or just plain untrue; she hated to lie but for some reason she felt the need to keep up this persona that she had started. She really wanted to just be herself, though, the more she got to know him. But she figured since she wouldn't be seeing him anymore after leaving Barbados in a few days, it wasn't really hurting anybody.

"When is your birthday, Toni?" Troy asked her.

"September ninth." *True.*

"I have a birthday coming up," he informed her as he played with her fingers.

"Yeah? When?"

"May second."

"That's just a few weeks from now. Any plans?"

"Not really," Troy shrugged. "I never do all that much."

"You should do something special for your birthday," Tonette suggested, using her free hand to rub his chest. "How old are you going to be?"

"Thirty-four."

"Oh, so you're a few months older than me, then. I turn thirty-four this year, too."

"And what will you be doing for *your* birthday?" Troy asked her.

Still wishing you were with me in Atlanta. "Haven't thought that much about it, really."

The hours ticked by as they continued to talk and get to know each other. There were times when one would kiss the other and things would start to get hot and heavy, but one of them always cooled things down before they lost their heads. They were both still very aroused and tried to stay on opposite ends of the bed from each other, but that never lasted very long.

After a while, they both dozed off. Tonette woke up first and glanced at the clock on the bedside table, shocked to see it was almost three in the morning. She looked over at Troy and couldn't help smiling; he was even adorable when he slept. Her fingers grazed over his eyebrows, ran lightly down the bridge of his nose, and traced his moist lips. That something washed over her again, and intensified the longer she looked at him. *Why couldn't I meet a man like him back home?* She thought to herself wishfully. *But would he even have noticed me as myself?*

Feeling the need to clear her head, she eased out of the bed and walked over to retrieve her dress from where she had tossed it the night before. She tried to be quiet as she slipped the dress over her head and tiptoed into his bathroom to wash her face and relieve herself. For some reason, she felt the need to get out of Troy's house; she felt like she was starting to fall into something she wasn't sure she was ready to fall into. Troy didn't live that terribly far from her hotel; she figured the walk would do her some good.

When she eased back into Troy's adjoining bedroom, she wasn't three steps into the room before Troy eased his eyes open, sitting up in bed.

"Toni?" he asked groggily, rubbing his eyes. Tonette ached at how cute he was. "What are you doing?"

Tonette had hoped to be able to leave without waking him up. She hesitated, trying to find a way to explain her trying to sneak out in the middle of the night. "I'm sorry for waking you."

"Where are you going?"

"I just...thought I'd head back to the hotel."

"Why?"

Thinking quickly, Tonette asked, "Don't you have to work?"

Troy glanced at the clock by the bed as he took a mint out of the nightstand and slid it into his mouth. "Not for hours, yet. Come back to bed."

Tonette wanted to dive into that bed with him. It was taking everything in her to resist. "I shouldn't."

"Why do you say that?"

Because I'm falling for you and it's freaking me out. "I just...umm..."

"Do you have someone else waiting for you?"

"No!" Tonette responded quickly.

"Do you have some other previous engagement?"

"No..."

"Then please don't leave. Stay with me."

He was looking at her with those intense eyes again, and Tonette knew it would take an act of God to resist him right then. Unless there was a sudden earthquake, a bolt of lightning ripping through the house, or a tornado sweeping it away, she knew she wasn't going anywhere, despite how much her heart might regret it later.

"Okay," she softly conceded.

Troy reached his hand out to her and she walked around to his side of the bed, placing her hand in his. He stood, the sheets falling from his naked body, and Tonette had to force herself to turn her eyes away; her arousal from the night before wasn't totally gone. Troy gently turned her around by the waist as he kissed her shoulder, then slowly slid the straps of her dress down, tracing a finger lightly down her spine.

"Interesting tattoo," he murmured, fingering the design at the base of her back.

"Oh, that old thing?" Tonette chuckled nervously. "Got it on a dare in college."

"Adventurous," Troy observed, turning her again by her waist to face him and pulling her close. "I like that."

"I have my moments," Tonette smiled. She slid her hands up and down his chest.

Troy leaned in and slowly ran his tongue along her ear, making Tonette shudder in pleasure. "Come back to bed," he requested again.

Tonette whimpered as he kissed her lips. Any residual resolve she had left was gone with every press of his lips to hers. Not having the strength to speak, she simply nodded and let him pull her down onto the bed with him.

A few hours later, they took a shower together. Tonette began getting dressed when Troy started to get ready for work, but he stopped her.

"You don't have to leave," he said.

Tonette looked at him, confused. "But you're going to work."

"Yes..." Troy eyed her as he buttoned his shirt. "But I will be back later."

"So you just want me to stay here in your house while you're gone?"

"Yes."

"Why?"

Troy came and sat on the side of the bed next to her, taking her chin in his hand. Looking right into her eyes, he said sincerely, "I would love to come home to you."

There went that feeling again. Tonette's hand that was holding the bedsheets to her chest tightened. She bit her lip, feeling heat flush her cheeks. "Wow."

"If you need to get some things from your hotel, I can quickly take you now to get it. But if it can wait, you are free to use my computer while I am gone to entertain yourself, and I have plenty of food in the refrigerator. I just..." he took her hand, blushing as he looked down momentarily, "I just would like to spend as much time with you as I possibly can before you return home, Toni."

"Oh, Troy..."

"If you do not want to stay, I will absolutely take you back to your hotel. But I would really, really love it if you stayed here." He leaned in and kissed her tenderly on the lips. "Please, Toni."

Tonette knew there was no way she could say no. She didn't even *want* to say no. Truth be told, he had her at *I would love to come home to you.*

She smiled. "Do you have an extra toothbrush?"

Troy grinned, causing her to smile wider. It did something to her when he smiled like that. "I have whatever you need," he assured her, taking her face in his hands and kissing her deeply. Tonette slid her arms around his neck as she felt her body heating up.

"How much time do you have?" she whispered against his lips.

Troy checked his watch. "About thirty minutes."

"Perfect." Tonette slid down to her knees and unbuckled his belt, grinning at him devilishly. Troy just bit his lip and leaned back on his elbows, leaning his head back as Tonette slid him into her mouth. He moaned loudly with pleasure.

"I could *definitely* get used to this," he whispered.

You and me both, Tonette thought to herself.

Tonette ended up spending the remainder of her time in Barbados at Troy's house. He didn't want her to leave, and she gave up on trying to get herself to want to leave. Even though she knew her heart would be aching for this man when she got on that plane back to Atlanta in a couple of days, she just decided to throw caution to the wind and enjoy it while it lasted.

She would get up and prepare breakfast for him before he went to work, then usually go running before going back to his place to read or watch movies before he came back.

And when he walked through the door, she always ran to him like she hadn't seen him in months, and sometimes she was wearing a sexy little teddy or a cute underwear set when she did so. They would fool around, either make dinner together or go out, go to The Gap and dance or just cruise, or take long walks along the beach, holding hands. He read her some of his poetry, which only endeared Tonette to him even more. She even allowed herself to imagine that Troy was her man and his house was their house, and they were happily living there together. Tonette felt like a character in the books she loved to read, and she had read enough of them to know how this would play out. She knew she was probably being foolish, allowing herself to get so wrapped up in Troy when she knew she would be leaving him shortly, but for the time being, she just didn't care. She wanted to be with him more than she wanted to be sensible.

Why did the first man to grab hold of her heart and turn her insides to molten lava have to live over two thousand miles away?

There still hadn't been any sex, even though Troy had long since replenished his condom supply. They were plenty intimate, but they put more of their energy into getting to know each other...at least, that's what Troy thought they were doing. He had no idea that Toni didn't exist. He didn't know that it was just plain Tonette pretending to be something she wasn't while on vacation, and that she had messed around and caught feelings for him and now didn't know how to stop herself. How would it look after all this time they had spent together for her to tell him the real deal? That she had given him a fake name and was doing things she never would have done as herself, and had told him so many lies that she had to sometimes struggle to remember everything? More importantly, why didn't she have enough confidence in herself to think that Troy would like her just as much as Tonette?

Knowing that she was deceiving Troy when he had been nothing but a sweetheart to her made her feel like dirt. She could only imagine that he would feel hurt or duped if he knew the truth. Which was exactly why she couldn't tell him. She couldn't look him in his face and tell him she had lied to him about her name and her occupation and whatever else. Once she went back to Atlanta, they would go back to their own respective lives like they had before she came to Barbados. In time, he would forget about her and Tonette would have plenty of memories to savor as she went back to her pleasantly quiet life.

Chapter 5

It was her last day in Barbados and Tonette had to tell herself not to be sad about it. She missed her friends and her students, but the bigger part of her knew she would miss Troy as soon as she got on that plane.

Trying not to think about that, she busied herself with just trying to focus on enjoying on her last day on this beautiful island. She and Troy were supposed to spend the entire day together, and then he would take her to the airport in the morning. Tonette had to repeatedly tell herself not to get sad at the thought of leaving Troy; she didn't even care that she hadn't seen or done half the things she had planned on seeing and doing while on the island. Spending that time with Troy had been more than worth it.

While Troy ran to the store, Tonette finally called Olarion, who happened to be hanging out with Blue. They both cursed her out for waiting until she was about to leave Barbados before calling them.

"What the hell took you so long to call us, heffah??" Olarion shouted. "You're getting ready to come home tomorrow!"

"I sent you guys texts," Tonette defended weakly.

"*Texts??* So you're there nine days and all you send us are some whack-ass texts, then you wait until day *ten* to call and you think that's sufficient??" That was Blue. "No, Boo-Boo."

"We were worried about you, Tonette! The *least* you could've done was checked in with us regularly. The couple of raggedy texts you sent were from when you first got there."

"Look, I'm sorry, y'all...I didn't mean to make you worry about me. I've just been enjoying myself and I really haven't even been on my phone at all that much."

"Yeah?" Olarion was clearly intrigued. "What have you been doing? Did you meet somebody?"

Tonette saw Troy's car pull up from the living room window. "I can't talk about that right now."

"Excuse me? Bitch, you go over there and get all scarce and wait 'til the last minute to call somebody, now you wanna be tight-lipped, too? What the hell??"

"Blue, look, I'll give you all the dish and the tea and whatever else it's called nowadays when I get back, I promise. But for now I've gotta go. You have my flight information, right?"

"Yeah, I got it," Blue grumbled. "I oughta just leave your ass at the airport, though."

"You know you love me too much to do that," Tonette said with a smile. "I love y'all."

"Yeah, yeah, whatever," Blue scoffed. Tonette just laughed. Blue could be a real drama queen when he wanted to be.

"Cut that out, Blue. You know we love you, too, girl," Olarion said to Tonette. "But we're still gon' kick your ass when you get here."

"Duly noted. Now bye." Tonette hung up the phone right as Troy came through the front door. He smiled upon seeing her, as he always did; his face would just light up.

Tonette knew she was going to miss that when she got back to Atlanta.

"Hey you," Tonette greeted him, grinning as she rushed over to him with her arms outstretched. She wrapped her arms around his neck, closing her eyes and trying not to sigh out loud at the contentment she felt whenever he wrapped his arms around her in return as he was doing then.

"My Lovely," he replied, using the term of endearment he sometimes called her. It made Tonette tingle every time he said it. "Are you okay?"

"Yeah, I'm great."

"Well, I am not."

"What's wrong?"

"A dear friend of mine was in a car accident early this morning. I just found out about it on the way back home."

"Oh my goodness!" Tonette exclaimed, her fingertips flying to her mouth. "Are they okay? They're not..." Her voice trailed off, not wanting to say it.

"No, thankfully, it was not fatal. But it was still very bad, from what I hear."

"Oh, Troy I am so sorry," Tonette said sincerely, placing her hands on his chest. He rubbed her arms, giving her a faint smile. "What do you need me to do?"

"I must go see her in the hospital. She does not have much family and I don't want her to be there alone until her aunt can make it to her."

Tonette froze. *She?* The jealousy consumed her before she could even think about trying to stop it. She fought hard to keep her face even. "Of course. Of course, you should do that."

"Unfortunately, that means we will not be able to spend today together as we planned," Troy said, his face pained. It was clear he didn't want to say it, and Tonette didn't want to hear it. But it would be totally selfish to ask him to not go to see about his friend just because this happened to be her last day in Barbados. The timing sucked, but she knew she couldn't try to stop him from doing what he needed to do.

"Well, I can't say I'm not disappointed," Tonette said honestly. She dropped her hands from his chest. "But I totally understand. I'll, um, I'll hurry up and get my things."

"Toni..."

"Do you have time to take me back to the hotel?" She couldn't look at him. "If not, I'll find my own way back." She turned away from him but he caught her hand, stopping her.

"Toni, don't be silly. Of course I'm taking you back myself."

She had hoped he would say *Of course I'm taking you with me to the hospital*, even though she knew that was unreasonable. Now wasn't the time to bring strangers around. How would he even introduce her? It wasn't like she was his girlfriend or anything, despite how she had been imagining she was just that over the past few days.

"Thanks," she croaked. Clearing her throat, she gently eased her hand from his. Might as well start weaning herself off his touch, like she probably should have done days ago. "I'll be quick so you can get going."

"Toni, wait," Troy gently grabbed her arm and turned her to him. He tried to make eye contact with her but she kept her eyes averted, trying her best to appear indifferent or at least, not as upset as she was. 'Cause inside, she could feel her heart breaking and the echo of every piece as it shattered to the bottom.

"You have to leave," she said, as much to herself as to him. "Don't let me hold you up."

"Please look at me."

Forcing herself, Tonette looked up into his eyes that she always got lost in. They were now filled with concern, regret, and pleading with her to understand.

"Are you upset with me?" he asked her.

Yes. "No, of course not," she made herself say. "You're just, um...you're just doing what you have to do. I totally understand that."

"Believe me, Toni, it's only something this dire that would make me leave your side when I know this is your last day here," Troy assured her, pulling her closer to him. His eyes bore into hers, and she forced herself not to look away. He pressed his forehead against hers as he wrapped her in his arms. "I do not want to leave you. But they said she was asking for me, and I need to go by her place to get some of her things."

Swallowing hard, Tonette just nodded. "You don't need to explain, Troy."

"And I would love to take you with me, but—"

"Troy, please," Tonette interrupted, taking a step back. His eyes looked anguished as he tried to hold on to her hand, but she slipped it behind her back. "I get it, really. You need to be there for your friend and not worrying about bringing a stranger around at a time like that, being all awkward. It's fine."

He just looked at her, his eyes still pleading with her.

Not trusting herself to say anything else without breaking down, she quickly turned on her heel and headed to Troy's bedroom to gather her things, hoping he didn't follow her. She needed a minute to get her head together. It was almost as if she was in a daze as she threw her things into her suitcase, not even bothering to fold anything as she usually did. When she came across the sheer black teddy she was going to wear that night, hoping to finally get some lovin' from him, she had to bite her lip to keep from crying. Looks like she was never going to get the chance to experience making love to Troy. It's not like she could ask him for a quickie before he went to check on his friend in the hospital.

It was already going to be hard enough knowing she would have to leave him in the morning, but at least she had a whole day to prepare for that. Now, it was ending just like that, and she wasn't ready. Tears pricked her eyes but she knew there was no way she could cry in front of him. How would she even be able to explain that? This wasn't supposed to be anything serious; they hadn't made any declarations. It was an island fling; at least it was supposed to be. Toni wouldn't get this upset over a man she met on vacation. But Tonette knew it was already too late for that.

After many deep breaths and a splash or two of cold water to her face, Tonette checked to make sure she had everything before steeling herself and walking back to the living room where Troy was waiting for her. She was thankful that he had stayed there while she packed, because she had at least been able to pull herself together somewhat while she did. Her mind told her that she couldn't let this ruin what had ultimately been a great vacation, but her heart hadn't quite caught up to that reasoning yet.

"I'm ready," she announced, heading straight for the door.

Troy had immediately stood upon her entering the room and intercepted her beeline for the door, removing the suitcases from her hands. She just gave him a tight smile as she went ahead of him out to the car, not even waiting for him to open the door for her as she slipped into the passenger seat while he loaded her bags into his trunk. She tried not to watch him in the rearview mirror, but her eyes kept straying to him. When he got into the car, though, she made herself look out of the window.

He started the engine, then paused thoughtfully before turning to look at her. "Toni, I really am sorry."

She shook her head. "You don't have anything to apologize for."

"You're upset."

"I'll get over it."

"I won't."

She looked at him, and there was something in his eyes that frightened her. Not in a bad way, but in a heart-melting, this-wasn't-just-a-fling-for-me kind of way. Her gaze fell down to her lap. "Yes, you will."

"I promise you I won't."

She could feel the tear prickles again. She knew she wouldn't be getting over it herself any time soon, but she didn't want to tell him that. She wasn't supposed to care this much, even though it was clear he did. "Let's go. You need to get to your friend."

Pursing his lips together, Troy put the car in gear and started backing out of his driveway. The drive to the hotel was only about fifteen minutes but to Tonette, it felt like an hour. She couldn't bring herself to say anything and Troy was looking like he was trying to find the right words to say. He kept looking over at her with that pained expression on his face, as if he was trying to get as many glimpses of her in as he could before he dropped her off.

When they got to her hotel, he insisted on taking her bags to her room. Tonette had just wanted them to say good-bye at the car, but Troy didn't want to leave her any more than she wanted him to. They were both quiet as they rode up the elevator to her room, and once inside, Tonette just went over to the window and looked out at the beautiful view of the beach, not being able to bring herself to appreciate it as she had been doing any other time. She wanted Troy to just put her bags down and go, but she knew he wouldn't do that. Sure enough, she felt his arms encircle her from behind, and her eyes slid closed, squeezing shut.

"I do not want to leave you, Toni," he whispered into her hair.

Tonette just nodded, not knowing what to say.

"Please say something."

Tonette's mouth opened, but nothing came out. She hung her head.

Troy turned her face him, taking her face in his hand and bringing her face to meet his. He lowered his lips to hers in a deep, intense, almost desperate kiss that had Tonette's knees melting like butter on a hot skillet. Troy wrapped his strong arms around her and lifted, bringing her over to the bed.

"Troy," she whispered against his lips, giving a half-hearted push against his chest, "We can't..."

"Yes," he insisted, laying on top of her. "We must."

"You have to go," she whimpered.

"I have to take in all of you once more, Toni...I don't want us to leave things like this," he pleaded, stroking the underside of her chin with his finger as he looked into her eyes. He lowered his head, planting wet kisses to her neck. "Do you want me to leave?"

Hell no! Yes! Ugh, I don't know what I'm doing!! Tonette's mind was all over the place as she fought back tears, both at how good he felt and how much it was going to hurt when he had to stop.

"It doesn't matter what I want," she managed to say.

"*You* matter, Toni."

"You know what I mean."

Troy kissed her again, this time with his hand sliding up her baby tee and grabbing her breast before grazing her nipples with his fingertips.

"Tell me what you mean," he whispered, kissing her chin. "Tell me what you want."

Tonette moaned as she arched her back, wanting to tell him to get inside of her, to give her something else to remember him by, but she didn't. It would just make it that much harder when he had to get up and leave afterwards.

Troy whispered her name over and over as he savored her neck, her breasts, her stomach, and then unbuttoned her jeans. Tonette wanted to tell him to stop, but what he was doing felt *so* good...

An anguished moan escaped her lips when Troy placed his mouth between her legs through her thin panties, then pushed them aside to stick his tongue inside of her. Tonette's hands gripped the sheets as she slowly thrust her hips against his face, not being able to help it. Her arms slid above her head as she surrendered to the moment, turning her head to the side and biting her lip in pleasure, her eyes closed.

She felt Troy's weight on her again as he climbed back on top of her, turning her face to his and kissing her again, deeply and hungrily. At some point he had pushed his pants down, but kept his briefs up. His hardness pressed into her, and she immediately wrapped her legs around him, grateful that there was at least the barrier of underwear between them. He seemed to know as well as she did that this was not the ideal time or situation to consummate their...whatever this was. They slowly ground their hips together, easily matching their rhythms, moving together as smoothly and as naturally as they had the first night they met at that club on The Gap.

They wrapped around each other, kissing and moaning as they looked into each other's eyes, each not saying what they wanted to say, just being content at the moment to try to give each other one last moment of pleasure.

"Toni," Troy breathed, a hand coming up to grab the side of her face.

"Yes, baby," she moaned.

"Do something for me?"

"Anything."

He slid his other hand between them, eliciting a gasp from Tonette when his fingers entered her. "Come for me." He flicked his tongue between her still-open lips.

A rush of breath escaped her. "Troy..."

"Come for me, baby."

"Oh my god..."

"Please come for me."

His fingers were driving her into oblivion. Her hips bucked his hand, feeling the rumble of the orgasm coming like a far-off freight train. When she felt alternating nips, licks, and long, slow suckles to her breasts, the force increased, as did her hips.

"Yes," she groaned loudly. "*Yes*, Troy..."

"Is this good to you?"

"Oh god yes..."

Troy moaned as he pushed her breasts together, flicking both nipples at once, and Tonette was literally about to start speaking in tongues. She felt convulsions start to take over her body.

"You coming, baby?" Troy asked her, teasing her with his fingers.

"Yes...please don't stop, Troy," she begged, her hips lifting off the bed on their own. "*Please!*"

"I'll never stop, baby," he assured her, looking up into her eyes. "I can *promise* you that."

Tonette didn't have time to contemplate what he meant by that; she could only bite her lip as her eyes rolled to the back of her head, and she clutched his shoulders. The orgasm train was coming right at her full force, and she screamed with it hit, Troy whispering in her ear to keep going, and her body shook like she was electrocuted.

"Get on top of me," she half ordered, half pleaded.

Troy quickly obliged her, fitting himself between her legs as if he belonged there. His fingers were still teasing her breasts.

"Take it out," Tonette said.

Troy looked at her and bit his lip.

"I need to at least feel you up against me," she whispered, reaching between them to do it herself. She grunted in pleasure at the feeling of his bare hardness against her bare wetness. Troy groaned when she reached down to grab his bottom, pulling him into her as her hips continued winding.

"Baby," he managed, the look of restrained pleasure on his face, "Are you sure?"

"I just need to feel you..."

His hips started to move against her as if they couldn't help it. "What if I..."

Tonette placed a finger to his lips. "Don't think...just move with me, baby." She eyed him seductively.

"You feel so *good*...and *so* wet..."

Tonette shuddered; his words seemed to have the same effect on her as his fingers and tongue did. "It's all for you. Now," she rolled on top of him, her hips immediately resuming their winding, "*You* come for *me*."

Troy's hands slid up her thighs and gripped her bottom hard. "You are so sexy, Toni...my Lovely..."

Biting her lip to avoid getting choked up at hearing his pet name for her, she started winding her hips harder, and faster. Pretty soon she had Troy hissing and growling, his hips coming up to meet hers, his fingers digging into her flesh. Without a word, he flipped her back over, sliding his rock-hardness against her slick womanhood, both of them taunting and urging each other to the proverbial mountaintop.

When he slipped inside of her, they both froze, their eyes snapping to each other's, their chests heaving. Neither of them made a move to remove him; it was clear they were both fighting the urge to just take advantage of the moment they had clearly both been waiting for since they met.

As if on cue, their hips began to move together. It felt so good that Tonette actually wanted to cry. This was ecstasy. Her mind screamed for her to stop, and she knew she should.

"Toni," Troy moaned.

"We should stop," Tonette whispered, even though her hips were still slowly moving.

"I know." Troy's hips continued to thrust. "I know..."

"So why aren't we stopping?" she breathed.

"Because we can't." He kissed her, nipping at her lips.

"But we should."

"I know. I know this isn't how it should be."

"No," she whimpered when he leaned down to suck her neck. She grabbed the back of his head, the pleasure being almost too much for her to bear. She squeezed her eyes shut. "It's not."

With that, they both slowly grinded to a stop, but Troy stayed inside of her for a few long moments, pushing himself as deep inside of her as he could, and her hands gripping his bottom to keep him there. They shared deep, tender kisses as Troy slowly extracted himself from her, both of them groaning in frustration as he did so.

"I apologize, Toni," he whispered, burying his face in her neck.

"Don't do that. I'm not complaining. We *both* did it."

"But I should have more self-control."

"Troy, stop."

"I just..." He raised his head to look in her eyes. "I don't want to mar our last moments together."

Looking back into his eyes, she bit her lip. "Did you come?"

Troy blinked in surprise, then gave her a slow, lazy grin. "I came close, but no."

"Well, I have some more work to do, then," Tonette announced before pushing him onto his back and sliding down. It was Troy's turn to grip the sheets as Tonette took him into her mouth, not stopping until she made him feel as good as he made her feel. Twice.

When it came time for Troy to leave, a sadness fell over the room again and Tonette had to fight to not tear up again.

Troy grabbed his keys and looked at her for a long moment before reaching and taking her hand, pulling her off the bed. Reaching into his back pocket, he pressed a piece of paper into her hand as he looked into her eyes.

"This is my contact information," he said, closing both his hands around hers and bringing it to his lips. "Please use it, Toni. Okay?"

Knowing she wouldn't, Tonette just nodded. Troy had no idea that once she got back to Atlanta, Toni would no longer exist.

Taking her face in his hands, he kissed her deeply, tenderly, and for several minutes. He didn't want to leave; it was evident. But they both knew he had to, so when the kiss eventually tapered off, he just ran his fingers down her cheek, placed one last lingering kiss to her forehead, and left.

Tonette just stood there as if in a daze, watching the door as if he was going to come bursting back through it. But several minutes passed and that didn't happen; he was gone. Tears sprung to her eyes at that realization, and she folded her arms across her stomach as she turned to look at the bed they were just rolling around on twenty minutes before. Her heart hurt and her body ached. Now what?

She had a whole day left in Barbados and didn't feel like going anywhere or doing anything; she just wanted to fling herself onto the bed and mope. She glanced down at the paper Troy had given her with his name, phone number, and email and home addresses, and immediately went over to stuff it into her purse. She thought about throwing it away, but couldn't bring herself to do it.

Knowing she would drive herself crazy thinking about Troy if she stayed in her room, she went to the bathroom to take a quick shower, threw on the first sundress she could yank out of her hastily-packed suitcase, and headed for The Gap, hoping to find some kind of distraction. Within the next thirty minutes, she found it.

"Toni, I am so glad to see you."

Tonette smiled. "Hello, Emmitt."

"I have been hoping I would run into you again," he said, stepping closer to her. "I wanted to apologize to you for what happened during our date. You know, with Eva and Corina?"

"Yes, I remember very well. And thank you for apologizing. Congratulations on your—"

"Please don't," he cut her off, holding up his hand. "It's not necessary, trust me."

Tonette didn't know what he meant by that and she didn't care. Emmitt was just the person she needed to run into. Despite their disastrous date and her overall lack of attraction to him, he was still incredibly fine. And she still had some residual sexual frustration to burn off.

"Okay, then," she shrugged, smiling at him as she shielded the sun from her eyes with her hand. "If you say so."

"Yes, I do. I am surprised you're still here...I thought you might have gone home already."

"I leave tomorrow."

"Oh? Well, it is a good thing I ran into you today, then."

"Yeah? Why is that?" She grinned flirtatiously.

"Maybe I can finally spend some one-on-one time with you. Do you think we can make that happen, Toni?" He stepped even closer to her, giving her a better view of his sculpted chest. The tank top he was wearing clung to it like it had adhesive on it. She bit her lip.

"None of your groupies are going to come jumping out of the shrubbery, are they?" Tonette asked, only half-joking.

Emmitt scoffed. "I do not have groupies. Just women who don't listen. Anyway, right now all I care about is you," he said in a low voice as he tweaked her chin.

Yeah, he's still full of it, Tonette thought to herself. But she wasn't looking for anything but some physical release from Emmitt, so it didn't matter how much of an asshole he was. She was using him, again, just as much as he thought he was using her.

"Would you like to go back to my room?" she asked seductively.

Emmitt licked his lips. "Very much so."

Without another word, they headed back to her hotel. Tonette didn't even care if the front desk attendants noticed that she was coming in with a second man not even two hours later than she had come in with the first. It wasn't any of their business. Thankfully though, they just nodded graciously at her and Emmitt as they passed before going back to what they had been doing.

As soon as they were inside Tonette's room, she tossed her key on the floor, whirled around, and planted a kiss on Emmitt, pushing her tongue into his mouth. He was a little caught off guard but he quickly recovered, wrapping his huge arms around her and lifting her off the ground. Feeling a strange sense of deja vu, Tonette wrapped her legs around Emmitt's waist, mumbling against his lips for him to take her against the wall. He backed her up as they continued to kiss wildly, Tonette's hands rubbing his bald head and gripping his shoulders. Once her back was braced against the wall, he hastily yanked her dress aside, revealing her bare breasts. He grunted in appreciation and took one into his mouth, sucking so hard Tonette thought he was trying to draw milk.

"Not so hard, Emmitt," she breathed, squeezing his shoulder.

"I'm sorry," he glanced at her. "I'm just so excited..."

"Do you have condoms?" Tonette asked. "*Please* tell me you have condoms."

"Of course," he ran his tongue down the valley of her breasts as he started unbuckling his pants. "I always have condoms."

Tonette was trying her best not to compare every little thing Emmitt was doing to Troy. She tried her best to just block everything else out and lose herself in the moment. What Emmitt was doing to her felt good, but it couldn't touch what Troy had done. She could only hope that changed in the next few minutes.

After covering himself and pleasantly discovering that Tonette wasn't wearing any panties, Emmitt thrust into her, releasing a guttural grunt as he did so. He proceeded to pump into her, no longer kissing her; just concentrating on what he was doing. His eyes were focused on himself going in and out of her most of the time.

When he was done with that, he threw her onto the bed, flipped her over, and entered her from behind. Grabbing her hips possessively, he had his way, not once asking how she felt or if it was good to her. Tonette suspected he didn't care, as long as he got his. There was no longer any affection; it was all just *banging*.

"Oh *god*, you feel so good!" he grunted, sweat dripping off his face onto her back. At some point he ripped off his shirt and her dress, and pushed his pants off, kicking them across the room. His naked body was big and strong, and he had no problem putting all of his weight on her when he flipped her onto her back and mounted her. He pushed her legs up to her shoulders, pounding into her, his eyes still focused on himself more than they were on her. Tonette didn't mind the rough stuff sometimes, but she still needed a little tenderness thrown in somewhere.

"Come here," she whispered, holding her arms out. He lowered himself to her and she wrapped her legs around his waist. "Now kiss me."

Emmitt obliged her, digging his tongue into her mouth so deep it seemed like he was trying to play Tap the Tonsils. Their teeth clanked together and after a few moments, Tonette gave up and attempted to push him onto his back, but he resisted.

"What's wrong?" she asked breathlessly.

"I do not allow women to get on top of me," he stated. And he was serious.

Boy, I sure know how to pick 'em, Tonette thought to herself. "You don't *allow* it?"

"No, I don't."

Frowning, Tonette placed a fist against her hip. "Dare I ask why?"

"Because whoever is on top is dominant. And no woman will dominate me."

Tonette couldn't stop the laugh that spewed out of her mouth like spoiled milk. She didn't bother asking if he was serious because she knew he was. "Well, I'll tell you this," she said, her voice strong and clear. "Either I get on top or you get out."

Emmitt's eyes bugged. "Really?"

"Yes, really. You're not going to be using me as your life-sized blowup doll and then tossing me aside when you don't have any left. I need to get mine, too."

"I'm sorry, Toni, but I just don't do that."

"And let me guess...you don't go down on women, either. But I bet you expect them to go down on you."

Emmitt blinked. "Of course," he said matter-of-factly, as if he didn't see the problem.

Shaking her head, Tonette climbed off of him and went to retrieve her dress from the floor. She tossed his clothes back to him, as well. "You can take that nonsense back to Corina."

He looked at her, dumbfounded. "You are really kicking me out?"

The look on his face was comical. "Yes, I'm really kicking you out. And please hurry up 'cause I have a vibrator that's more attentive than you are."

Shocked, Emmitt slowly started getting dressed, as if he expected her to stop him at any moment. It was clear he wasn't used to being put out, and not getting his way. But Tonette wasn't one of his groupies, and was only using him to eat up some time and release some frustration. But he just cared about getting his, and Tonette wasn't up for that. They were either going to use each other equally and fairly or not at all.

Well, she thought to herself after he was gone and she dug her big purple vibrator out of her suitcase, *Thank goodness I put some fresh batteries in this thing 'cause I'm about to get my money's worth.*

Chapter 6

Tonette grinned when she saw Blue waiting for her at the airport back in Atlanta. She loved her time in Barbados but was glad to be home and see her friends.

"Girl, you look like somebody that done got their world rocked," Blue greeted, opening his arms to her. He pulled her into a strong hug that lifted her off the ground, causing Tonette to squeal.

"It is so good to see you!" Tonette gushed, squeezing him.

"It better be! I had to sit in traffic coming over here to get you!" Blue teased, swatting her on the bottom before setting her feet back on the ground.

"I certainly appreciate it."

"And what the hell is this shit?" Blue asked, his mouth twisted, as he flipped Tonette's hair with his hand. "When did you get this??"

Tonette tried to suppress a smile. She knew Blue wouldn't be happy about her going to someone else to get her weave in. "You don't remember putting this in before I left?"

"Don't try to play me! My memory ain't *that* bad!"

Not being able to hold it any longer, Tonette burst out laughing.

"Oh, so you cheatin' on a brother now, huh?" Blue asked, frowning down at her. "It's like *that*?"

"Blue, come on," Tonette pleaded, not being able to tell if he was really upset or just messing with her. "Don't take it personally. I had my reasons."

"Uh-huh." Blue snatched her suitcases off of the carousel and stalked ahead of her.

"Blue!" Tonette exclaimed, hurrying to catch up with him. "Seriously??"

"You know I don't play that!" Blue admonished, never breaking his stride.

"Come on! I told you, I had my reasons."

"And the reasons *are*?"

"I'm going to tell you and Olarion all about it when we get home. Now can you please stop walking so fast?"

Blue looked at her and shook his head, slowing down to a more casual pace. "What am I gonna do with you?" he mumbled.

Tonette just grinned, grabbing onto one of his strong arms as they walked.

Olarion met them at Tonette's apartment, and they wasted no time getting all the details from Tonette about her trip.

"Girl, you look amazing!" Olarion gushed, hugging Tonette excitedly. "You didn't have all of this going on when you left!" She eyed Tonette's hair and outfit as she waved a hand up and down.

"Yeah, I know," Tonette confirmed, doing a playful twirl before plopping down onto her couch. "I wanted to go over there and just be somebody else completely different. *That's* why I went to someone else to get my weave in, Blue," she said pointedly, looking at him.

"That doesn't explain anything. You could've done all that with me doing your hair," Blue protested. "It's not like I was gonna be there to bust your groove up."

"Blue! Stop being stubborn!" Olarion admonished. "It's not like whoever did it did a bad job. If I didn't know better I would think this was her real hair."

Blue just sucked his teeth, not wanting to admit that.

"Girl, don't pay any attention to him," Olarion said, waving a dismissive hand at Blue. "I'm just glad you went over there and enjoyed yourself. You *did* enjoy yourself, right? You didn't just go over there all cute just to sit in your room the whole time, did you?"

"Absolutely not," Tonette insisted. "I had an...*unforgettable* time." A wistful smile came to her face.

"Wow, really?" Blue marveled, observing the look. "You must have done *something*, the way you're over there smiling like that. Did you get to see a lot of the island?"

"Some, yeah."

"Just some? You were there for ten days."

Tonette's smile automatically spread into a grin and Olarion gasped excitedly, grabbing her arm. "Oh my god, you met somebody, didn't you??" She squealed when Tonette just continued to grin goofily. "*Hell* yes! Tell us about him!"

"His name is Troy," Tonette began, still smiling, "And he...he really, *really* showed me a good time while I was there."

"Awww snap! Somebody went to Barbados and got her back blown *out*!" Blue exclaimed with a hard clap of his hands at the word *out*. "I love it! Tell us what he was working with!"

"Blue!" Tonette exclaimed, but she was still smiling. "It wasn't about all of that! He was definitely attractive but it wasn't just about the physical with him...we actually got to know each other. We met on my first night there and just clicked right off the bat."

Olarion looked absolutely transfixed. "Girl," she hedged. "Did you go over there and fall in love?"

"No," Tonette quickly replied, her smile vanishing. "I didn't say that."

"But the look on your face and the wonder in your voice say otherwise."

Tonette didn't know how she had looked or sounded, but she kicked herself for it internally, anyway. "I'm *not* in love. We just had an awesome time, that's all."

"That's all, huh?"

"Yes, that's *all*."

Olarion looked at her skeptically. "So he showed you around?"

"Not really," Tonette replied thoughtfully, playing with the hem of her shirt. "I didn't even think to ask him to show me around, come to think of it."

"Mmm-hmm, you must've been too busy getting your sugar cube sucked on," Blue said mischievously.

"Blue!" Olarion and Tonette admonished.

"Whatever! You gonna try to tell us you didn't? 'Cause that glow you got going on ain't *all* from the island sun."

"For your information, we never even had sex," Tonette said defiantly.

"Aww, hell," Blue sucked his teeth, waving a hand dismissively as he leaned back in the armchair. "Where's the damn remote?"

"What, because I didn't have sex with him you don't want to hear anymore?" Tonette asked, amused.

"Pretty much."

"Y'all *seriously* didn't get busy?" Olarion asked Tonette. "Why the hell not?"

"It wasn't about that, y'all, I told you," Tonette defended. "We certainly fooled around but we just...never took it all the way. Well, not really," she added, remembering their last encounter.

Blue's eyes snapped to her. "What do you mean, *not really*? Either you got your salsa stirred or you didn't."

"Okay, well we did kind of slip up for a minute, but since he wasn't wearing any protection, we stopped."

"Oh my gosh! Are you pregnant?!" Olarion exclaimed.

Tonette scoffed. "No! This *just* happened yesterday!"

"So what??"

"I am not pregnant."

"You hope you're not."

"I'm *not*."

"So you went over there for ten days and didn't get busy once. What a damn waste," Blue shook his head, resuming his search for the remote.

"I didn't say I didn't *at all*. It just wasn't with Troy," Tonette admitted in a low voice.

"What??"

"After the way Troy and I left things, I was just looking for a way to work off some frustration. So I hooked up with this other guy that had been trying to get with me."

"And? How was it?" Blue asked expectantly.

"*That* was a waste. He was fine but he was just all about getting his."

"Aww damn, I hate that," Olarion shook her head. "I *hate* men that are selfish in bed!"

"Yeah, me too. So I just kicked him out and broke out the vibrator."

"Girl..."

"So tell us some more about this Troy," Blue said, locating the remote under his chair and holding it in his hand. "There had to be something about him that has you over here looking like a lovesick puppy."

Tonette tried not to smile, but she couldn't help it. She told them all about Troy and her time with him, from how they met on the dance floor her first night in Barbados to how they had to part sooner than expected the day before she left. The only thing she didn't tell them about was how she had been pretending to be someone named Toni the whole time. Part of her was still a little embarrassed about that.

"Girl, that is beautiful," Olarion gushed when she finished. "This sounds like a true island romance."

"It was definitely something I won't be forgetting for a while," Tonette admitted.

"So when are you gonna call him? You want us to go so you can have some privacy?"

"Please! She can talk to him with us here," Blue scoffed. "Just put him on speakerphone for a minute or two so I can hear the accent. I've always had a thing for island accents."

"I'm not going to call him."

"*Fine*, dammit, we'll go, then," Blue grumbled, starting to stand up.

"No, I mean I'm not going to call him at *all*," Tonette clarified. "There's no need to."

Olarion frowned. "What do you mean, there's no need to? Why don't you want to call him?"

Tonette shrugged. "I just...figure that what happened in Barbados needs to stay in Barbados. It's done."

"Why? Are you mad at him or something because he didn't spend that last day with you?"

"No! I mean, I was upset about that but I definitely understood it...that was something that couldn't be helped. I just don't want to fool myself into thinking that what we shared over there can turn into something now that I'm back here. It's just not realistic."

"Girl, him being in Barbados doesn't mean that you two can't have something; there are planes going back and forth between here and there all the time," Olarion said. "And especially since it sounds like you two developed some real feelings for each other...when was the last time you felt like you feel about Troy for *anyone*?"

Tonette knew it had been a while; years, even. She hadn't even been on a decent date in months. That was mostly by choice, though, and she knew it...she just didn't put much effort into meeting men. She had honestly been content with being on her own, not feeling like she was missing anything.

But after her time with Troy, she was thinking differently. It had only been a little over a day since she had seen Troy but she already missed him something terrible, and she knew that wasn't something that was going away any time soon.

But like she had tried and failed to do in Barbados, she knew she needed to just make herself get used to being without Troy. Her vacation was over...it was time to get back to reality. Toni was gone, and Toni was who Troy had really been so taken with. Tonette figured that now that she was back home and didn't have to worry about Troy showing up out of the blue anymore, getting over him would be a lot easier.

"I can answer that," Blue piped up. "Since I thought I still liked women."

"It hasn't been *that* long, Blue, stop exaggerating!" Tonette protested.

"But it *has* been a while, Tonette, and I don't see why you would want to just throw this away like that," Olarion said with concern in her voice. "You two could make it work if you really wanted to. From what you told us, he sounds sincere and like he really fell for you. And you definitely have feelings for him. I mean, what's holding you back?"

I'm not who he fell for, Tonette thought to herself. *He fell for Toni, and I'm just Tonette.*

"It's just...best to leave well enough alone," Tonette evaded, turning her eyes to the television Blue still hadn't turned on. "We had a great time but...now it's over. I can just be happy with the memories."

"Humph. Those *memories* aren't gonna be doing anything for you when you're rolling around in your bed at night with that vibrator of yours," Blue scoffed. "Ain't nothing like the real thing. And you *can* have the real thing, you know."

"I know."

"Seriously," Blue's deep voice dropped as he turned to fully face her, resting his elbows on his knees. "What's up, baby? I can tell there's something you're not telling us."

Tonette bit her lip. Part of her wanted to divulge everything to her friends; surely they would understand why she had done what she did, with the whole Toni persona. She had already said she wanted to go over there and be someone else. But there was another part of her that just felt silly about all of it, not to mention guilty. It would have been one thing if she had just had a one-night fling with Troy and left it at that, but they had spent extended time together, had spent hours talking and getting to know each other, and he thought he was getting one person when he had really been getting someone who didn't even exist, and Tonette couldn't pretend that wasn't the case. She didn't want to keep in contact with Troy and keep up the whole Toni charade any longer than she already had. It was best to just leave things as they were.

"I'd rather just put my energy into meeting someone that I can actually see more than once every few months or so," Tonette replied, even though she hadn't even thought about such a thing. Now that she said it, though, it wasn't such a bad idea. She would love to meet someone with whom she shared the same connection and passion that she had shared with Troy in Barbados. But something told her that wouldn't be as easy as she hoped it would.

"But you don't even have any prospects here, do you?" Olarion asked gently. "You really only go out with us and you never pay the men that approach you any attention."

"I've even offered to set you up a few times and you weren't trying to hear it," Blue added. "I thought you just *liked* being by yourself or something."

"I wouldn't say that...I'm just comfortable with my life the way it is," Tonette replied, her spirits sinking slowly. It was the first time the fact that she had no prospects was actually pointed out to her and to her surprise, she felt a little dejected. She had really never even given it any thought before then.

"Tonette, girl," Olarion shook her head. "I just don't see how you can come back to *nothing* after what you shared with Troy. That sounds like something out of a love story. A connection like that is rare, girl. It's the kind I hope to have with whoever I end up with. Speaking of that, I'm going to this bridal show next weekend. Can you go with me?"

"Sure," Tonette replied distractedly, still lost in her thoughts.

"Two single-ass women going to a bridal show," Blue shook his head, finally turning on the television. "I still don't get that shit."

"The right man is coming, Blue. And when he does and puts that ring on my finger, I'll already know how I want our wedding to go," Olarion explained, as she did every time her friends teased her for her constant wedding planning even though she had no man. "Doing all of this now is going to save me a whole lot of stress and headaches later."

"Uh-huh. Or you'll be even *more* of a pain whenever you actually *do* get engaged. Your ass is just obsessed with weddings."

"I am not!"

"The hell."

The two of them continued to go back and forth while Tonette pondered her own love life, or lack thereof. When she thought about it, she *didn't* want to go back to just nothing but her friends and her work and books occupying her time; she didn't want to go back to plain old Tonette. She had enjoyed being Toni; being bold and flirtatious and confident and comfortable in her own skin had been a refreshing and welcome reprieve. But for whatever reason, she didn't know if she knew how to do that now that she was back home.

Tonette didn't have to go back to work for another week, and she fell right back into her regular routine of getting up, working out, running errands, and then either hanging out with Blue and Olarion or spending the evenings at home reading or watching movies. It was something she did without thinking; her earlier declarations to herself that she was going to put more effort into meeting someone to spend her time with were temporarily forgotten. She had already settled back into being Tonette. The only thing that remained of Toni and her Barbados vacation was the weave that she still wore, which she didn't have taken out until it was time to go back to work.

Despite how much she might have wanted to, Tonette couldn't make herself stop thinking about Troy. Every day and hour they spent together was constantly replaying through her mind as if it were on repeat. She saw those eyes of his that always seemed to sear into her every time she closed her eyes. Truth be told, she would have loved to have talked to him again; she missed him more than she dared to admit. In what she hoped would be an exercise to deal with her feelings, she wrote him several letters, none of which she planned to mail. She just wanted a way to get her feelings out, in a way that she still didn't feel comfortable expressing to her friends. Thankfully, the process worked some, even though she knew she could write a thousand letters and still miss Troy a great deal. Nothing but time would help her get over that.

What she did do, though, was get him a birthday card, remembering him tell her his birthday was coming up. She figured she could send it without a return address or even a name; part of her figured he might know it was from her (or Toni). But as she signed the card with a simple 'Happy birthday from you-know-who' and stuck the card in the pale purple envelope, she hesitated as she adhered a stamp to it. His contact information was sitting right there on her desk, staring up at her. He had given her his phone number, email address, home address...several ways to get in touch with him. He hadn't even asked her for any of her information. It had been over a week since she returned from Barbados; she wondered how much time would have to pass before he forgot about her.

Biting her lip, she wrote out Troy's name and address, and mindlessly scribbled her address in the top left corner. She hadn't really planned on doing that, but figured there was no harm in it...she wasn't even sure if she was actually going to mail the card, anyway. She lightly ran her fingers over Troy's name and released a long sigh. The yearning for this adorably sexy man with the intense brown eyes hadn't waned yet. She wanted him to have the card, and smiled when she imagined the look on his face when he received it. But would sending it be opening a can of worms she was trying her best to close?

Not wanting to think about it anymore, she stuck the card and Troy's contact information in her desk.

It was nearing the end of the school year, and Tonette was glad to see her students again. She was back to her own natural hair, her own regular clothes, and her own life as it was before Barbados.

"How was your trip, Ms. Andersen?" Joey, one of her students, wasted no time asking her.

"It was wonderful," Tonette smiled. "I had an awesome time. Barbados is a beautiful island; it was *so* much fun."

"Did you do like that author lady that made that movie did and bring some man back with you?" another student asked.

Tonette laughed at the reference to one of her favorite authors, Terry McMillan. "No, I didn't bring anybody back with me."

"Did you get married?"

"Absolutely not."

"Do you even have a boyfriend?"

Tonette wasn't comfortable with where this line of questioning was headed. "I think we need to get on with the lesson for today, guys," she averted, actually embarrassed for some reason to admit to her students that she was single. "Go ahead and take out your textbooks..."

"Aww, are you gonna make us do *work* today?" Amy asked with a groan. "This is the end of the year; we should be taking it easy!"

"I can't be sure you're ready for the seventh grade if I do that, now can I?" Tonette winked, standing from where she had been perched on the edge of her desk. "Now who can tell me what you went over while I was away?"

The simple question 'do you even have a boyfriend?' stayed on Tonette's mind the rest of the day. It had been asked as if there would be something wrong with her if she didn't at *least* have a boyfriend to speak of, since she hadn't gone and brought a husband back with her from Barbados like Terry McMillan had from Jamaica. It was almost as if Tonette was a failure or something or her vacation had been a waste since she hadn't gone and gotten her proverbial groove back.

After work, Tonette went to the gym, even though she had already worked out before work that morning. She knew Blue and Olarion were busy, and she didn't want to just go back to her apartment so she could sit and stew about Troy and her lack of a love life. As she slipped a t-shirt over her head and some sweats over her legs, she noted how different her workout clothes were from Toni's...Tonette didn't quite feel comfortable showing off the great body she had worked so hard for, but Toni had flaunted it. Tonette knew she would never have the nerve to walk up in her gym here at home in nothing but a sports bra and some teeny-tiny shorts like she had worn in Barbados.

"Hey, I haven't seen you around lately," a guy she sometimes worked out with, Stanley, greeted her. He draped his towel over the weight bench next to hers and set his jug of water down on the ground, smiling at her as he adjusted his workout gloves.

"Oh, yeah I've been on vacation," Tonette responded, returning his smile before refocusing on her form in the mirror as she did dumbbell curls.

"Where'd you go?"

"Barbados."

"Yeah? I've been there; I bet you had a good time, huh?"

Tonette couldn't help but smile wider. "Yeah, I had a great time. You've been doing all right?"

"I can't complain. Hasn't been the same here without my workout partner, though," he winked at her, taking a seat on the bench.

Tonette felt her cheeks flush. Was he flirting? *Nah, couldn't be*, she internally dismissed.

She and Stanley continued to make small talk as they worked out, each spotting the other and even getting on side-by-side treadmills. When they were winding down, Stanley did something Tonette totally wasn't expecting; he asked her out.

"Hey, you want to go get something to eat?" he asked her when she had emerged from the locker room, her duffel bag thrown over her shoulder.

It was a casual enough question but it still sent Tonette's nerves into overdrive. She hadn't been prepared for this and found herself totally flustered.

"Oh! I umm...thank you but I can't. I mean, I should get on home. Stuff, uhh...stuff to do, you know?"

Stanley looked a little taken aback, but nodded. "Yeah, it's cool. No problem. Just thought I'd ask..."

"Sorry. Um, see you later," Tonette stammered, rushing past him towards the exit. As soon as he was behind her, she squeezed her eyes shut in embarrassment. She had acted like a complete idiot just because he had asked her out to eat. It's not like he was asking her on a real date. He probably thought she was some kind of novice who had never been with a man before, and Tonette wished she could hit the rewind button and do that whole scene over again. Toni was always so smooth when she dealt with men; why couldn't Tonette be the same way?

Chapter 7

"Girl, it was so embarrassing," Tonette confided in Olarion the next day as she was leaving work. She was recanting the episode with Stanley from the previous night, still blushing at how flustered she had become. "I still can't believe I reacted like that. You would think I'd never been asked out before."

"Maybe he just caught you off guard," Olarion suggested. "Could your mind have been on a certain Bajan named Troy, perhaps?"

"This has nothing to do with Troy," Tonette quickly insisted, even though she suspected Olarion knew better. She held her cell phone to her ear as she deactivated the alarm on her car. "Stanley and I usually just work out together whenever we happen to be at the gym at the same time but that's it; we never try to do anything outside of that. Like you said, I was just caught off guard."

"Well, I'm sure it's not as bad as you're making it sound like," Olarion said. "You know we usually think we make bigger fools out of ourselves than we actually do. I'm sure he hasn't thought any more about it."

"I don't know if that makes me feel better or worse."

"I wouldn't worry about it, girl. I'm sure he'll ask you out again and when he does, *accept*!"

"It was a reflex! It's not like I *planned* to say no!"

"Well, there's nothing you can do about it now. But let me ask you this; are you even attracted to him?"

Tonette started her car engine but made no move to put it in gear. She just turned up the air conditioning and sat back in the driver's seat. "Honestly? I've never really looked at him like that. He was always just a guy at the gym."

"Okay, well start looking. He might be just what you need to get back out there, girl."

"Maybe," Tonette said thoughtfully, though she didn't quite believe it. Stanley was a nice guy, and she could even say she enjoyed his company as they worked out, but once she left the gym, she never thought about him again until she saw him there the next time. There were no sparks, no butterflies, no raw magnetism sucking her in like there had been with...

"But anyway, how was your date last night?" she asked, trying to deter her thoughts from its pointless destination.

"Girl, it was great! Aaron took me to see that comedy show at Philips Arena. I'm tired as hell today but it was worth it."

"Y'all got back late?"

"Yeah, girl, you know those shows hardly ever start on time. We were waiting for damn near an hour for the first set to start. Then there was some accident on the way home so we got stuck in traffic, and decided to just stop and get something to eat instead of sitting on the highway. I didn't get home until almost three in the morning."

"But you enjoyed yourself, though, right?"

"Oh yeah, I'm not complaining. I've had about three Crunk Juices, though," Olarion chuckled. "Good thing I own my own business and can take a nap during the day when I want to."

Tonette giggled. "So when are you going to see him again?"

"Hell, hopefully tonight! He might be coming by after we all meet Blue's new boo."

"Blue has a *new boo* every other month."

"Now you and I both know that Blue has it going on. Sometimes I still look at him and shake my head that no woman gets to enjoy all that."

"I can't argue with you there," Tonette agreed. When she had first met Blue years before, she was extremely attracted to him with his smooth dark skin, tall strong body and lips that automatically made you want to lick yours, but she was shocked when she found out that he was probably more into men than she was. She and Olarion often joked that they wanted to at least get to feel what those lips of his felt like one time.

"You gonna go on to the gym? I'm on my way to Zumba now," Olarion said.

"Zumba? I thought you would be doing Crossfit today."

"Please, I don't have the energy for Crossfit. I'd drop a damn kettlebell on my foot or something, as tired as I am. Zumba will do it for me today."

"Oh okay. Well yeah, I had planned on going to the gym but I admit I'm kind of nervous about possibly seeing Stanley."

"Girl, you don't have to be nervous. If you see him, just act like you always do; don't even bring up what happened last night. If you don't treat it like a big deal, he won't either."

"Maybe you're right."

"I'm sure I am. Call me when you get home."

"All right, see you later. Love you."

"Love you back."

They ended the call and Tonette leaned her head against her headrest, sighing. Olarion had a point; if she saw Stanley, she didn't have to bring up her blubbering episode from the previous night. Hopefully he wouldn't use that as an excuse not to speak to her or ask her out again. If he did, Tonette told herself she would accept his invitation and hope for the best.

To her disappointment, though, Stanley never showed up. Tonette worked out for close to two hours, but she never saw him. She was a little embarrassed that she had even been looking for him, and told herself not to get all paranoid and think that he wasn't there because he was avoiding her.

She headed home so she could get showered and changed before Olarion, Blue, and his new man came by. When they arrived, Tonette immediately took in the brown sugared hotness that was Blue's current flavor of the month. For the life of her, Tonette would never understand where Blue always pulled such fine men from.

"This is Corey," Blue introduced, clamping a hand on his date's shoulder. "Corey, these are my girls, Tonette and Olarion."

"It's nice to meet you ladies," Corey greeted, taking each of their hands and kissing it. Tonette and Olarion shared a look among them, sharing their silent approval as far as his looks went. His hazel eyes sparkled as he and Blue stood closely next to each other, each with their hands in their pockets. Blue had long ago told them that he didn't go for effeminate men; you would never look at either Blue or Corey and think that they were anything but straight.

"Come on in and sit down; I'm heating up some turkey meatballs I made, if any of y'all are hungry," Tonette offered.

"We'll definitely stay for that; I love those things," Blue said. "We're going to be going to a party in a while, though, so we won't be here all that long. I just wanted to bring him by so he can meet my people."

They all sat and made small talk as Tonette and Olarion did their usual routine of subtly goading information out of Corey, just like they did whenever Blue brought his dates around to meet them. He would never say it out loud, but he liked to get their approval for whoever it was he was seeing; he loved Olarion and Tonette like they were his own blood and sincerely cared about what they thought. Plus, he always joked that he wanted them to know who to look for if he ever came up missing.

"Whatever happened with that dude you blew off?" Blue asked Tonette, popping another meatball into his mouth. "Was he at the gym when you went today?"

"No," Tonette replied, trying to keep the dejection out of her voice. "And I did not blow him off."

"That's what it sounded like when you described it to me."

"Well, I didn't."

"He's gonna ask her out again," Olarion chimed in confidently. "And when he does, Tonette is gonna say *yes*." She looked at Tonette pointedly.

Blue sucked his teeth. "Do you even like the man, Tonette?"

"I like him okay, yeah," Tonette replied with a shrug of her shoulder. "He's all right."

"Wow. And you mean to tell me you didn't knock him off his feet with all of *that* eagerness??"

Tonette rolled her eyes at his sarcasm but she couldn't resist chuckling. Corey was trying to suppress a smile, also. "Shut up, Blue."

"I'm just saying. I hope you have more enthusiasm than that when you're around buddy. 'Cause that sounded about as dry as these meatballs would've been if Olarion had tried to make 'em."

Olarion gasped as Corey laughed out loud, not being able to help it. "Excuse you! I can cook, damn it!" Olarion exclaimed.

"Your shit gave me food poisoning, O. Don't act like you forgot that."

"That was *one* time!"

"How many times do you need??"

"I'm sayin', I've gotten a whole lot better since then. You don't have to keep holding that over my damn head."

"And *I'm* sayin', if you want to get a husband you better learn how to cook stuff that won't send him to the damn E.R."

Tonette had been trying her best not to laugh, but she couldn't hold it in anymore. She and Corey fell against each other on the couch, laughing hysterically. Olarion just glared at them with her arms folded.

"All three of y'all can kiss my beautiful yellow ass," she mumbled. "And Corey, you are no longer cool with me. Get out."

"Hold up, this is *my* apartment!" Tonette reminded her, still laughing. "You can't be kicking folks out!"

"Whatever!"

"Bitch, save that saltiness for your pasta and come over here and give me some sugar," Blue teased, grabbing Olarion's arm and playfully yanking her over to him. She rolled her eyes, but couldn't resist grinning when he wrapped his arms around her and planted a big kiss on her cheek.

Everyone left a while later, and Tonette was again alone with her thoughts. As she cleaned up the dishes, her mind again drifted to Troy. He would fit in so well with her friends, she thought...she already knew Blue and Olarion would like him. Everything in her wanted to hear his voice again; she didn't know what it would take to fully get him out of her system but she knew she wasn't anywhere near that point yet. He had managed to dig himself a deeper place inside of her in the ten days she had been in Barbados than other people had managed to do in months or years.

Wandering into her office, she got the paper with his contact information on it out of her desk and bit her lip, turning it around in her hands. She picked up her cell phone and started to dial his number, then stopped. What would she even say? If she called, she would have to continue the whole *Toni* charade, and she didn't want to do that. Ideally she would like to just come clean with him, but doing that over the phone after the time they had spent together would seem cowardly. And since it wasn't like she could just hop on a plane and fly back to Barbados to tell him to his face, she figured it was best to just leave things as they were. Especially since she didn't think she would have the nerve to be honest with him in person, either.

Sadly, she put her phone back down and stuck the paper back in her desk drawer. She knew she would just have to be satisfied with her memories.

Chapter 8

Tonette was just about to head out to work when she got a call from Olarion.

"Hey," Olarion greeted breathlessly. "You left yet?"

"I'm on my way out the door now. What's wrong?"

"I'm in the middle of filling this order and my stove went out," Olarion explained. She had a small baking business on the side, mostly just for family and friends. She might not have been much of a cook but she was an awesome baker. "I still have a hundred cupcakes I need to make by the end of the day."

"Girl, you know you're welcome to come over here and use my stove if you need to. It's no problem at all."

"Thank you *so* much, T! You are saving me!"

"Please, it's nothing. You have a key so just let yourself in whenever."

"I owe you, girl."

Tonette went on about her day, doing only a marginally better job of keeping her mind on what she was supposed to be doing rather than daydreaming about Troy or obsessing over messing up with Stanley. She looked forward to hanging out with her friends later on that evening at Chili's. She didn't know what she would do without them, as they had been her main support system for years. Her parents lived out of state, and she had no siblings. Tonette hadn't even realized how much she had grown to depend and lean on her friends until recently...she was the only one out of the three that didn't date regularly and always kind of felt like the odd one out because of it. And there was a small part of her that feared that they would each find someone and she would end up being alone, the tolerated fifth wheel.

Later on that day, Olarion called.

"Hey, I'm almost done here. Thank you again, girl."

"No problem at all. You got everything done?"

"Just about. Over a hundred German chocolate cupcakes; I'm exhausted. I still have a few more to frost and then I'm boxing them all up. I'll have everything cleaned up just the way you left it."

"I'm not worried about that. I'm just glad you were able to finish everything. Feel free to leave me a couple of those," she joked, though she meant it.

"You know I got you. They're already in the refrigerator."

"Yes, thank you! I'll have to put in some more time on the treadmill at the gym 'cause I *will* be scarfing those down later on."

Olarion chuckled. "Enjoy. You need me to do anything around here before I leave?"

"Nah, not really. Oh, come to think of it, there *are* a few bills in my office that I forgot to take by the post office. Can you run those by there for me?"

"Of course! Everything you need to be sent out is in your desk?"

"Yep, right in the top drawer. I appreciate it."

"No sweat. I don't know why you don't just get with the times and pay these things online, though."

"Guess I'm old school," Tonette laughed. "I still prefer letters to emails."

"Lord help her," Olarion joked. "Well regardless, I've got it covered. See you later on?"

"Yep, seven o'clock, right?"

"Yep. See you then. Love you."

"Love you back."

Tonette was feeling pretty good when she went to the gym and changed into her workout clothes. She was adjusting the heart rate monitor on her arm as she exited the locker room when she looked up and saw Stanley. She froze, her mouth opening to say something, but he just smiled at her as he kept on walking towards the cardio machines. Tonette blew out a breath. He didn't *seem* upset with her. Maybe Olarion had been right; maybe he hadn't thought much else about her bumbling refusal of his invitation the other night. She still wanted to apologize, but found she didn't quite know what to say. She didn't want to make it a big deal if he wasn't.

She proceeded with her workout, and eventually Stanley ended up next to her in the weights section. Tonette immediately tensed, but told herself to get it together and channel some of that Toni-esque confidence.

Eventually, Stanley spoke to her. "Hey, you done with the bench, Tonette?"

Get it together, girl, she admonished herself. "Yeah, I'm done."

"You mind spotting me?"

"Sure."

She waited for him to push the weight plates onto the bar before moving behind the bench as he laid down. She glanced down at him, trying to start really noticing his looks, as she never had before. He was rather good-looking; almond-brown skin, neatly trimmed goatee, deep-set dark eyes. As he repeatedly lifted the weights over his chest, Tonette allowed her eyes to drift to his muscles, which were nice and defined. A thin sheen of sweat covered his body, and Tonette could appreciate the stark contrast of his white tank top against his skin. He just kept lifting and those muscles just kept contracting over...and over...and over...

"Tonette?"

Startled, Tonette blinked in surprise. Her face flushed with embarrassment. *Could he tell I was checking him out?* "Huh?"

"That was twelve reps, right?"

She hadn't even been counting. "Yeah."

Stanley returned the bar to the stand and sat up, wiping his face with a towel. "You all right, girl?"

"Yeah, I'm fine," she replied quickly. "Why do you ask?"

"You just seem a little distracted, that's all."

"Oh. It's nothing...just wondering what I'm gonna eat when I leave here."

She was trying to lead him into asking her out again, figuring she didn't have all that much longer until he would be done with his workout. She didn't want the night to end without making some progress towards seeing or at least establishing contact with Stanley outside of the gym. It had become her mission without her even realizing it.

"Yeah, I'm gonna need to grab something, myself. I haven't eaten since breakfast."

"Me, either."

Stanley wordlessly laid down for another set, and Tonette tried to keep her concentration on spotting him instead of his physique. Actually counting his reps this time, she noted how his pace started to slow as his muscles began to fatigue, and she readied her hands under the bar as he pushed out the last couple of reps, gritting his teeth as he did so.

Nice teeth, she noted.

Sitting up again, Stanley took a long gulp of water from his jug and glanced at his watch. Tonette bit her lip and tried not to look as anxious as she felt.

"You all done?" she asked after a few moments.

"Yeah, I think that's gonna do it for me. It's been a long day," Stanley replied, wiping his face as he stood up.

He looks to be about 6'3 or so..."Oh, okay then."

"You have some more to do?" he asked her.

"Oh," Tonette paused, glancing at the weights behind her. She actually did, but didn't want to say so for fear that he might not want to hang around and wait on her. "Just...another couple of sets." *Toni wouldn't cut her workout short for a man*, she surmised silently. *She would be confident that he would wait for her.*

"That's cool. How 'bout I go get my stuff together and then we go grab something to eat? If you have time," Stanley offered, pulling off his workout gloves.

Yes! "Sure, that sounds good," she replied, temporarily forgetting about her plans to meet her friends at Chili's.

Stanley smiled, causing Tonette to smile. "Okay, great. Take your time; I'll meet you up by the front."

"Okay."

Tonette had to resist the urge to squeal in delight as Stanley headed off to the locker rooms. She tried to get her mind right to finish her workout, even though she now had no more interest in doing so. But she made herself go through her reverse flies and incline crunches as she would have done any other time, being sure not to rush. She felt so relieved that Stanley had invited her out again, and she was looking forward to going out with him and hopefully speeding up the getting-over-Troy process.

After her workout, she sent a text to Olarion to let her know she wouldn't be meeting her and Blue before she quickly freshened up in the locker room then headed towards the front of the gym, hoping Stanley hadn't grown impatient and left. But there he was, talking and laughing with one of the guys at the front desk. When he saw her approaching, he straightened up and smiled.

"You ready?" he asked her.

"Yep," Tonette smiled at him.

They both said good-bye to the front desk attendant before walking outside into the cool evening air, their respective duffel bags slung over their shoulders.

"You have a taste for anything in particular?" Stanley asked her.

"Not really." *Am I being too indecisive?*

"Okay. There's a Waffle House down the street. Is that okay?"

"Yeah, that's cool."

"Okay. Follow me," he said with a smile. "I'll walk you to your car, though."

They went on to the restaurant and had a nice enough time, but Tonette could admit that she didn't feel any butterflies like she had with Troy. Stanley was nice company, and she could even say she was mildly attracted to him, but he didn't conjure up the immediate impure thoughts that Troy had. Troy had her panties wet within the first few minutes without even trying; Tonette was wondering if she would even let Stanley kiss her good night, if he tried to.

But she told herself to get a grip. It was her first time hanging out with Stanley; this wasn't even a real date. He could very well grow on her over time, if they continued to hang out. Plus, he was cute, local, and better than nobody. And he knew her and seemed to like her as Tonette.

Most importantly, though, Troy was in Barbados. And he was going to remain in Barbados. So it didn't do any good to keep comparing everything to him, especially since she had a feeling nobody would be able to measure up.

Before they parted ways, Tonette and Stanley exchanged numbers, and Stanley suggested they get together the following weekend. Tonette agreed with a smile, telling herself to think positively.

A couple of days later, Tonette, Olarion, and Blue were hanging out at her place, eating pizza and watching movies. Blue had brought over some beers, and they all lounged on Tonette's couch, their legs entangled, pigging out as they talked about their latest respective dating tales. Even though Tonette's post-workout meal with Stanley hadn't been an official date, she was glad that she had something to contribute to the conversation, for once.

"I cannot believe y'all have got me up in here watching some *You've Got Mail*," Blue grumbled, taking a swig of his beer.

"What? This is a good movie!" Olarion defended. She nudged him with her bare foot. "Stop complaining. Oh, speaking of mail, Tonette, I got that stuff sent off for you like you asked."

"Thanks, girl, I appreciate it."

"Yep. I sent off that purple envelope, too, since it was all stamped and addressed and everything."

Gasping, Tonette shot up straight on the couch, a cold fear ripping through her body. "What? Are you serious??"

"Yeah," Olarion said slowly, confused as to what the big deal was. "It was with everything else so I figured it was supposed to go out, too. What's the problem?"

"Oh my god," Tonette muttered frantically, untangling her legs from her friends'. The purple envelope contained the birthday card she had gotten for Troy. "Oh my god, oh my god..."

She ran to her office and yanked open the top drawer, panic engulfing her when she realized the card was in fact gone. "*Oh my god!!*" she shrieked.

Blue and Olarion rushed into the office, both looking concerned and confused. "Girl, what's wrong?" Olarion asked.

Tonette had her hands in her hair, pacing the small room frantically. "This isn't happening," she kept repeating.

"You're gonna have to fill us in on what the issue is," Blue said, glancing around the office as if looking for anything that might explain Tonette's behavior. "'Cause you are seriously freaking out right now."

"Yes, Blue, I'm freaking out!" Tonette exclaimed, starting to feel herself hyperventilate. She placed one hand over her heaving chest and the other on her stomach, 'cause she felt like she might throw up. "Why did you do that??" she screamed at Olarion.

Olarion blinked, obviously surprised. "I...you *asked* me to send the bills out for you."

"Yes, *bills*! The purple envelope was obviously *not* a bill! That wasn't supposed to get sent!"

"I didn't know!"

"You should've *asked*!!"

"Tonette!" Blue grabbed her by her arms, trying to get her to stop pacing back and forth. "Tonette, look at me!"

Eventually, Tonette turned her eyes to her friend, her breathing still erratic and heavy.

"Calm down, baby," Blue instructed gently, cupping her face in his large hand. When Tonette's breathing returned somewhat back to normal, he asked, "Now what's up?"

"Yeah, girl, what did I do that was so terrible?" Olarion asked from behind Blue.

"That card..." Tonette began, trying to control her quivering voice, "Was to Troy."

"Troy? I thought you weren't going to contact him, though," Olarion said. "I admit, I didn't even look at the name on it."

"Hmph," Tonette scoffed, taking a seat on the edge of the desk. She buried her face in her hands.

"Baby, if you didn't want the card sent off, why did you buy it and address it and put a *stamp* on it?" Blue asked, hoping he wasn't sounding sarcastic.

Heaving a heavy sigh, Tonette dropped her hands. "I got him the card 'cause I knew his birthday was coming up, and thought it would be a nice surprise from me. But I changed my mind about actually sending it."

"Why?"

"Because it wouldn't actually be *from me*."

Olarion and Blue looked at each other, as confused as ever. "What in the world are you talking about?" Olarion asked.

Suddenly exhausted, Tonette trudged back into the living room, her friends right on her heels. Flopping down onto the couch, Tonette debated internally whether she should go ahead and come clean about her whole Barbados Toni persona. It was still a little embarrassing, but it was probably the only way to explain her reaction to Olarion mailing off that birthday card. Deciding there wasn't much point in continuing to hide it, she told them everything.

"Are you serious?" Olarion asked when she finished.

"So you weren't kidding when you said you wanted to go over there and be somebody else, huh?" Blue quipped. "Here I thought you were just talking about your hair and your clothes; I didn't know you meant *literally*."

"That wasn't my intent, either," Tonette insisted. "I didn't go there thinking I was going to give out a fake name and all that. But when I met Troy, *Toni* just came out when he asked what my name was. And I was too attracted to him to correct myself 'cause I didn't want to look silly. Then we started spending more time together, and I kept piling on the lies about certain things, and after a while I just didn't have the nerve to tell him the truth." She looked down at her hands shamefully. "And to be honest, I still don't."

"Girl," Olarion blew out a breath, putting an arm around her friend, "That's some wild stuff."

"Yeah."

"You can't just call him and tell him the real deal?" Blue asked. "It would probably be easier over the phone."

Tonette shook her head vehemently. "He deserves better than that," she replied wistfully. "Troy is...he's such a nice, good man. And he treated me with nothing but respect. I can't tell him over the phone that the time we spent together was basically one big lie. That just seems like a cowardly way out."

"But how else are you going to tell him, though? It's not like you're going back to Barbados any time soon," Olarion countered.

"I was just going to leave things as they were," Tonette answered. "I know it's still punking out, but at least we would both be left with good memories of each other. Our time together was special and beautiful...I don't want to mar it with all this."

"Tonette," Blue hedged, "Are you still gonna try to deny that you love this man?"

Tonette's eyes shot up. "I don't!"

"Why do you keep denying it? There's nothing wrong with it if you do."

"I care about Troy, a *lot*," Tonette admitted. "But I don't think I'm in love. I *can't* be. I was only there for ten days!"

"So what? Girl, love at first sight exists. And sometimes, you just *know*." Olarion squeezed her shoulder encouragingly.

Tonette looked at her friend, then looked away. That feeling that she got whenever she thought about Troy was spreading over her again. But even if she *was* in love with Troy, what difference would it make? She wouldn't even be seeing him again.

She sighed, feeling defeated.

"Look here, boo," Blue said, clasping a hand on her thigh. "I can feel where you're coming from with all this. And I guess I can see why you freaked out about Olarion mailing that card. But I really don't think you have anything to worry about, though. Was your name on the card?"

"No," Tonette grunted. "But my address was."

"Okay, well, still...he might know it was from you—"

"You mean *Toni*," Tonette corrected.

"Okay, fine. But what are the chances of it going beyond that? He'll read it, appreciate it, and keep jacking off to the thoughts of his time with the Georgia peach he tasted on. You're *good*. So please stop worrying and chill, okay?"

Tonette nodded, trying her best to believe Blue's words. She hoped with everything in her that they came true, and that somewhere between Atlanta and Barbados, that birthday card got lost in the mail.

Chapter 9

Tonette tried to steady her hands as she got ready for her date with Stanley. It wasn't her first date ever but it had been a while, and she was surprised at how nervous she was. She'd lost count of the number of times she told herself to calm down.

She knew her nervousness wasn't just about the date with Stanley, though; a large part of it was about Troy and what would come of it if and when he got that birthday card. She had no idea if he had any other acquaintances in Atlanta; he had never mentioned any. So the chances were pretty high that he would know it came from her. Would he just write her back? Tonette loved getting letters, but she didn't know if she wanted to start being pen pals with Troy, either. Maybe if it was as herself, but it wouldn't be; it would be as *Toni*. And she wouldn't have the heart to ignore him if he started trying to contact her. She groaned. She just couldn't help worrying that a can of worms had been opened that she wouldn't be able to close.

Taking a deep breath, she shook it off. There was no need in stressing over something she couldn't do anything about. And she wanted to concentrate on the man she was spending the evening with, not the one she *wished* she was spending the evening with.

Stanley came and picked her up, and they went to an outdoor concert where Stanley provided a blanket and a light meal he had packed of chicken salad, crackers, fruit, and sparkling cider. As they sat and nibbled and enjoyed the music, they talked about their backgrounds. Tonette had to admit it was a relief not having to conjure up things to say to try to make herself seem more interesting; everything she told Stanley about herself was the truth. He seemed interested, though, and it only made her wonder if Troy would have been just as interested in her as herself as he had been with her as Toni.

"Can I admit something?" Stanley asked, popping a cracker into his mouth and dusting the crumbs from his hands.

"Yeah, sure."

"I've actually wanted to ask you out for a while," Stanley said, leaning on his elbow and looking up at her. "You were always just so cute to me but I never really had the nerve to step to you like that."

Extremely flattered, Tonette blushed. "Really? I couldn't possibly make you nervous."

"You just kind of seemed like you didn't want to be bothered," Stanley revealed. "Not in like a mean way or anything, but like you were just there to handle business and that was it. You know how a lot of people spend more time socializing and taking selfies in the mirror than they do actually working out...you weren't about that. Guess I just didn't want to hear you tell me to leave you alone." Stanley chuckled.

"Wow," Tonette marveled, still blushing. She had no idea Stanley had been looking at her like that. When she thought about it, she couldn't even really remember when they started working out together; it had just kind of happened.

"But I'm glad I finally asked you out, though," Stanley said, gazing up at her with a look that made Tonette blush even harder and avert her eyes. "I'm having a good time with you."

Making herself turn her eyes back to his, Tonette gave him a timid but sincere smile. "I'm having a good time with you, too."

They continued to enjoy the music and each other's company, and Tonette found her attraction to Stanley slowly growing. There were a couple of times she started to compare him to Troy and she quickly stopped herself; doing that wouldn't get her anywhere. Stanley might not have ignited the fire in her that Troy did, but she still found him attractive and nice to hang out with.

When the concert was drawing to a close, Stanley asked Tonette if she wanted to go out dancing, which she immediately declined.

"I just have to get up really early tomorrow, and it's already kinda late," she said. "Sounds like fun, though."

"No problem. Maybe another time, then?"

"Sure. Maybe."

The truth was, Tonette was too self-conscious to dance in front of him. This wasn't Barbados and she couldn't rely on the island air and rum to boost her confidence. *Toni* might not have had a problem tearing up the dance floor, but that was something Tonette had never been all that comfortable doing.

Stanley took Tonette home and walked her to her door. Tonette had her hands clasped nervously in front of her, nervous about what was going to happen when they got there. Would he try to kiss her? He hadn't really tried any kind of displays of affection all evening; the most he had done was place a hand at the base of her back when they were walking to his car after the concert. Tonette might've been attracted to Stanley but she hadn't thought about what it would be like to kiss him, and when they arrived at her door and he leaned down to plant one on her, she turned her head at the last second so his lips ended up somewhere between her cheek and her temple.

Stanley looked mildly surprised, but he recovered quickly. "Did you enjoy yourself tonight?" he asked her.

"I really did," Tonette replied sincerely. "Thank you for such a nice evening. I've never been to an outdoor concert before."

"I'm glad you had a good time," Stanley said, sliding his hands into his pockets. "I did, too."

Tonette smiled up at him, not quite knowing what to say to that.

"I'll call you?" Stanley said after a few slightly awkward moments.

"I'd like that."

Cupping her chin in his hand, Stanley placed a soft kiss on her forehead before stepping back. "Good night, Tonette."

"Good night. And thanks again."

Stanley just winked at her before walking back to his car. Tonette watched him for a moment, then entered her apartment with slightly shaking hands, letting out a relieved breath.

That went well enough, she thought to herself, kicking her shoes off and tossing her purse onto the couch. Overall, she had enjoyed her time with Stanley. He had showed her a nice evening, he had been a gentleman the entire time, and he respected it without protest when she declined his invitation to extend the evening together. But what was that mess at the door? Why didn't she just go ahead and kiss him? Was it because he didn't intrigue her and arouse her like Troy did? Stanley was not at all hard on the eyes...kissing him wouldn't have been a bad thing. *Toni* certainly would have laid one on him.

"Oh well," she muttered, scratching her scalp thoughtfully. "Nothing I can do about it now." She could only hope that Stanley didn't take it as too much of a snub and use that as an excuse to not call her again.

Any worries she had about that were assuaged the next day when Stanley called her after work, inviting her out to dinner. Mildly surprised, thinking he might be upset with her (even though he seemed fine when he had called her the previous night after he got home), she accepted.

It was going to be an early dinner, though, and Tonette didn't have time to go home and change into anything cuter than what she had worn to work. Immediately self-conscious, Tonette wondered how it would look if she called and pushed the date back, or postponed it altogether.

But that would be silly, doing that just because of her outfit; surely Stanley would know she was just coming from work.

She was chewing her lip, wondering how she was going to handle this self-induced crisis when Olarion called.

"Hey girl," she greeted. "You want to hang out tonight?"

"I thought you were going out with Aaron tonight." Aaron was Olarion's new man.

"I was, but he got called in to work. You wanna come over?"

"I can if you'll let me borrow an outfit; Stanley invited me out for an early dinner but I don't want to wear what I have on, and you live closer."

"Ooh, snap! The second date already?" Olarion squealed excitedly. "He must really like you!"

"Kinda looks like he does, huh?" Tonette said with a small smile.

"Do you like *him*?"

Tonette shrugged at the question. "So far, yes. He's a nice guy and good company."

"A nice guy and good company," Olarion repeated. "That sounds very...generic."

"Well, what am I supposed to say?"

"Ask me that same question about Aaron, if I like him or not," Olarion urged.

"I figure you do, considering you're in a relationship with him."

"Just ask me."

Tonette sighed, knowing where she was going with this. "Okay, fine. Do you like Aaron?"

"Girl, *yes*!" Olarion enthusiastically replied. "I *love* spending time with him! Every time he calls me it just brightens up my day!"

"Okay, okay, point taken. No need to get all Hallmark on me."

"I meant everything I said, though," Olarion assured her. "And I know you've only been out with Stanley on one *real* date so far and things take time, but I just don't get that vibe that you're really interested in him, you know? Its like he's just someone to hang out with or something."

Tonette was quiet as she pondered her friend's words.

"Tonette?" Olarion called out. "You're not just seeing Stanley because you don't think you can find anybody else, are you? I mean, if you don't like the man..."

"I like him," Tonette protested. "But like you said, we've only been on one real date. Sometimes the attraction and stuff takes time to build. And anyway, weren't you the main one urging me to go out with him since I didn't have any other prospects?"

"Yeah, I meant give him a chance, not lead him on if you're not sincerely interested after you have."

"I'm not!"

"Okay, good; I'm glad to hear that. 'Cause that's not doing either one of you any good. And you're right; sometimes people have to grow on you. It can't always be instant fire like you said it was with Troy."

Tonette closed her eyes, the image of Troy coming towards her on dance floor her first night in Barbados playing in her mind like a tortuous tease. She shook her head to clear the image. "I plan on giving Stanley a real chance;

I'm actually looking forward to seeing him later. So can I borrow something to wear from you? This school-maiden outfit is a little less cute than I want to be on a second date."

Olarion chuckled. "You know you can borrow something, girl. Come on."

Tonette felt a lot better donning the cute orange maxi dress, light denim jacket, and sandals that she had borrowed from Olarion. She remembered her friend's words about giving Stanley a sincere chance, which she had begun to question if she had actually been doing, despite her insistence that she was. Telling herself to put everything else out of her mind and just concentrate on Stanley, she met up with him at a Japanese restaurant for dinner.

It was another pleasant evening. Stanley was a gentleman, as usual. They talked about their childhoods, their jobs, various likes and things that they had in common. Tonette found herself laughing a lot, genuinely enjoying herself. She even let him talk her into trying some kind of sushi that she wouldn't have dared try otherwise; he fed her from his chopsticks, his other hand hovering underneath, as he watched her face for a reaction.

Chewing thoughtfully, Tonette slowly nodded. "It's actually not bad. You didn't tell me it was this spicy, though." She reached for her water.

"I thought you might like it spicy."

Tonette almost choked on her water and Stanley immediately reached over and patted her hard on the back. She grabbed a napkin and covered her mouth with it, hoping that the flush she felt in her cheeks wasn't noticeable. Stanley's comment might very well have been totally innocent, but she couldn't help but take it as some kind of flirtatious innuendo. And she wasn't sure how she felt about that. But she wasn't going to waste time over-analyzing it, like she had a tendency to do with things.

"You all right?" Stanley asked her, concerned.

"Yeah, I'm fine, thanks," she smiled sheepishly, giving her lips another pat with the napkin before placing it on the table in front of her. "Guess it just...went down the wrong pipe."

"Oh, okay," Stanley eyed her as he played with his chopsticks. The look on his face was thoughtful.

"What's wrong?" Tonette asked self-consciously after a few moments of him staring, figuring maybe something was on her face or something else on her was amiss.

"Nothing at all." He paused, as if hesitating whether or not he should say what he wanted to say next. "I...I like you, Tonette. A lot."

An automatic smile came to Tonette's face, and she felt her cheeks heat up again. *Toni never blushed this easily.* "Stanley...I am *so* flattered by that," she said sincerely. "I like you, too."

Smiling, Stanley's shoulders relaxed some in relief. "I really look forward to getting to know you better."

"I feel the same way."

His smile widening, he reached over and took her hand. "Good."

Tonette smiled at him, telling herself that she really meant everything that she had just said.

Stanley had a very early meeting the next morning, so they called it a night not too long after that. He walked

Tonette to her car, and Tonette was very aware of how close he was to her. And how good he smelled. Getting closer to Stanley wouldn't at all be a chore; he might not have been the one she yearned for and fantasized about, but she tried to have confidence that that would change over time. Why wouldn't it, if they continued to spend time together? She really did like him; she just wasn't on fire for him yet.

"I have to get up early tomorrow but I'll give you a call before I go to bed, all right?" he told her when they reached her car.

"That sounds good," Tonette smiled up at him. "Thank you for another lovely evening."

"My pleasure." He gave her a firm hug then gazed down at her, his eyes straying to her lips, and Tonette knew he was going to try to kiss her again. Preparing herself for it, she told herself not to turn her face away if he did.

Sure enough, Stanley leaned down and pressed his lips against hers. Tonette allowed it, even enjoyed it a little, but she found herself subtly pulling her head back after a couple of seconds. Stanley looked at her with question in his eyes, but she smiled at him, hoping he wasn't taking it personally.

Stepping back a little, Stanley stuffed one hand in his pocket and scratched the back of his head with the other. "Tonette, I hope you don't mind me asking but in light of what we talked about a little while ago...are you seeing anyone else?"

Her eyes widening at the unexpected question, Tonette's heart quickened. She felt caught, even though she certainly *wasn't* seeing anybody else. Could he possibly tell that another man was on her mind at times when they were together?

"No, I'm not," she managed to answer evenly. "Are you?"

"No. I *hope* to only see you." He looked at her intently and she tried not to squirm under his gaze. "I just wanted to be sure if I was up against anything."

Tonette bit her lip. He *was* up against something, but she didn't want to not date at all simply because her heart and body still yearned for Troy. That was something she would have to deal with herself; Stanley didn't need to know about that. It's not like it would become a real problem between them.

"You don't have anything to worry about, Stanley, in regards to that," Tonette assured him, placing a hesitant hand on his chest. "I wouldn't waste your time. I enjoy spending time with you and I look forward to more of it. I just...I guess I just like to move kind of slowly, that's all. Is that okay?"

Stanley looked at her for a few moments before a slow smile eased onto his face, and his hand closed around hers. He seemed satisfied with her explanation. "I can get with that. As long as I know we're on the same page, I can move as slowly as you need me to."

Actually relieved to hear that, Tonette smiled up at him. "Good."

They parted ways a few minutes later, and Tonette drove home thoughtfully. She was glad that he was willing to go slow, but she couldn't help but wonder if he would eventually get bored with her. There were many times when she was with Stanley that Tonette simply just didn't know what to say, and that made for several awkward lulls in the conversation. She didn't know if Stanley noticed that or not, or if it bothered him, but Tonette hoped that they, or *she*, would get past this initial awkward phase and she would loosen up some more around him. She wished for that Toni-Troy connection and rapport, but knew she would have to make the best of what she had.

Stanley's kiss had been nice, but not skin-tingling. She hadn't felt much of anything, really, and tried not to take that as a bad sign. That didn't have to mean anything. Maybe she just had so much going on in her head that she *couldn't* enjoy it like she might have otherwise. She couldn't help but wonder if and when Stanley would try to get her into bed. Tonette's sexual experience was existent, but not vast. Her partners could be counted on two hands, and that was including the little tryst with Emmitt before leaving Barbados. But her relative lack of experience didn't mean there was a lack of desire; she had *plenty* of that. She thought and fantasized about sex way more than she actually had it. Tonette had never been one for one night stands (Emmitt excluded) and she just never felt comfortable with most of the men she dated to go there with them. Maybe it was due to her somewhat conservative upbringing; her mother always emphasized being respectable and being a lady and all of that. Sleeping around just didn't seem to fit into that kind of teaching.

Getting physical with Stanley had yet to cross her mind. But there had yet to be a night where she hadn't thought about all of her passionate times with Troy, and pleasured herself to the image of them finishing what they started. She could only hope that subsided in time, but she was fully intent to enjoy it while it lasted.

Chapter 10

Over the next couple of weeks, Tonette and Stanley continued to date and get to know each other. They worked out together, either went to the movies or watched DVDs at each other's place, or met up for dinner somewhere after work. Tonette even cooked for him once, which seemed to only endear her to Stanley more. Tonette could admit she was enjoying the time with Stanley; a smile would come to her face when he called her, and she always looked forward to seeing him. She and Stanley seemed pretty similar, personality-wise...he was pretty low-key like she was. Some might even call him boring, as Olarion had hinted at when Tonette would recount their dates to her. Olarion might have needed a little more excitement and creativity when it came to dating, but Tonette was fine with the quiet evenings at home and somewhat predictable dinners, at the end of which she always thanked Stanley for a lovely evening. That's what she always called it; a lovely evening. Lovely...like Troy referred to her.

Maybe she needed to come up with another adjective.

As far as the physical with Stanley went, kissing was as far as they had gone. Maybe some very, very light petting on occasion, but that was about it. Tonette had hoped that by now some kind of internal embers for Stanley would start lighting, but that hadn't happened yet. She didn't understand it. It wasn't like she wasn't physically attracted to Stanley; he was definitely handsome and she knew from all the workouts they had done together that he took care of himself. She remembered how she had wanted to give her body to Troy the first night she met him. What made him so different? She hated to compare the two men, but she felt that might be the only way to figure out why she couldn't seem to get over one and focus on the other.

One night, while she was bit her nails and half-watched a movie alone in her apartment as she mulled for the millionth time over her situation, Olarion and Blue called her on three-way to insist that it was time they meet Stanley.

"Absolutely not," Tonette immediately protested.

"Why the hell not?" Blue exclaimed.

"Because it's not time for all that yet. Stanley and I are really still just friends at this point. We haven't become official or anything."

"So what? You still spend more of your evenings with him than you do without him. Y'all are *dating*. That counts," Blue countered.

"Yeah, but...still."

"Tonette, it's not like we're going to interrogate the man," Olarion chimed in. "We just want to meet him, that's all. Just something casual, like when Blue brought Corey over."

"Oh yeah, that's over with, by the way," Blue interjected.

"Aww, hell. *Already*??"

"I don't waste time when I know it's not right," Blue stated simply.

"We'll get back to you in a minute," Olarion told him. To Tonette, she said, "Girl, for real. Is there some reason you don't want us meeting Stanley?"

"I told you already. We're just friends."

"Don't try that. You and I are friends. Do you kiss me like you do him?" Blue asked.

"Umm...do *I* need to remind you that you're gay?"

"That ain't my point. Folks that are *just friends* don't do all that kind of kissing."

"Fine, Blue. Come over here and I'll lay one on you right now."

"Girl, bye."

"I'm serious. It'll be worth the trip; I'm a better kisser than you probably think," Tonette continued to tease him, only half-joking. Olarion giggled. Truth be told, Tonette wouldn't have at all minded kissing Blue, even though she knew it wouldn't mean anything. She just wanted to satisfy her longstanding curiosity about what those lips of his felt like.

"Shut up; stop playin'," Blue replied, sounding uncharacteristically uncomfortable.

"See there. You're the one that started it. I can kiss you but it's not my fault you'd prefer one from Stanley more than you would from me."

"Why don't you let me be the judge of that. I don't even know what the man looks like."

"He's very nice-looking."

"There go those dry and generic descriptions again," Olarion muttered. "Do you even notice that you do that?"

Tonette felt herself becoming frustrated; not even so much at her friends but at the point she couldn't deny they were making.

"Y'all, look," she sighed, rubbing her temples. "I don't want to give him the wrong impression by introducing him to folks already. He might think that means more than what it does."

"Well then let him know what it does and does not mean. Problem solved," Blue said.

"Just tell him that we're all going to be having dinner and he's welcome to join us, if he wants," Olarion suggested. "Or the next time he invites you out, say you already have plans with us and he can just join you. Then it's not like so much of an actual *meeting* and more of a casual get-together. That wouldn't be so bad, right?"

"You *have* told him about us, haven't you?" Blue asked.

"Of course I have. I talk about y'all all the time."

"Good. Then I'm sure he'd be smart enough to know we'd want to put a face with the name, since he's the man you're seeing. It's not like we're your parents and you're getting our approval. We ain't gon' dog the man. Just wanna meet him, that's all."

"Yeah, but still—"

"Just ask him, see what he thinks about it," Olarion cut her off. "You're the one making this a bigger deal than it has to be. If he's not comfortable meeting us yet, then fine; so be it. But if he's down with it..."

"Then it's on," Blue finished her sentence.

Tonette sighed again, letting her head fall against the headboard on her bed. She knew there was nothing she could say to get her friends off this track they were on. They were set on meeting Stanley and weren't going to leave her alone about it until she agreed. Maybe she was over-analyzing again, but she still felt it was a little soon to be introducing Stanley to loved ones. She certainly didn't feel ready to meet any of his. But to appease her friends (and shut them up), she agreed to ask Stanley what he thought about it, hoping that he wouldn't be any more ready for all that than she was.

But...no such luck.

"Sure, I'd love to meet your friends," Stanley eagerly responded when she hesitantly broached the subject with him a couple of days later.

Tonette had been afraid he'd say that. "Really?" she asked, trying to keep the disappointment out of her voice.

"Absolutely. Why wouldn't I?"

"I don't know," she tried to reply casually. "I just...didn't want you to feel put on the spot or anything."

"As much as you talk about them, I feel like I know them already," Stanley said with a chuckle. "They seem like they'd be a trip."

"That's putting it mildly," Tonette replied with a chuckle of her own.

"Yeah, so just let me know when and where."

"Okay, sure," Tonette managed to say as cheerfully as she could. She told herself to think positively, even though part of her still worried about Stanley reading more into this invitation than she intended.

Lighten up, she chided herself. *Toni wouldn't make this such a big deal. She'd just treat it like a casual meet-up and keep it moving.*

Tonette tried to remember that as she returned Stanley's anticipatory smile.

Yawning, Tonette turned on the light in her bathroom and groaned, looking at her thick, brown natural hair. She was tired but knew if she didn't twist it up before going to bed, she'd have a tangled mess on her hands in the morning.

Sighing, she grabbed some hair moisturizer and proceeded to start the often-dreaded part of her nightly routine, gazing at herself in the mirror as she did so. It was so much easier in Barbados when she had the weave in; sometimes she missed that. She missed looking like Toni, in general. Toni was brazen...Toni was unapologetically sexy...Toni didn't worry about what other people thought. As soon as she had gotten back to Atlanta, Tonette had put all of her vacation clothes in a box and stuffed it in the back of her closet, not having the nerve to wear any of it now that she was back home. It wasn't like the clothes were even inappropriate; they were just sexier and more revealing than Tonette usually wore. Her style geared more towards the cute and comfortable. The most revealing things she usually wore involved shirts that showed her abs; that was about it.

She lifted her arms higher to reach the hair at the top of her head, and her short nightshirt rode up her thighs. Her eyes dropped to the birthmark a little below her hip, and automatically thought of how intrigued Troy had seemed by it when he saw it for the first time:

"It is in the shape of the sun," he had said, lightly tracing a finger around it.

Tonette, who was sitting up in Troy's bed as he laid eye-level with her hip, had never really noticed that before; it always just looked like a splotch to her. "Yeah, it kinda is, huh?"

"Beautiful," Troy said in a low voice, still admiring it.

Tonette smiled. She never saw any beauty in it; it was just a birthmark to her. But the fact that Troy seemed to love it so much made her take pride in it. "Thank you."

Troy leaned over and placed a slow, wet kiss on the mark, sending a shudder of pleasure through her and a heated laser of arousal straight to her core. Her gut clenched all on its own.

"You continue to amaze me, Toni," Troy said, looking up at her as he continued his kisses, slowly progressing them along her hip. Every time his lips touched her skin it sent a fresh wave of body-rocking shivers through her, as if she was being zapped repeatedly with a taser gun. "I just cannot get enough of you."

That had been music to Tonette's ears; the feeling was certainly mutual. "Good," was all she had been able to whisper in response.

Troy's kisses traveled up her hip, across her abdomen, and up to her opposite breast, snaking his body around hers, his hands sliding up her bare back. Her eyes had rolled back in her head in pleasure, her body, mind, and heart all either on fire or too jumbled to think straight...

"Oh!" Tonette gasped, catching herself as she felt herself actually swaying. She shook her head to clear it of those memories that were making her thighs squeeze together. Just the *thought* of Troy did more to her than Stanley's hands or lips on her did. Releasing a long, frustrated groan, she knew she had to find *some* way to get past all this; it had been weeks since she returned from Barbados and she still yearned for Troy as if she had just seen him yesterday.

"Snap out of it!" she scolded herself, frowning at her reflection in the mirror. This was getting ridiculous. "It was just an island fling, that's *it*! Get that man out of your head!! Barbados is *over*!"

She was practically yelling but she didn't care. Tonette felt almost helpless against this hold Troy seemed to have on her, and she knew it was that hold that was keeping her from really moving on. This fantasy of him was consuming her more than she sometimes realized, and even though it was an enjoyable one, she knew she'd never be able to really commit to the possibility of anyone else until she let go of it.

She *had* to find a way to let go of it.

It was the night of Stanley meeting her friends, and Tonette told herself not to be nervous or negative. Like Blue said, he and Olarion weren't her parents; she didn't need their approval. And it wasn't like this was anything new; any time any of them started dating someone, the other two always insisted they meet him after a while, both for safety and curiosity's sake. This didn't have to be a big deal; she hated that she had to keep reminding herself of that.

Olarion, then Blue arrived at her apartment first. Stanley had already let her know he was on his way.

"Where is he?" Olarion asked.

"He's coming."

"See, dude's late," Blue shook his head. "Starting off on the wrong foot already."

"Hush, Blue. He is not late; y'all are just early." Tonette took the bottle of wine he had in his large hand and went into the kitchen.

"What smells so good?" Olarion called out behind her as she kicked her shoes off and dropped onto the couch.

"Roasted veggie pizza."

"Yum. Homemade?"

"Kind of. Its refrigerated dough; I didn't make it from scratch or anything."

"I have an early appointment in the morning so I won't be able to be here all night," Blue informed them, flipping through Tonette's copy of *Ebony*.

"I thought you didn't take really early appointments anymore," Olarion said.

"It's an exception; the daughter of a friend of my mama's. Plus she wants some damn microbraids so that's gonna take me most of the day."

"Well, I sure appreciate these things you put in my head," Olarion commented, running a hand over the expertly-braided cornrows that Blue had put in. He added extensions that extended down her back and to look at it, you'd never guess Olarion's real hair was only half as long. They looked completely natural. "I love not having to worry about my hair for a while."

"Yeah, I know. Folks' laziness is what keeps my car note paid."

"Shut up, Blue!"

The three of them continued to talk about various things until Stanley showed up a little later. Olarion shot Tonette a look of approval behind Stanley's back as he and Blue shook hands, and Tonette couldn't help but smile as she slightly shook her head.

"What do you do, Stanley?" Olarion asked him a little later, after they had begun eating.

Stanley wiped his fingers on the paper towel that was draped across his thigh. He finished chewing the bite of pizza he had just taken before replying, "I'm an operations manager."

"Yeah? Do you enjoy that?"

Stanley shrugged. "It's cool. Can't say it's my dream job or anything but I don't hate it."

"I can understand that; I was like that before I went into business for myself."

"Really? What kind of business?"

"I own a little cafe. Things were kind of shaky the first year or so but we're doing really well now."

"Yeah, she owns a cafe but can't cook," Blue quipped, nudging Tonette.

Olarion narrowed her eyes at him.

"She can bake her tail off, though," Tonette countered, nudging Blue back. "My girl makes cupcakes that melt in your mouth."

"Oh, you're automatically cool with me, then," Stanley said with a smile, looking at Olarion with a wink. "I have an embarrassingly big sweet tooth."

"Really? I didn't know that," Tonette commented, intrigued.

"Yeah, it's why I have to stay in the gym so much," Stanley joked.

"Well, I guess we have that in common, then. I'm a sucker for her german chocolate cupcakes."

"I'm sure we're going to find a lot more things we have in common," Stanley replied flirtatiously, gazing at her. Tonette immediately blushed, not being able to resist the smile that shot across her face. Olarion and Blue shared a *Do you see that?* look over their heads.

The rest of the visit went very well, with Stanley and Blue bonding over a shared love of the Atlanta Hawks and Olarion promising to bake him some walnut brownies. Tonette was actually pleasantly surprised with how well things went; she had expected her friends to grill Stanley or do something else to put him off, but that didn't happen. They all got along really well, and Tonette couldn't help but be glad about that and take that as a good sign. While she and Stanley weren't an official couple and her seeing him certainly wasn't contingent upon her friends' approval, she had to admit to herself that everyone getting along made her feel better about continuing whatever it was she and Stanley had started.

Olarion hung around after the men left, and she wasted no time letting her opinion of Stanley be known.

"Girl, *marry* that man!" Olarion exclaimed emphatically. "He is *perfect* for you!"

"What?" Tonette balked, even though she couldn't resist smiling. "How do you figure that?"

"You two just...*go* together, you know?" Olarion replied, placing some dirty plates in the sink. She grabbed her half-empty glass of wine and leaned against the counter, wrapping one arm around her waist. "I can really see you two being together for the long haul. He's kind, he's considerate, he's patient. The way he looks at you...girl, he's smitten."

"You think so? I guess I haven't noticed," Tonette shrugged, turning on the water in the sink.

"Maybe you should pay more attention, then. Get your head back in Atlanta," Olarion commented, taking a sip of wine as she looked at her friend pointedly.

Tonette turned to her. "What does that mean?"

"You know what it means. Stanley is a perfectly good man; handsome, tall, gainfully employed, straight, and sincerely interested in you. Unless you just don't like him, there's should be no reason why you won't give him a fair shot."

"I told you I was, though."

"Yeah, that's what you *said*. But I'm still not seeing it, girl. You don't act like a woman interested. To look at you tonight with Stanley, I wouldn't be able to tell if you were his date or his cousin."

"Olarion, come on..."

"I'm serious, girl. Be for real...are you still hung up on Troy?"

Tonette mindlessly played in the growing suds in the sink. "I don't want to be," she answered softly. "I *so* want to get over Troy, Olarion, for real...I know I won't be able to fully commit to getting to know Stanley until I do. I'm really trying."

"Are you?" Olarion asked with a raised brow.

"Yes!"

"I'm just saying, girl, from the outside looking in, I can't really tell," Olarion admitted. "Whenever he tried to hold your hand or put his arm around you tonight, you looked *so* uncomfortable."

"I did?"

"Yes, you did."

Tonette sighed, turning to lean against the counter next to her friend. "I don't know what my problem is, girl," she admitted wearily. "I mean, I like Stanley, a lot...but I haven't been able to make myself really...*go* there with him, you know?"

Olarion peered at her. "You're not physically attracted to him?"

"Yeah," Tonette replied slowly. "I am. We've kissed a bunch of times and I honestly enjoy it."

"Do you fantasize about him? Do his kisses make you want to do other things with him? Can you imagine his body on top of yours, sweaty and—"

"Olarion!"

"I'm just saying, Tonette. What about any of that? Or do you just plan to kiss him forever and that's it?"

"No..."

"But even more importantly than the physical stuff, how does your *heart* feel when you're around him? Do you get the tingles when you know you're going to be seeing him? Do you want to be around him more than you don't? I could say yes to those questions if you were to ask me that about Aaron."

"I just...I can't put my finger on it. I know there's nothing wrong with Stanley but..."

"I'll say it again. Don't waste the man's time if you're not really interested." Olarion drained her glass and set it on the counter next to the sink.

"I *am* interested!"

"Well, which is it? 'Cause one minute you're insisting you're interested and the next, you can't pinpoint why you can't really let go and really get into him. It can't be both."

Tonette chewed her lip as she pondered her friend's words.

"Tonette," Olarion said, linking her arm with hers, "You really need to figure out what it is you're doing. If you're still hung up on Troy, there's nothing wrong with that but just admit it...and let Stanley go so he can find someone who will give him their undivided attention. If you just want to be friends with Stanley, then let him know that. I'm just saying be honest with him, and with yourself. But don't miss out on a good thing because you're still hanging on to a fantasy." She squeezed her arm. "Or because you're too afraid of having something real of your own."

Tonette looked at her friend thoughtfully, and nodded. "You're right, girl...I really need to check myself, huh?"

"Yeah," Olarion replied with a smile. "You do."

Chapter 11

After her talk with Olarion, Tonette gave a lot of serious thought to her friend's words. She couldn't necessarily deny that she had been holding on to the fantasy of Troy, whether she had been trying to or not. It was the memories of him and the yearning for him that she couldn't make herself let go of that was hindering her progress with Stanley. She missed Troy; it was as simple as that.

But, Troy was in Barbados. She hadn't gotten any response to that birthday card that Olarion had sent off, so Tonette figured that it really was over and she needed to get over it. It wasn't fair to Stanley for her to not be all in, and the more she thought about it, the more she realized she really did want to put sincere effort into getting closer to him. She had been avoiding him in the couple of days since he had met her friends because she wanted to figure out what it was she really wanted, and she decided she sincerely wanted to give Stanley a real chance, for real this time. The thought made her smile, and sent her right to her phone to call him. Besides, what did she have to lose?

After she finally and really resigned herself to getting over Troy, Tonette found herself loosening up with Stanley considerably. She had actually asked if she could come over the night she came to that realization, which she knew threw him for a loop. But as soon as she saw him, she threw her arms around his neck. Another loop thrown.

"You all right?" Stanley had asked, wrapping his arms around her.

"Yeah, everything's great," Tonette replied, tightening her hold on him. "I'm just...really happy to see you, that's all."

"I'm glad to hear that, Tonette," Stanley said, his hands roaming her back. They finally separated after several more moments and he looked at her, a faint smile on his lips. "I was wondering why I hadn't heard from you since the other night."

"I'm sorry about that, Stanley...I've just had a *lot* on my mind. But..." she slid her hands up his chest, "I do look forward to us spending more time together. I'm ready to kind of...kick things up a little bit."

Stanley smiled, clearly glad to hear that. His hands rubbed up and down her arms. "You sure? I thought you wanted to move slowly."

"Yeah, but," she leaned up and placed a soft kiss on his lips. "We can step on the gas a little bit, can't we?"

His smile widening, Stanley looked at her, his eyes clearly wondering what was up with the sudden change of attitude but glad about it, regardless. "As much as you want."

Now, Tonette sat curled up on her couch, smiling as she updated her friends on her progress with Stanley. She honestly felt good about it, and the happiness was all over her face.

"Girl, you are glowing!" Olarion observed happily. "I am so glad to hear that you are finally giving this thing with Stanley a real chance."

"Me too," Tonette replied, still smiling. She actually felt giddy.

"So what else happened when you went over there?" Blue asked. "During booty call hours, I might add."

"It was not."

"Yes, it was."

"Well, regardless of what hour it was, that is *not* what we did," Tonette informed them. "We talked, we cuddled, we did a little kissin'..."

"*A little kissin'*, huh? And that's it?"

"Well...I can say that things *did* go a little farther than they have any other time," Tonette admitted, blushing.

"Whaaat?" Olarion exclaimed. "Girl, I wish you could see your face right now."

"I know, I can't seem to stop smiling, huh?"

"And I'm glad about it! *This* is how a woman with a crush is supposed to look."

"Well, I can finally admit that's me," Tonette said, her smile widening.

"So you're over Troy now?" Blue asked with a raised brow.

"I won't lie and say I'm completely over him, no; but I'm on the way there," Tonette replied honestly. "I just had to realize that I was wasting time letting the memories of him hold me back from something that could be really good for me."

"Really?"

"Yeah. My time with Troy was great, but it's over...I left that in Barbados. I need to focus on what's happening here and now."

"It's about time," Blue teased, tweaking her nose. "But seriously, Boo, I'm glad to hear that, for real. Stanley seems like good people."

"Yeah, he does. So are y'all an official couple now?" Olarion asked.

"Not yet, but we talked about that. Thankfully he understands that I'm not *quite* ready to go there yet but...it's coming," Tonette said, still smiling.

"Well, that's progress!" Olarion grinned. She reached over to hug her friend. "I am *so* happy for you, girl."

"You know what? I'm pretty happy about it, myself," Tonette said. "That talk you and I had the other night really helped. I appreciate that, O."

Olarion grabbed her hand. "Anytime."

The three of them continued to talk for a while until there was a knock on the door. They all looked at each other questioningly.

"You expecting somebody?" Blue asked.

"No..." Tonette replied curiously, moving the pillow she had been holding in her lap and standing.

"Maybe it's your soon-to-be man," Olarion suggested teasingly.

"It shouldn't be...he's down in Macon visiting his parents," Tonette replied as she padded over to the door.

She quickly checked the peephole, but couldn't really see who it was; she could only tell it was a man. With a slight frown, she glanced over her shoulder.

"Who is it?" she called out.

There was a pause. "Troy."

No...it can't be. Tonette felt her heart rate speed up automatically. She quickly tried to recall if there was *anybody* else she knew named Troy as she glanced at her friends again, hoping she didn't look as freaked out as she was starting to feel.

"Who is that?" Olarion asked, clearly not having understood the name.

Blue stood up as Tonette slowly opened the door, and her stomach dropped to her knees, which actually started to buckle. She could not believe her eyes; she simply could not believe her eyes.

Troy was standing right in front of her.

"Good evening," he greeted, that voice automatically setting her skin on fire. He looked at her curiously, then his eyes eased to her friends before going back to her. Those intense eyes of his were focusing on her questioningly. "I am sorry to bother you unannounced; my name is Troy Anton."

"Oh my god..." Olarion gasped.

"I am looking for Toni," Troy continued. Tonette was still staring at him, her mouth agape and her throat as dry as a bone. "She and I met in Barbados a few months ago. Again, I apologize for the impromptu visit; she is not expecting me. But I...haven't been able to get her off of my mind and had to come to her. Is she here?"

Tonette, Olarion, and Blue just stood there staring at him for several more moments before Olarion finally snapped out of it first, stepping around Tonette, who was still frozen. "Hi, Troy, I'm Olarion," she introduced herself, a hesitant smile on her lips.

Troy took her offered hand in his and bowed his head to her graciously. "A pleasure to meet you, Olarion."

"Uh, I'm Blue," Blue said, stepping forward also. He and Troy shook hands, and Blue motioned towards the bags at his feet. "Looks like you're planning on staying a while."

"Yes, it's a bit presumptuous of me, I know," Troy said shyly, glancing down at them. "I have some time off of work and just decided to throw caution to the wind and come see the woman I hadn't been able to get out of my head since she left Barbados." His eyes were on Tonette again, who still hadn't moved.

"That is so romantic!" Olarion gushed. "Here, come on in...Blue, get his bags."

Blue looked at her with a clear *What are you doing?* look but stepped forward to bring Troy's bags into the apartment. Troy stepped in as Olarion closed the door behind him, his eyes lingering on Tonette as he did so.

"I'm sorry," he said, facing her. "I cannot help but notice that you look so much like Toni..."

"I...umm..." Tonette managed to stammer, placing a hand to her throat.

"*Just* like her," Troy marveled, his eyes roaming her face. "I take it you're of some relation?"

"I'm her twin," Tonette blurted, then resisted squeezing her eyes shut as she internally kicked herself.

Blue and Olarion were looking at her like she was crazy. Troy looked intrigued. "Really? I didn't know she had a twin. She actually said she had no siblings."

"Oh, yeah...I, uhh, I'm not surprised. We're not terribly close," Tonette said weakly, her heart racing a million miles a minute. *What am I doing??* she berated herself.

"Oh, I am sorry to hear that," Troy commented sincerely. He held his hand out. "Well, regardless, I am pleased to meet you...?"

"I'm Tonette," Tonette answered his unspoken question, hesitantly placing her hand in his. The fire immediately shot up her arm and spread over her body in record speed. She could feel her friends' eyes on her but she didn't dare look at them. "Tonette Andersen."

Troy frowned, confused. "Andersen? Toni told me her last name was Andrews."

Tonette had forgotten all about that...a clear indication she had no business lying. But for whatever reason, she began continuing to dig her latest hole. "Well yeah...I'm, I'm divorced."

Troy's eyebrows shot up. "Oh?"

"Yeah...from Blue." Tonette glanced at her friend, who shot her a look that clearly let her know he didn't want to be dragged into her charade. Tonette silently pleaded with him to play along. Olarion coughed, turning away.

"And you are friends now? That's good," Troy commented with a small smile.

"Well, you know...sometimes it just doesn't work out. We are *definitely* better friends than lovers," Blue replied smoothly, looking at Tonette pointedly.

"Definitely," Tonette muttered.

"I see," Troy said, turning back to Tonette. Tonette tried not to notice how good he looked in his green V-neck t-shirt, his firm pecs peeking out at her. His hair looked freshly cut, he actually seemed taller than she remembered, and his cologne had already given her nose multiple orgasms. Tonette tried her best to keep her facial expression even, even though her insides were screaming. *He's just as adorably gorgeous as I remembered.*

"Is Toni not here?" Troy asked.

"Oh, um...actually, no, she's not," Tonette replied, nervously scratching her neck. "She left. This is the address she gave you, huh?"

"She sent me a birthday card with this address, yes. I apologize for the imposition..."

"No imposition," Tonette quickly insisted.

"When do you expect her return?"

"I'm not sure, actually...it's, um...she actually must have forgotten that she was only temporarily staying with me while her house was being renovated. Mold and stuff, you know."

Olarion grabbed Blue's arm, clearly embarrassed for her friend.

"I agreed to take her in at the insistence of my...I mean, *our*...parents," Tonette continued. "They're always on us to get along better. She stays gone more than she stays here, though; I'm the homebody twin." She chuckled nervously, rambling, still not believing all of this was happening.

"Oh okay," Troy said, seeming to buy her story. "Well, hopefully I can catch up to her soon. In the meantime, can you recommend a nearby hotel? I came straight from the airport and would like to get some rest."

"Oh, how long will you be staying?" Olarion asked.

"Well, I teach school and our term recently ended, so I have a while before we start back," Troy explained. "I'd like to stay as long as I can to see Toni, if possible."

"Oh, okay. Well, there's a few hotels about ten or fifteen minutes from here," Olarion suggested.

"But there's a Motel 6 right down the street," Tonette blurted without thinking. For some reason, she wanted Troy closer to her, even though she knew it was probably smarter for him to be farther away. Her friends were shooting daggers at her but she refused to look at them. "It's not terribly fancy but it's clean and not all that expensive..."

"Thank you, Tonette...I will check that out." Troy smiled at her, and she bit her lip as she returned it with a shaky one of her own. Her head was swimming and she was still trying to figure out if this was some kind of dream.

"No problem," she said.

"I will head over there, then," Troy said, slinging his duffel bag over his shoulder. "Do you mind if I come back later? I do not know anyone else in Atlanta."

"Of course not," Tonette replied quickly.

Troy smiled, relieved. "Thank you. May I give you my number? You can let me know when it's okay for me to return."

Tonette almost told him she already had his number, but thankfully caught herself. "Sure," she said, retrieving her cell phone from the end table. She entered his number into her phone as he recited it and smiled. "Got it."

"Good." Troy headed for the door and opened it, then paused and turned to her thoughtfully. Tonette held her breath without even trying. "I feel a little silly for asking this but...has Toni mentioned me at all?"

"Oh!" Tonette debated how to answer; should she give the impression that he meant nothing to Toni and send him on back to Barbados or make it seem like she had been missing him as much as he had been missing her? Looking into those eyes, though, she knew she wouldn't be able to say anything to disappoint him. "Yes, she did mention you, actually."

Troy's face brightened.

"She said you showed her a really good time when she was in Barbados."

Actually looking like he was blushing, Troy grinned harder, glancing at the floor shyly. *It just isn't fair for this man to be so damn cute.* "I am glad to hear that," he said.

Tonette smiled at him, wishing she had another excuse to touch him.

"Well, thank you for your time, and I apologize for interrupting you," Troy said, his accent like music that made Tonette's heart dance.

"No apologies necessary. I'll be sure to let...Toni know you're here," Tonette replied, again without thinking. Behind her, Olarion coughed again.

"It was nice meeting the two of you," Troy said to her and Blue.

"You too," they chorused.

Troy treated Tonette to another smile, his eyes lingering on her for a moment before grabbing his bags and walking out. Tonette closed the door behind him, releasing a long, shaky breath as she collapsed against it, her hand over her racing heart.

"What the hell?!?" Blue exclaimed immediately.

"Girl! What the hell were you thinking??" Olarion demanded, stalking over to her.

"I don't know!" Tonette shrieked, sticking her hands in her hair. "I'm still in utter shock that he even showed up here! I mean, did that really just happen? Was that *really* Troy from Barbados right here in my living room? In the flesh??"

"Yeah, girl," Olarion confirmed, looking like she couldn't quite believe it herself. "That was him, apparently. And can I just say, I can *definitely* see why you were so hung up on him. That man is beautiful. And he seems so *nice*!"

"He *is*! He's a sweetheart and I've just fed him a whole new batch of lies!" Tonette groaned, trudging over to her couch and dropping down onto it. "Oh my god..."

"You most certainly did, telling him you and I used to be married," Blue said, crossing his strong arms over his chest. "Even if I was straight, that wouldn't have happened. You're too uptight for me."

"Shut up, Blue! Tonette, I don't even know what to say about all this," Olarion mused, going to join her on the couch. "I mean, okay; I can understand why you were thrown for a loop. He just shows up out of thin air and you weren't expecting it; I get it. But girl...you really aren't good under pressure, huh?"

"I know, I know," Tonette said wearily, shaking her head. Her eyes floated up towards the ceiling as she leaned against the back of the couch. "I've just made an already convoluted situation worse."

"Yes, you did. And I can even understand why. But wouldn't it just be easier to go ahead and tell him the real deal so he can stop chasing a woman that doesn't exist and go on back home?"

"No, that would *not* be easier," Tonette quickly answered, looking at her. "It might be the right thing to do, but it wouldn't be *easier*."

"Okay, but still. He came all the way here from *Barbados*, girl...unless you're planning on transforming yourself back into Toni, he needs to go ahead and learn the truth. Otherwise, it's just...cruel."

Groaning again, Tonette covered her face with her hands. She didn't want to keep leading Troy on. One thing that had given her solace finally was that she wouldn't be seeing Troy again so it would be relatively harmless to let him remember Toni as he did. But now that he was in Atlanta, within reach again, she didn't want to lose him so soon, either. If she told him the truth about everything, that there was no Toni and never had been, he would surely be on the first thing smoking back to Barbados, thinking the worst of her. Tonette didn't want him to leave and she didn't want him thinking ill of her. But how could she avoid that and be honest with him?

"Well, you sho' 'nuff put your foot in this one," Blue observed.

"You don't have to remind me of that, Blue," Tonette droned, her arm over her eyes. "I'm well aware, thank you."

"I'm just saying. How is all of this gonna affect things with Stanley?"

Tonette sat up; she had temporarily forgotten all about Stanley just that quickly. "I don't know," she replied. "Who says it has to affect things with him at all?"

"Well, if Troy ends up staying here for any extended period of time, who else is he going to be trying to spend time with?" Blue asked, looking at her pointedly. "Like he said, he doesn't know anybody else here."

"But that doesn't mean he can't go out and meet anyone else," Tonette retorted weakly, not liking the idea of that as soon as she said it. She didn't want Troy meeting anyone else.

"He came all the way here to see *Toni*; he wouldn't have flown all this way and showed up unannounced if all he wanted to do was go out and meet somebody else."

"Yeah, girl...he might be wanting to hang out with you as long as he thinks *Toni* is off doing whatever it is you're pretending she's doing," Olarion commented. "You can't ignore him; he knows where you live."

"I don't want to ignore him," Tonette said softly, playing with her shirt.

"So...you're going to be entertaining Troy at the same time you're kicking things up a notch with Stanley? A while ago you were all gung ho about that."

"Nothing has to change about that. Troy isn't going to be here forever."

"But while he *is*—"

"Look, y'all, I don't *know*, okay??" Tonette exclaimed. "I'm clearly flying by the seat of my pants here...I have *no* idea how all of this is going to play out. It's not like I knew Troy was just going to show up at my door today. I'm still tripping about *that*! Give me some time to get my head together!"

Olarion looked at her friend sympathetically. "I feel for you, girl. I wouldn't have anticipated this in a million years."

"Hmph," Tonette shook her head. "Believe me, neither would I."

"Well, I just need to make sure I have a whole lotta popcorn and a front row seat," Blue commented. "'Cause this is about to be one interesting show."

Chapter 12

The next morning, Tonette was still hoping that Troy showing up had been some kind of dream, but she knew it wasn't.

He was really there, in Atlanta, mere blocks from her. He had really gotten on an airplane and come all the way there just to see her. Or rather, just to see *Toni*. And she had stupidly told him that stuff about being Toni's estranged twin. Olarion was right about her not being good under pressure. But it's not like this was a scenario she could have anticipated. She had no idea Troy would just show up. At the most, she thought he might have just written her or something after getting that birthday card, which he apparently clearly received. She tried not to focus on how romantic it was that he missed her (or Toni) so much that he flew all this way to be with her and concentrate on how she was going to get out of this latest mess she had gotten herself into.

Olarion called, curious as to whether Tonette had heard back from Troy yet.

"No, not yet," Tonette replied with a yawn. It was Saturday morning and she was still lounging in bed. "He doesn't have my phone number, remember; he gave me his. I never called him after you and Blue left last night."

"I'm kinda surprised to hear that. I figured you might be anxious to be alone with him again."

"Maybe if I wasn't caught up in this web of lies I'm in, I would have. But I know I'd just be a nervous wreck if I was alone with him."

"What are you gonna do, though? He's obviously going to want to see you again 'cause he's going to want an update on Toni."

"I still haven't worked all that out yet."

"Girl," Olarion said slowly, "I know your head is probably still spinning but please do. No need in making all of this more complicated than it already is."

"Yeah, I know. I'm going to tell him the truth. I have to."

Olarion paused. "You really think you can?"

"I'm gonna *have* to," Tonette repeated, more to herself than to her friend. "Like you all said, he deserves to know."

"True," Olarion agreed. "But let me ask you, woman to woman...how did you feel when you opened that door and saw him again?"

The smile came to Tonette's lips all on its own. "Honestly? It was just like I felt whenever I saw him in Barbados. Just the sight of him does something to me, O. I can't even explain it."

"I can. But I know you're just going to deny it again," Olarion said. "But like I said, he is so good-looking! You didn't tell us he had it like *that*! And you got to be all over that for ten days in Barbados, huh?"

Tonette chuckled. "And I'll never forget it."

"He's like a milk chocolate-dipped Allen Iverson."

"Yeah he is, isn't he?"

"What if he makes a move on you here?"

"He won't," Tonette insisted. "He's smitten with *Toni*, and I'm not like Toni. I'm like the *opposite* of her."

"I don't know, girl," Olarion countered, doubt in her voice. "You didn't see the way he kept looking at you."

"Only because I look so much like who he thinks he came to see," Tonette said, trying to ignore the butterflies that emerged in her belly at the thought of Troy being interested in her as herself. "I certainly can't let myself get deluded into thinking he would be interested in me like that."

"Why would you say that? Why *wouldn't* he be interested in you?"

"I'm not Toni."

"You *are* Toni," Olarion countered. "You created her, Tonette. Did you forget that?"

Tonette sighed. "You don't get what I'm saying."

"No, I *do* get it. And it sounds like you're intimidated by your own alter ego. Girl, some weave and some new clothes doesn't change the woman you are inside. Troy had to see that to be so enamored with you."

"It wasn't just the hair and the clothes; it was Toni's personality, too. She was bold, she was confident..."

"Why are you talking about her like she's a real person?"

Tonette didn't even realize she was doing that. "Can we not talk about this, please?"

"Why are you getting upset?"

"I'm not upset. I'd just like to change the subject. And anyway, let's not forget that all of this wouldn't even be happening if you hadn't sent off that birthday card."

"So you're trying to blame me? How about none of this would be happening if you had just been honest with Troy from the beginning?"

Even though Tonette knew Olarion was right, her words still stung. "I have to go," she mumbled, hanging up the phone and dropping it on the bed beside her. She rubbed her eyes wearily before grabbing her extra pillow and burying her face in it.

Later that evening, Tonette tried to get her mind right for the date she had with Stanley. She was trying her best to recapture some of the anticipation and excitement she had been feeling about their budding relationship before Troy showed up, but so far she hadn't been able to do it; her mind was now again preoccupied with Troy. She hadn't spoken to him yet, even though she had played with the thought of calling him all day. She didn't want to just leave him hanging, but she didn't know what to say to him. While she knew she needed to just tell him the truth, it was way easier said than done.

She had to remember that even though Troy was here, she was still supposed to be concentrating on Stanley. Stanley wanted *her*; Troy wanted Toni. Tonette didn't want to admit that she still wanted Troy; all those feelings that she was just starting to finally suppress came rushing back full force as soon as she saw him again. Her heart flipped at the thought of him being so close to her. Yes, she was happy to see him; she just wished it was under different circumstances.

Stanley came and picked her up and took her out to dinner, and Tonette had to fight to keep her mind on him and what he was saying to her. Regardless of how hard she tried, she just couldn't keep her mind from straying to Troy; she wondered what he was doing right then, what he thought about the fact that he still hadn't heard from her, how long he would stay once it was evident he wouldn't be seeing Toni. She was clearly preoccupied, and Stanley noticed.

"You all right?" he asked her, putting down his fork and leaning back in his chair. "You seem like you've got something on your mind."

Tonette's eyebrows shot up. "Oh...I'm sorry, Stanley. I guess I do."

"Everything okay?"

"Yeah, everything's fine. It's just...something that's come up, is all."

"You wanna talk about it?"

Tonette shook her head. She most certainly did *not* want to talk about it; not with him. "It's nothing for you to worry about."

"You're clearly worried about it, so I'm worried about it," Stanley retorted. "And maybe you just need another perspective on whatever it is."

"It's nothing like that. Just...an unexpected visitor came into town last night and it's thrown me off, that's all." At least that was true.

"Why is it throwing you off?"

"Long story. It's just a really complicated situation."

"Well, who is it? An estranged relative or something?"

"It has something to do with that," Tonette said lightly, taking a long swallow of her white wine. In a *very* twisted way, that was kind of the truth too, at least as far as the story she concocted for Troy.

"I get it. But try not to let it worry you so much," Stanley advised, reaching over and rubbing her arm. "I'm sure everything will work itself out."

Tonette gave him a weak smile. *If only*, she thought to herself. "I sure hope you're right."

"Let me know if there's anything I can do, all right? I'm here for you," Stanley said sincerely.

Tonette's smile widened. "I appreciate that."

They left a little while later and Tonette did a somewhat better job keeping her mind on the man she was with during the ride back to her apartment. She didn't want Stanley thinking she hadn't meant everything she had said about wanting things to progress between them. Her interest in Stanley hadn't waned just because Troy was there...it was just that her interest in Stanley couldn't touch her feelings for Troy with a thousand-foot pole.

"You want me to walk you up?" Stanley asked her, pulling up to her building and parking the car.

"That's all right; I just want to get up there and get in the bed. I'm kind of drained," Tonette replied honestly. She smiled at him. "Thank you for a lov—um...it was a great evening."

"My pleasure."

"And I'm sorry about being so preoccupied," Tonette continued, reaching over and running her hand along his arm. "I promise I'll make it up to you."

"I want to tell you not to worry about it but I'd be a fool to turn that down," Stanley said with a smile, placing a hand over hers. He leaned over and placed a lingering kiss on her lips. "You sure you're gonna be all right?"

"Oh yeah, I'll be fine," Tonette assured him. "Like you said, everything will work itself out."

"Well, if you need anything, you know what to do. I'm just a phone call away."

"Thank you so much, Stanley."

"No problem. All right, woman, let me get my hug," Stanley said, opening his door. He walked around to her side and held the door open for her, offering her his hand as she eased out of the car in her relatively-short dress, and wrapped her up in his arms tightly. Tonette closed her eyes as she rested her head on his shoulder, smiling at how nice it felt to be held like this. She was getting more and more used to Stanley's affections, and didn't shy away from it like she had in the beginning.

After several leisurely moments, Stanley eased back and cupped Tonette's chin in his hand, leaning down to kiss her. She kissed him back without discomfort, opening her mouth to allow his tongue to play with hers for several moments. Soft tingles of arousal flittered throughout her body, to her surprise.

"I'll call you, okay?" Stanley said after the kiss tapered off.

"Okay." Tonette softly replied, the smile still on her lips.

"You *sure* you don't want me to walk you upstairs?"

"Yeah, I'm sure. I'll let you know I made it inside safely."

Stanley gave her lips one more peck before getting back into his car and driving off as she headed inside. The smile was still on Tonette's face as she wandered up to her apartment, taking her time, twirling her keys in her hands, temporarily forgetting all about the situation with Troy.

That is, until she got to her door and saw Troy waiting outside of it.

"Troy!" she gasped, clearly jarred.

"Good evening, Tonette," Troy greeted her pleasantly.

"H-How long have you been here?"

"Not very long. I don't want to bother you but—"

"It's no bother," Tonette insisted, then blushed at her eagerness. "I mean, um...would you like to come in?"

Troy smiled at her. "Only if you are sure it is not an imposition."

"I'm sure." Tonette discreetly took a deep breath and tried to quell her jumping nerves as she stepped around him and unlocked the door, her hands shaking slightly. Just that quickly, she forgot about Stanley as her body filled with liquid desire all by itself, as it always did whenever she got around Troy. She was just thanking God that she had declined Stanley's invitation to walk her to her door.

Once they were inside her apartment, Tonette double-locked the door and turned to Troy, smiling nervously. "So...what brings you by? I hate to say Toni hasn't been back yet."

"I figured as much, since I had not heard from you."

"Oh," Tonette blushed. "I'm sorry about that, Troy..."

"You don't have to apologize. I *did* just show up unannounced." His eyes roamed her up and down, making Tonette's cheeks flame with the heat of a dozen ovens. "You look very beguiling this evening."

"Thank you, Troy," Tonette said softly, crossing one leg over the other as the arousal shot straight to her core and sent a soaking rush to her new pink panties.

Troy's eyes lingered on her legs for several moments before he looked away suddenly, as if realizing what he had been doing. Tonette's heart raced at the thought of him being attracted to her. She had just bought the sleeveless, peach-colored dress a couple of days prior, thinking Stanley would like seeing her in it. But the fact that Troy liked it also made her want to go out and get more of them in every color they made.

"Would you, um, like something to drink or anything?" Tonette asked after a few moments of them both trying not to look at each other. "You're welcome to hang out...you know, unless you have something else to do..."

"That would be nice, thank you. I have absolutely nothing else to do," Troy replied with a smile. He eyed her again. "Are you sure it's no bother?"

"Absolutely. Let me just...go change into something more comfortable. Make yourself at home; I'll be right back."

"All right."

Tonette had to resist the urge to run to her room, cautious excitement giving her the energy and jitters of five Red Bulls. Troy was in her apartment again, and this time they were all alone...she couldn't deny being excited about that. As she quickly changed into a tank top and a pair of blue cotton shorts, she played with the idea of just going ahead and telling Troy the truth about the whole Toni thing. She knew he deserved to know. But as she went to the bathroom to check her appearance in the mirror, she realized the bigger part of her wanted to just enjoy the evening with Troy, with no interruptions. She could worry about telling him the truth tomorrow.

Fluffing her twist-out, she took another deep breath as she flipped off the bathroom light and headed back to the living room, making herself stop nervously wringing her hands as she entered.

"So...what would you like?" she said brightly, rubbing her hands together.

Troy looked up from the magazine he had been flipping through. "Some juice would be nice, if you have any."

"Coming right up," Tonette said with a smile. "Is apple okay?"

"Yes, thank you."

"Sure." Suddenly remembering she hadn't let Stanley know she had made it inside as promised, she grabbed her phone from the end table and sure enough, there was already a text from him, checking on her. She sent him a quick message, letting him know that she was fine and calling it a night, and that she'd talk to him the next day. She turned her phone on vibrate before setting it on the counter and getting the juice from the refrigerator.

"Here you go," she said a few minutes later, each hand holding a tall glass of apple juice.

"Thank you, Tonette," Troy said with a smile, taking the offered glass from her as she sat down next to him on the couch.

"No problem."

"So..." Troy hedged, taking a long sip of the juice before setting it on a coaster on the coffee table. "Did you let Toni know I was here?"

"I did..." Tonette looked away, scratching her head. She could feel Troy looking at her expectantly and she turned to face him. "Look, Troy, I have to be honest with you..."

"Yes?"

"Toni isn't..." She blinked before she got totally lost in his eyes again, "She isn't going to be here for a little while. She had to leave unexpectedly for work this morning. Some kind of...bone emergency," she added, remembering telling Troy that Toni was a paleontologist.

"Really?" Troy replied, clearly disappointed. Tonette looked away again, feeling like the scum of the scum of the earth.

"I'm sorry, Troy," she said softly.

"Well, I know it was a bit impulsive for me to fly all the way over here without a word...I cannot fault her for not being here," Troy said, rubbing his hands together. "There is no telling what you must think of me."

"Oh, I think it's really romantic, you coming here to see Toni like this," Tonette assured him. "She must have really made an impression on you."

"Yes," Troy agreed, smiling to himself. "That is putting it mildly. Ever since I met her, she had me captivated. She became all I thought about, and I wanted her all to myself the entire time she was there. I admit I often found excuses to go see her, before I finally got her to just stay with me for the last few days of her stay. Those days were...and please don't laugh at me for saying this..."

"Of course not," Tonette said softly, anxious to hear what he was about to say.

"I realize this might sound corny or silly considering that Toni and I hadn't known each other that long, but those few days she stayed with me were honestly some of the best of my life," Troy admitted, looking down at his hands. "Every time I told myself that I should not let myself get so into her because she would be leaving in a matter of days, I was never able to do it."

So it wasn't *just me*, Tonette thought to herself excitedly.

"When she came back home, I figured it would be best to try to move on; try to get over her," Troy continued. "Then one day I got a birthday card out of the blue."

"Really?"

"Yes. There was no name on it but I knew it was from her when I saw the address; as I mentioned, I do not know anyone else in Atlanta. I took it as a sign and before I knew it, I was buying a plane ticket to Atlanta." Troy looked at Tonette from under his lashes. "Do you think I'm mad?"

"No! No, absolutely not," Tonette said emphatically. "I could only *wish* a man was so taken with me that he would go to such lengths to see me. That's a...a beautiful thing. Toni is a lucky woman."

"I am a lucky man for having met her."

Tonette blushed, extremely flattered. Her heart swelled in her chest. Then she remembered that he wasn't talking about her; he was talking about Toni. The woman he had flown over two thousand miles for wasn't her. The woman he had fallen for wasn't her. It was a little deflating remembering this, but she plastered a smile on her face, not wanting to let on how disappointed she actually was.

"Well, um..." She tucked her feet under her, then mindlessly played with her thick socks. "Are you going to go back to Barbados now that you know Toni isn't here?"

Troy leaned forward and rested his elbows on his knees, slowly rubbing his hands together. "I suppose I should," he said thoughtfully. "Especially if you are unsure of how long she will be gone. And I don't want to keep bothering you..."

"You're not bothering me, Troy," Tonette interjected.

"But I have a while before school starts back—I'm a teacher—and I at least want to stay a while, in case she comes back early," Troy continued. "And I don't suppose there is a way to reach her while she is away?"

"Unfortunately not," Tonette replied quickly with a shake of her head. "She insisted that she wouldn't be able to be reached while she was gone. I'm not even sure where she went, to be honest; we're not all that close so she would only tell me so much, you know."

Troy nodded as if in understanding before looking ahead of him with slightly narrowed eyes. "I still cannot believe I am here," he said after a few moments. "I don't know what I expected to happen when I decided to come...all I knew was that I really, really wanted to see Toni again."

"Since she isn't here, do you feel like you...wasted a trip?" Tonette asked, looking down into her almost-empty glass. She steeled herself for his answer.

Troy looked at her over his shoulder. "I suppose that remains to be seen," he replied in a low voice that made

Tonette's breath hitch. "I do appreciate you spending this time with me, though."

"It's my pleasure. I feel like...like I know you already." Tonette looked at him, then looked away in a bashful shame.

It was several moments before she realized Troy was still looking at her with those intense eyes that had been haunting her dreams ever since she had left Barbados. "I have gotten that feeling, myself."

They gazed at each other before Tonette made herself turn her eyes away. Some strange mix of nervousness and arousal was swirling through her body. She felt incredibly guilty for lying to Troy, but at the same time, she ached to reach out and touch him. He sat mere inches from her, right where she had wished he would be for weeks and weeks, and she couldn't put her hands on him like she wanted to; there would be no way for her to explain that. More importantly, she didn't want him to reject her because she wasn't who he really wanted.

"So..." She bit her lip.

"I should go," Troy said softly.

"What?" Tonette hoped she didn't sound as panicked to him as she sounded to herself. "Why?"

"It is getting late, and I don't want to overstay my welcome."

Tonette started to insist that he could stay as long as he wanted, but didn't want to sound desperate. "Oh."

Troy drank the remainder of the juice in his glass before standing up.

"What are you doing tomorrow?" Tonette asked, quickly standing up herself.

"I don't have any plans," Troy replied, turning to face her. "Why do you ask?"

"If you want, you can...hang out with me," Tonette suggested shyly. "I'm pretty much free all day, myself." It might not have been the smartest idea, but she told herself it was too late to take it back.

"I would like that, Tonette, thank you," Troy replied with a smile. "Only if you're sure—"

"Troy," Tonette cut him off, placing a hand on his arm and ignoring the lightning bolt that rocked her body when she did, "Can we go ahead and agree that you are *never* imposing or bothering me so you don't have to keep feeling like you are? I'm glad to entertain you while you're here...it's the least I can do, given the circumstances."

Troy placed his hand over hers, and Tonette had to fight to keep her knees from buckling.

"I really appreciate it, Tonette," Troy said, his voice thick with sincerity.

"And you don't have to keep thanking me, either," Tonette added, nudging him playfully.

Chuckling, Troy nodded. "Understood," he nudged her back.

The two of them gazed at each other for a moment before bursting out in simultaneous laughter. Some of the tension of the moment lifted and Tonette almost felt like she had when she was on the island with Troy. They always had such a good time together.

The smile still on his face, Troy gently grabbed Tonette's wrist and pulled her in for a hug. It wasn't one of the close, intimate hugs that she shared with him in Barbados, but she still had to will all of her senses to calm down, as well as her heart, which was now beating a thousand beats a minute. Closing her eyes, she treated herself to a concentrated inhale of his scent, a soft grazing of his muscles with her fingers, and a subtle pressing of her body against his. Yearning overtook her body and caused it to pulse like the speakers at a rave, and she wished with everything in her that she had the nerve to do *something* to let him know how she was attracted to him, to get his desire for her to match hers for his, and to get his mind off Toni and onto her.

"Good night, Tonette," Troy said softly into her ear.

"Good night," Tonette whispered.

With a tight smile, Troy released her and walked out.

Tonette remained in that spot in the middle of her living room, her hand over her heart, knowing she was falling all over again but also knowing there was absolutely nothing she could do to stop it.

Chapter 13

"So you still didn't tell him, huh?"

Tonette adjusted the Bluetooth in her ear as she grabbed the eggs from the refrigerator, glad that Blue wasn't able to see her blush automatically at his question. "No, not yet."

"I don't know why you're saying 'not yet' like you plan on telling him at all."

"I *do* plan on telling him!"

"Well, what are you waiting on? You could've told him last night when y'all were drinking juice and making eyes at each other."

Tonette cracked some eggs in a bowl and added the onions and peppers she had already cut up. "Maybe I should have—"

"There's no *maybe* about it, T."

"Regardless, you and Olarion act like this is just the easiest thing for me to do. It's not."

"I'm not saying it will be easy, baby, but it's necessary," Blue said honestly. "You're just making it worse with every day you let pass without being real with him. If you care about him like I know you do, you'll just go ahead and do it and get it over with."

Tonette knew he was right. But she just hadn't been able to work up the nerve to tell Troy the truth yet.

"And you never know, it might not even be as bad as you think," Blue continued. "Who's to say that he won't appreciate your honesty and decide he wants to be with you, anyway? 'Cause when you think about it, T., what you did isn't all *that* bad...yeah, you were dishonest, but it wasn't on some malicious shit. Maybe he'll realize that and forgive you."

"That's wishful thinking," Tonette muttered, pouring her egg mixture into a pan.

"But it's possible."

"I guess it's *possible* but...I don't know, Blue. I just hate the thought of hurting Troy or him not wanting anything else to do with me."

"Well, baby, you started making this bed when you first introduced yourself to him as Toni," Blue reminded her. "I know you had no way of knowing how all of this was going to play out; you didn't plan to fall for the man like you did..."

"I didn't—"

"Don't even bother telling me that lie, okay? You fell for Troy hard and you're still on the ground. There's nothing wrong with that. Obviously he fell for you, too."

"For *Toni*, you mean," Tonette reminded him.

Blue paused. "Do I need to remind you that *you're* Toni?"

"Yeah, but still—"

"But still, what? You might've been playing a part but the base of it is still *you*. Was *everything* you told him about yourself a lie?"

"No, not everything."

"Okay, then."

"But Blue, it's not the same...I created this whole new persona. You and Olarion probably wouldn't have even recognized me, the way I was acting over there. It's nothing like I really am. That's obviously what Troy likes. And that's not me."

"So you don't think Troy would like you like you are now? Is that what you're saying?"

Tonette quietly stirred her eggs, silently confirming his statement.

"Damn. I've never known you to have low self-esteem."

"I don't have low self-esteem. I'm fine with the way I am. But Troy might not be."

"How would you know until you give him a chance to get to know the real you?"

"Well, he'll get to do that today," Tonette countered. "I'm supposed to be meeting up with him in a couple of hours."

"And you're gonna let a whole 'nother day go by without telling him the truth, I bet."

"I don't know."

"I do. Why don't you just admit you don't want the man to leave?"

"Okay. I *don't* want him to leave. Is that so terrible?"

"*That* isn't, but letting him continue to believe something that isn't real *is*."

Tonette sighed. She knew he was right.

The conversation with Blue weighed heavily on her mind as she ate her breakfast and started getting ready to meet Troy. It was still kind of surreal to her that he was even there. There had been plenty of times when she had actually pinched herself, not believing that her wishes to lay eyes on Troy again had actually come true. She would be lying if she said that she didn't want to do anything to send him back to Barbados sooner than he planned to go...she just wanted to enjoy him for as long as she could.

Her nerves started to dance with increasing speed as she got ready to meet up with Troy, feeling giddy and nervous all at the same time. She couldn't wait to see him and spend time with him, but she worried about saying something to tip him off. Her mind tried to remember everything she had told him in Barbados, and she just hoped that she didn't end up putting her foot in her mouth before the day was over with.

Finally, Troy came and picked her up in his rental car and they proceeded to explore Atlanta. Tonette took him to the Georgia Aquarium before showing him some of the other major tourist attractions like the Martin Luther King Jr. center, the World of Coca-Cola, and the Foxx Theater, along with some popular local spots, and Troy seemed fascinated by all of it.

"I did not realize there was so much here," he commented, looking at all the buildings as they passed them.

"Yeah, there's certainly plenty to keep you entertained," Tonette concurred.

"You must feel very fortunate to live here."

"It's a great city to live in. I guess I don't appreciate it as much as someone who doesn't, though. You kinda take it for granted."

"I can understand that. It is the same with me back home."

Tonette remembered him saying something like that back in Barbados. "I guess it's easy to kind of slip into that after a while, not appreciating what you have."

"That is a mistake I try not to make," Troy mused thoughtfully, stopping the car at a red light. He glanced over at Tonette, his gaze lingering for a moment before turning his eyes back to the road ahead of him. Tonette subtly placed a hand to her stomach, trying to still her bouncing butterflies, as she wondered what was behind that look but not having the nerve to ask.

They stopped for lunch at The Vortex and Tonette couldn't help but giggle at Troy's reaction to the atmosphere and the unusual burger combinations.

"I can honestly say I've never seen anything like this," he commented, looking around him. "I don't think I've ever seen so many tattoos in one place in my life."

Tonette laughed. "Yeah, it's certainly something else," she replied, smiling as she watched him take in his surroundings. "They don't even allow children in here."

"Really? I guess I can understand why that is."

"Now, Troy, don't laugh at me but after I finish eating all this, I'm going to want to go home and lay down, so I hope you don't want to go and do anything else after we leave here."

Troy looked at her. "Are you serious?"

"Yep. We call it having the 'itis," Tonette explained, pronouncing it EYE-tus.

"The 'itis'?"

"Yeah, where you stuff yourself then just lay down 'cause you're too full to move. You'll see."

When their orders arrived, Tonette laughed out loud at how big Troy's eyes got at the size of his burger that featured pulled pork, cheddar cheese, and bacon, along with the side of tater tots.

"My goodness," he marveled, looking like he didn't even know how to begin eating it.

"I told you."

Troy's eyes strayed to Tonette's plate. "Are those eggs on your burger?"

"Yep. Fried eggs, four slices of bacon and three pieces of cheese. It's *so* delicious but I'm going to have to move into the gym to work off all these calories. It tastes too good to care right now, though."

Troy chuckled. "It's nice to see that you're not obsessed with your weight and things like that."

"Oh no. I try to take care of myself but I'm not fanatical about it. If I want a burger or some pizza or whatever, I have it. It's all about moderation, for me. Life is just too short to be worried about every little calorie."

"I agree. From what I can see, though, you do a very nice job of maintaining yourself." His gaze swept over her and her face immediately flushed. "A *very* nice job."

Tonette's face was on fire. "Thank you, Troy."

They proceeded to eat and talk, taking their time and enjoying themselves. Troy asked a few questions about Toni but for the most part, he asked Tonette about herself, becoming intrigued when she told him she was a teacher. They swapped stories about their jobs and their students, both clearly sharing a love for what they did, and before they knew it, two hours had passed. Several times Tonette had noticed Troy giving her these looks, but again, she didn't have the nerve to ask him what was behind them.

"I am stuffed," Tonette said as they headed back to her apartment.

"You and me both," Troy concurred, smiling. "I wouldn't mind taking a nap, actually."

"That's that *itis* kicking in!" Tonette excitedly teased as she playfully patted his shoulder. "I'm right there with you on that. I cannot *wait* to get to my couch."

Troy chuckled.

When they got to her apartment building, Troy parked the car and immediately got out, going around to open Tonette's door for her.

"You don't have to walk me upstairs if you don't want to," Tonette commented as she got out of the car, placing her hand in his offered one. "I know you're probably tired."

"A gentleman always sees a lady to her door," Troy insisted, closing her door behind her. He didn't immediately let go of her hand; as they walked towards the building, their hands just kind of fell apart, to Tonette's chagrin.

"Well, that's very sweet of you."

They headed upstairs to her apartment in relative and comfortable silence. Troy gave her another one of those thoughtful looks again, and Tonette finally worked up the nerve to ask, "Is something wrong?"

"Not at all," Troy replied, still looking at her.

Not knowing what else to say, Tonette just nodded and continued up the stairs, her legs suddenly shaky.

When they arrived at her door, Tonette turned to face him with a smile on her face. "I had such a good time with you today, Troy. How did you enjoy the somewhat-condensed tour of my city?"

"I loved it," Troy said, licking his lips and smiling. Tonette's stomach clenched at the sight, remembering the things that tongue did to her in Barbados. "I know you said not to keep thanking you, but I must. I really do appreciate you showing me around and keeping me company today. It was very enjoyable."

"I'm glad you enjoyed yourself."

"Immensely." Troy gazed at her for a moment before stepping forward and pulling her into a hug. It was slightly tighter than the hug they had shared the night before, but still not nearly as intimate as the ones they shared in Barbados. Tonette wanted to get as close as she could to him, but she had to resist the urge to just mash her body into his. That would cause questions she wouldn't know how to answer.

The hug lingered for several moments before Troy pulled back and set those intense eyes on her face again, as if he was searching for the answer to something. Tonette fought to keep her eyes from averting away from his; instead, she took advantage of the opportunity to enjoy the up-close-and-personal view of his adorably gorgeous face. Everything in her wanted to feel those lips of his against hers again; her body was literally starting to ache, being this close to him. Thoughts of pulling him into her apartment and immediately just start taking clothes off clouded her mind; that's what *Toni* would have done. But Tonette didn't have the nerve.

"I just got the strangest feeling of déjà vu," Troy softly informed her, his hands maintaining their light hold on her waist.

Tonette's throat felt like cotton. "Really?"

"Yes. Maybe it is because you are Toni's twin but...I just feel very, very close to you."

Her face on fire, Tonette reluctantly stepped back, feeling the need to break up this moment before she either made a complete fool of herself or said something to blow her cover.

Troy looked down, stuffing his hands into his pockets. "I apologize," he said in a low voice. "I did not mean to make you uncomfortable."

"Oh no," Tonette rushed to assure him, not wanting him to never try touching her again, "You didn't—"

"I should go, Tonette."

"Troy, I..." Tonette's voice trailed off, not wanting to insist that he come inside like she was about to. She wanted him to stay, but knew it was probably best if he didn't. She looked down at some spot on the floor. "Okay."

"What were you about to say?" Troy asked, stepping closer to her. Anxiousness tilted his voice.

"Nothing." Tonette's voice caught in her throat at her quick reply. "It was nothing."

Pursing his lips, Troy nodded. "I will call you."

"Okay."

With one last thoughtful and curious gaze, Troy turned and walked away. Tonette forced herself to go ahead and go inside her apartment and not stand there watching him until she couldn't see him anymore like she wanted to. Once inside, she leaned against the door in relief, thankful that she hadn't said or done anything stupid.

After Tonette took a nap for a couple of hours, she got a call from Stanley, wanting to see her.

"Sure, yeah," Tonette yawned, sitting up. "I'd love that."

"You were asleep already? It's just a little after six."

"Oh no, I was just taking a nap, that's all."

"You okay?"

"Yeah, I'm great. What did you want to do?"

"I don't even know; it's been a long day. I really just miss you and want to be around you tonight; we don't even have to do anything."

Tonette couldn't resist grinning at his statement. "You sure know how to make a woman blush."

"Just speaking the truth," Stanley replied, the smile in his voice evident. "You need to get yourself together? I can come get you."

"You know what? Let me just meet you at your place; I've got to salvage my mashed hairdo."

Stanley chuckled. "Y'all ladies and your hair. Just be sure not to do anything too intricate to it 'cause all I'm gonna do is mess it up when you get here."

Tonette gasped. "Stanley!"

"What? You know I can't keep my hands out of your hair. I love it."

Grinning harder, Tonette shook her head. "Well, I certainly can't be mad at that."

They ended the call a few minutes later and Tonette played with the phone in her hands, still smiling to herself.

Tonette was on her way to run some errands the next day when she got a call from Troy.

"Hey, Troy, good morning," Tonette greeted him, the surprise in her voice evident.

"Good morning, Tonette," Troy's voice was rather somber.

"Is everything okay?"

"Unfortunately not. I must return home today; I just got word that a friend of mine has passed."

"Oh my goodness!" Tonette exclaimed. "I'm so sorry to hear that, Troy! What happened?"

"She was in a car accident a while back and it turned out her internal injuries were worse than everyone thought," Troy said, his voice sad. Tonette immediately wondered if it was the same friend that he had to go see about on her last day in Barbados. "She has had multiple surgeries since then and her body just couldn't take it anymore. She passed last night."

"Oh, Troy..." Tonette sincerely felt bad for him; he sounded so sad. She wished there was something she could do or say to comfort him but she knew there was nothing. "I am *so* sorry."

"I appreciate your concern, Tonette; thank you." Troy cleared his throat. "I am about to head to the airport to get the next flight out...I just wanted to let you know that I was leaving and to thank you for all of your hospitality these past few days."

"It was my pleasure; I enjoyed hanging out with you."

"And I you. If you speak to Toni, please let her know that I am sorry I did not get to see her."

It was Tonette's turn to clear her throat. "Sure."

"Hopefully she will reach out to me."

"Yeah," Tonette momentarily squeezed her eyes shut, kicking herself for her cowardliness. She knew she needed to bite the bullet and just tell him the truth, but she simply couldn't make herself do it. "Hopefully."

"Tonette..."

"Yes?"

Troy paused, then cleared his throat again. "I very much enjoyed meeting you."

Tonette couldn't resist her smile upon hearing that. Her fingers dug anxiously into the steering wheel. "The feeling is definitely mutual, Troy."

She wanted to ask him if he would be coming back, but she chickened out. She wanted to tell him to keep in touch, but she couldn't find the nerve. She had to remember that Troy wanted Toni, not her.

They ended their call a couple of minutes later, and an increasingly overwhelming sadness washed over her. It bummed her out knowing that Troy was on his way back to Barbados; she wasn't ready for their time together to be over already.

It was Olarion that had to remind her what a blessing Troy's leaving really was.

"Girl, you need to be thanking the Lord he left," she said. "I know you're going to miss him and everything, but this is a gift. Now you can stop with this whole twin charade and you don't have to worry about slipping up, since you apparently still can't tell him the truth."

"Olarion, it's not like I don't *want* to," Tonette said, her voice pained. "There were a few times yesterday when I started to just come out and tell him, but I punked out. I just couldn't make myself do it."

"Well, I know we've been on you to tell him the truth, but I certainly realize it's easier said than done," Olarion sympathized. "I can't even say with all certainty that I would have been able to do it myself, if I were in your situation. It's never easy hurting someone you care about."

"No, it's not."

A few silent moments passed by before Olarion softly asked, "Are you okay?"

Tonette knew she was asking if she was okay with Troy being gone. She wasn't. But she knew him leaving was probably for the best. And she could get all of her attention back on Stanley, where it needed to be.

"I will be."

Chapter 14

Over the next few weeks, Tonette and Stanley continued to date and get closer. He had grown on her considerably and she had gotten to where seeing him became the high points of a lot of her days. He still wasn't igniting the fire in her that Troy did, but she was beginning to wonder if *any* man could do that.

Troy still invaded her mind, but thoughts of him were slowly dwindling over time. She just tried to put him out of her mind the best she could; there was no use pining over a man she couldn't have, especially when she had a perfectly good one right in front of her that wanted her.

Since it was summer vacation, Tonette had a lot of free time on her hands. She always enjoyed the summer break, usually spending the majority of the time reading, having movie marathons, and spending time with her friends. She recalled one of the last assignments she had given her students before the school year ended. It was more of a 'just because' exercise; it wasn't anything she graded. She had told them to write about the person they wished they could be. When one of them asked her who she wished *she* could be, she immediately thought of Toni. While it was true that Tonette was happy with herself overall, she couldn't deny that there were some elements of Toni that she wouldn't have minded having, like her boldness and security with her sexuality. Toni wouldn't have let Troy go back to Barbados without making some kind of move on him, if that's what she wanted to do. The time they were in the hallway outside her apartment after they had gone sightseeing would have been the perfect opportunity. There were times when Tonette still kicked herself for letting that chance pass her by.

Stanley had invited Tonette over to his place for dinner, stating he wanted to cook for her. He poured her some wine and told her to relax, but Tonette couldn't resist wandering back into the kitchen where he was, her bare feet against the cool hardwood floor. She had grown to be very comfortable at his place.

"It sure smells good in here," she commented with a smile, as she watched him check a couple of pots on the stove.

He glanced over his shoulder at her with a wink. "Well, you know. I do what I can."

"What's on the menu?"

"You'll see."

"Ohh, keeping me in suspense, huh?" Tonette grinned, standing next to him at the counter as she took a sip of her wine.

"You know it."

"Hmm." She set her glass on the counter and looked at him, admiring the sight of him cooking a meal just for her. He didn't think it was that big of a deal, but she appreciated the gesture.

"You keep hanging around in here, I'm gonna put you to work," Stanley teased her.

"I don't mind helping. What do you need me to do?"

"I'm playing with you. You don't have to do anything."

"Seriously, though, I don't mind. It's the least I can do."

"Okay then, you wanna do something for me?"

"Sure."

Stanley suddenly reached over and grabbed her by the waist, pulling her to him, causing her to shriek in surprise.

"Come here," he said in a low voice.

Before Tonette could blink, Stanley swooped down and claimed her lips with his. He kissed her deeply and intensely, holding her even tighter to him, and to Tonette's surprise, her body responded in a way it never had to him before. Arousal warmed her, melting her insides to a puddle that gathered right between her legs. Her arms slid around his neck, welcoming the feeling and hoping this meant she had *finally* moved on from you-know-who.

Stanley backed her against the counter, moaning as his hands slid underneath her shirt. The intensity of their kiss built rapidly, and Tonette felt Stanley's brick-hard erection press against her. She gasped against his lips, not knowing why in the world she was surprised that he was aroused when she was, also.

"Tonette," he breathed, his kisses trailing down her neck. He buried a hand in her hair as he ground his hardness against her.

Tonette's hands gripped his shirt as he gently nudged her legs apart so he could get closer to her. Her head was spinning and she felt control slipping away from her, and she couldn't decide if this was a good or a bad thing. When Stanley's fingertips grazed across her breasts, she gently pushed him back.

"The food is burning," she panted as an excuse, her chest still heaving.

Stanley looked at her for a moment, the look in his eyes clearly indicating he didn't care about that food right then, but he stepped over and turned off the burners. He turned back towards her, but Tonette had already gone to the cupboard she knew the plates were in and was reaching up to get some. Stanley quickly went over to help her, reaching over her to get the plates as he pressed his still-solid erection into her backside.

Tonette was thankful that Stanley had grabbed the plates because she surely would have dropped them. She turned to face him as he set the plates on the counter behind her, his eyes still full of desire and set intently on her face. Her hands gripped the counter as she bit her lip, trying to mentally decide if she was ready to go where he clearly was ready to.

"What are we doing?" Stanley asked her, his voice low and deliberate.

Even though Tonette had an idea, she still asked, "What do you mean?"

"You and I. What is this?"

Tonette wasn't quite ready for this conversation but knew Stanley was well within his rights to ask. They had been dating for a while and he had been more than patient with her; of course he would be asking this sooner or later. "I'm not sure what to tell you, Stanley..."

Backing off of her, Stanley ran a hand down his face. That clearly wasn't the answer he wanted. "Tonette..."

"Stanley, look—"

"I want you all to myself," Stanley forged ahead, stepping closer to her. "I know we haven't made any declarations or commitments to each other, but I haven't been seeing anybody else. If you have, it's fine...I can't say anything about it. But I'm getting to where I don't like the thought of you with anybody but me. I want you to be my woman, Tonette."

Tonette's mouth fell open. She was flattered, even though she wasn't *quite* on the same page as he was. She really hadn't thought about Stanley with other women, and she could admit she didn't particularly enjoy the thought. But was she ready to be exclusive? With Stanley?

"Stanley, please know that I like you a *lot*," Tonette began, lightly grabbing his wrists. "And I love spending time with you. I want us to continue to get closer and get to know each other."

"But?" Stanley urged, sensing there was more.

"I can't even explain why, but I'm just not quite ready to be exclusive yet. Hey," Tonette urged, her grip on his wrists tightening when she felt him start to pull away. "Please don't be upset with me. I've come a *long* way since we first started seeing each other."

Stanley looked away, frustration marring his handsome face. "Is there someone else?" he asked, his face still turned away from her.

"No. I'm not seeing anyone else. This is just about me wanting to be fair to you, and it wouldn't be if I got with you before I was really ready to," Tonette said, her voice pleading with him to understand.

Several tense moments passed and Tonette started to think Stanley was going to say he was tired of waiting on her and kick her out, but to her relief his expression softened. He released a long sigh, taking her hands in his and bringing them to his lips.

"I guess you meant it when you said you wanted to move slow, huh?"

Tonette smiled, relieved that he wasn't angry with her. "So you understand?"

"Not really, Tonette, but that's just because I want you so much. But as long as you're being honest with me, I can be patient with you."

"Absolutely," Tonette insisted, even though honesty hadn't exactly been something she could brag about the past few months.

Stanley gathered her up in his arms, resting his chin on the top of her head. Closing her eyes, Tonette laid her head against his chest, hoping she wasn't being foolish for not snatching this good man off the market.

Later, after Tonette was home, she sat in her office with a note pad in front of her. She took a pencil and drew a line down the middle of the paper, and actually began to write out Stanley's pros and cons. It was an exercise she had heard about other people doing and had even seen Olarion do several times over the years, but she had never done herself. Part of her felt a little silly, but she figured it couldn't hurt. Maybe it would give her a nudge in the right direction.

She wrote diligently for over twenty minutes, and when she finished, she wasn't surprised to see that Stanley's pros far outweighed his cons. Sighing, she pushed the note pad away and sat back in her chair, tapping her fingers on the desk. Something was holding her back from being all the way in with Stanley. Even though she had gotten considerably more comfortable with him and cared deeply for him, she couldn't make herself jump off that cliff just yet. In the back of her mind, she knew what that something was. Or rather, *who* that something was. She just didn't want to admit it, even to herself, because she was supposed to be over him by now.

When Blue called a little later to check on her, he asked if she had heard from Troy since he went back to Barbados.

"No," Tonette replied simply.

"Are you okay with that?"

"It is what it is, Blue," Tonette shrugged, trying to sound more cavalier than she really felt. "I can't let myself obsess over him like I used to."

"Be real with me, baby. You miss him?"

Tonette sighed, knowing she would be glad when Troy was no longer her friends' favorite topic of conversation. "Yes, I miss him. But it doesn't matter. He's gone and I need to concentrate on Stanley."

"You say that like Stanley is some kind of consolation prize."

"Not at all."

"If Troy was here full time and you had a chance to be with him, as yourself, would you choose him or Stanley?"

Tonette didn't want to answer that question. They both knew the answer. "I don't know."

Blue knew she was lying. But thankfully, he didn't press her. "Okay, boo."

Chapter 15

Barbados seemed like such a far off place and time to Tonette; it was almost like none of her time there really happened, even though she knew it had. But thankfully, she was getting to where she could (cautiously) say that she was somewhat over Troy. Not completely, but for the most part. Stanley had come from behind and taken over the majority of the thoughts in her mind when it came to romance, and Tonette was enjoying fantasizing about a man that she could actually have.

Things with Stanley were going really well; she saw him two or three times a week, usually, and they always had a good time together. Tonette knew Stanley still wanted to take their relationship to the next level, but thankfully he wasn't pushing her. For the time being, he was satisfied with the title of being the only man Tonette was seeing, even if he couldn't officially call himself her man yet.

The two of them still hadn't slept together, even though Stanley had made it more than clear that he wanted to. One night when he was at her apartment, they began kissing and fooling around, and things got pretty hot and heavy. Stanley had a raw intensity in his eyes that Tonette hadn't seen from him before, but she very well knew what that look meant.

"I want you," Stanley needlessly informed her, his voice a growl. His hands were aggressively clawing at her clothes. "*Now*."

Her breath caught in her throat, all Tonette could do was moan, loudly, as Stanley lifted her shirt and helped himself to her heaving, aching breasts. He had never before been this aggressive or forward and Tonette wondered how he would take it when she told him that it wasn't going to happen.

"Stanley..."

"Baby, please don't turn me down right now," Stanley pleaded, sliding his hands between them to unbuckle her jeans. "I need you..."

"I can't—"

"Why do you keep pushing me away? Do you have any idea how much I want you??"

"It's not like that—"

"Then let me have you," he whispered against her lips, grinding hard against her. "Feel that," he ordered, grabbing her hand and putting it down his pants, which Tonette had no idea when he unbuckled. He was long and rock-hard, and Tonette felt herself clinch at the thought of that sliding inside of her.

"*That's* how much I want you, baby," he whispered before sticking his tongue down her throat.

They kissed hungrily for several moments, Stanley's hand guiding Tonette's as she stroked him, increasing his already sky-high arousal. He was sucking on her neck so hard that she knew she was going to need makeup to cover the mark he was surely leaving there.

"Take these off," he growled, tugging on the waistband of her skinny jeans.

"Stanley, wait," Tonette said firmly, grabbing his hands. "Let's ease up for a minute..."

Blowing a frustrated sigh through his moist lips, Stanley gritted his teeth and rolled onto his side, running a hand down his face. "Shutting me down again, huh?"

"No, I'm not—"

"What's your excuse this time, huh? Are we moving too fast again? Is this another major life decision? You need a few weeks to think about this, too?"

Tonette looked at him with hurt eyes before sitting up and yanking her bra and shirt back down in one swoop. Angry tears burned her eyes. Scooting away from him slightly, she re-fastened the button on her jeans.

"I'm on my damn period."

All of the color drained from Stanley's face, and remorse immediately replaced the frustration in his eyes. He reached for her but she moved away. "Tonette, baby, I am so sorry..."

Angrier than she had been in a while, Tonette jumped off the bed and stomped towards the kitchen. Stanley was right on her heels.

"I didn't know!" he exclaimed, trying to grab her hand but she wasn't having it. "Tonette, please..."

"No," she said strongly, whirling around to face him. "I don't appreciate that at all, Stanley."

"I know..."

"Just because we're dating and you've been patient with me, that doesn't give you the right to be nasty about it," Tonette continued, swiping a tear from her cheek and folding her arms. "If you want to be with someone that's more obliging to you, be my guest. But even if it *wasn't* my time of the month, I have *every* right to take my time deciding when I'm ready to have sex with you. I like you a lot, Stanley, but I don't *owe* you my body."

Sighing wearily, Stanley nodded. "You're right," he said earnestly. His eyes pleaded for forgiveness; it was the first time she had gotten really upset with him. "You're absolutely right, Tonette. Baby, I'm sorry...I shouldn't have come at you like that. Please forgive me."

Shaking her head, Tonette looked away from him. His words had really hurt her.

"Tonette!" Stanley persisted, stepping around her so he was in her line of vision. "Please. You have to know I would never say or do anything to hurt you on purpose. I just lost my head for a minute but I know that's no excuse."

"But you meant it, though," Tonette replied, sniffing as she cut her eyes at him. "That came from somewhere. You're tired of waiting on me."

"No—"

"I won't be pushed or pressured to do anything I'm not ready to do, so if you want to go, don't let me stop you."

"Tonette!" Stanley grabbed her shoulders and tried to get her to look at him. "Stop!"

"Matter of fact, why don't you go ahead and leave? I'm sure there are plenty of other women who are more than willing to let you between their legs in no time. Wouldn't want you waiting on any more of my *life decisions*."

"Tonette, please take a second and listen to me, okay?" Stanley pleaded, his grip on her tightening a little. "I was wrong, and I know it. You have every right to be upset at me. But please don't use this as an excuse to push me away. You *know* I care about you. Yes, I absolutely want to make love to you but if you need or want to wait, for *whatever* reason, I'm willing to do that. I don't want to lose you over this, Tonette." His eyes bore into hers, sincerity radiating from him with a warmth that started to melt the coldness she was feeling towards him right then.

Finally, she sighed. "Stanley, I don't have a three-month rule or a six-month rule. I'm not trying to be coy or play hard to get. This is just me; I take my time with things, especially when it comes to who I share my body with. That means something to me. It's not that I don't want you. I can't even say with all certainty that if I wasn't on my period that we wouldn't still be in my bed right now. But what you said hurt, like you were mocking me or something. And if this is going to keep being an issue—"

"It's *not*," Stanley insisted, pulling her closer to him. "I promise. Like I said, I just lost my head. I said something stupid, but I absolutely respect you. Tonette, I want you; not for sex, but for *you*. Can you please forgive me and give me a chance to prove that to you?"

Tonette looked at him, and she knew he meant what he was saying. Stanley had proven himself to be a good man to her over the previous couple of months, and he deserved another chance. And it certainly wasn't like she had never been guilty of saying something stupid.

"Okay," she finally said, sniffling.

Breathing a sigh of relief, Stanley pulled her to him and wrapped his arms around her, resting his cheek on the top of her head.

Even though Tonette forgave Stanley for his comments, she still opted to spend the rest of her evening alone, so Stanley left shortly after their reconciliation. Tonette got some raw carrots and hummus, poured herself some apple juice, and curled up on the couch. Her mind replayed the past hour or so as she ate, chewing slowly and thoughtfully.

Tonette wasn't upset about the fact that Stanley wanted to sleep with her; she had thought about them making love several times recently herself. What hurt her was that he seemed to mock the fact that she preferred to take her time with things, even though he had always insisted that he didn't have a problem with it. She had accepted his apology, but she still thought he meant what he said; he just hadn't meant to say it.

But Tonette also had to acknowledge the irony of the whole situation. She insisted on waiting with Stanley, but she had been ready to sleep with Troy the night she met him. Yes, she was under her alter ego of Toni at the time, but the feelings, emotions and desires she had been experiencing were all her. She had gotten close to making love to Troy several times, willingly, and she had known Troy a few days; she and Stanley had been dating for a few months and she still didn't really feel ready. What was the difference? And did it make her a hypocrite that she proclaimed to Stanley that she was one to take her time yet her actions with Troy clearly indicated he opposite?

The more she thought about her actions in Barbados, the more she began to feel that burn of desire and yearning for Troy again. The replay button on her memory was pressed all on its own, and she was whisked back to all those passionate moments they shared, recalling them as vividly as if they had happened yesterday. She bit her lip as she recalled their encounter in her room the day before she left Barbados; those few moments of him being inside of her were better than all of her previous sexual encounters combined. Just like that, Tonette felt herself starting to miss Troy again.

With a heavy sigh, Tonette let her head fall against the back of the couch. Confusion was starting to sprinkle over her mind, and that frustrated her. She had finally gotten to where she was happy with her relationship with Stanley and over Troy, setting herself free from the hold he had seemed to have over her. But now thoughts of him were starting to fill up her mind and longing for him spreading through her heart at a rate so fast she couldn't stop it. Tonette wanted to move forward with Stanley; she didn't want to go back to ping-ponging between trying to make herself want him more and trying to make herself want Troy less. She didn't want to move backwards.

"What am I doing?" she whispered to herself, already knowing she didn't know the answer.

"Hello, Tonette."

She almost dropped the phone. The last thing Tonette had been expecting was a call from Troy. She told herself to get a grip as she gathered herself to respond.

"Troy, this is a surprise," she replied lightly. Her hand automatically went to her chest, as it often did when Troy was involved. "How are you?"

"I am well, thank you for asking. And you?"

"I'm great."

"I know you're probably a little surprised to hear from me," Troy said. "After the memorial for my friend, I kind of shut down for a little while, but then it occurred to me that I was not doing myself any good by doing that. Her death was just another reminder that I needed to get on with my life, and also that I do not want to have any regrets as I do. So with that being said, I will be flying back in to Atlanta tomorrow."

Tonette almost dropped the phone again. "Y-you are?"

"Yes. I had to leave suddenly last time, sooner than I planned or wanted to. And I still have a little while before the new school term begins. So I am following my gut and coming back."

Immediately, Tonette was giddy at the prospect of seeing Troy again. But at the same time, she was anxious that she again had to face the dilemma of either continuing with the whole Toni charade or finally telling him the truth.

"Well, that's...that's great, Troy," Tonette said, trying to keep her voice from shaking. "It will be good to see you again."

"I look forward to seeing you, also," Troy replied in a voice that had Tonette's thighs squeezing together all on their own. "Would you mind picking me up from the airport? I hate to ask, but I was informed that there will not be any rental cars available yet and—"

"Sure, no problem," Tonette quickly confirmed, squeezing her eyes shut at her obvious eagerness. "I'd be happy to."

"I appreciate it, Tonette," Troy replied gratefully. "I can go ahead and give you my flight information, if you like."

"Yeah, just let me grab a pen." Tonette's hand gripped the phone as she scurried into her office, her head floating that she was actually going to be seeing Troy again in less than 24 hours. She grabbed a notepad and pen out of her desk and took a deep breath, telling herself again to get it together. "Okay, hit me."

Troy gave her his flight information and they ended the call, with Tonette promising to be there at the airport ready and waiting when his flight came in. Her hands were shaking and her heart thumped in her chest. Troy was actually coming back to Atlanta.

Tonette couldn't deny she was looking forward to seeing him. But she was also anticipating finally coming clean about pretending to be Toni in Barbados and then pretending to be Toni's twin after he came to Atlanta the last time looking for Toni. It wasn't going to be easy to look into those eyes and admit all this, and she already knew he would be upset with her, but she knew she could not keep putting it off. Every time she thought she was in the clear and would be able to get out of telling him the truth, he showed up again. It would just put her more at ease to have everything out in the open.

Later on that day, Olarion called and when she asked about her plans for the next day, Tonette almost didn't want to tell her about Troy coming in and her jumping at the chance to pick him up from the airport. She knew that would just start a whole new barrage of questions that she wouldn't want to answer, but she figured she might as well go ahead and bite the bullet.

"Oh, I have to pick Troy up from the airport," she said as casually as she could. "So, what are you gonna be do—"

"Hold up!" Olarion exclaimed, cutting her off. "Did you just say you were picking Troy up from the airport tomorrow?"

"Yeah."

"Why??"

"Because apparently there aren't any rental cars available, and he needs a ride..."

"Not *that*! Why is he coming back?"

"Oh. Because his visit was cut short last time, that's all." Tonette didn't want to get into all the stuff Troy had said about having no regrets and living life to the fullest and following his gut and all that.

"So he wants to come back and try to see Toni again?"

"He didn't mention Toni when I spoke to him. But what other reason could there be?"

Olarion was quiet for a moment. "You don't think he just wants to come back to see *you*? You said you two had a good time together and shared a moment—"

"I don't think I said all that."

"Yes you *did*, Tonette!"

"Well, even if I did, it doesn't make any difference. The only reason I agreed to pick him up was because I figured it was a good opportunity for me to finally tell him the truth about everything. Obviously, the universe is telling me I need to do it, since he keeps showing back up."

"Why didn't you just tell him over the phone and save him a trip?"

Tonette paused. The thought had never even occurred to her. "I don't know," she replied weakly.

"You're looking forward to seeing him, aren't you?" Olarion surmised.

"I didn't say that."

"You didn't have to say it."

"I'm with Stanley."

"Don't be trying to claim the man now when you're always so quick to remind us any other time that y'all aren't official yet. And I like Stanley, but this doesn't have anything to do with him, anyway. This is about your unresolved feelings for Troy that you are still for whatever reason trying to deny."

"This has nothing to do with that. I'm just trying to finally do the right thing."

"So, what, you're going to tell him in the airport so he can get right back on the next flight to Barbados? Or are you going to try to enjoy him for a while first and use the fact that he just got here as an excuse?"

Tonette pursed her lips. "You don't think very much of me, I see."

"Don't you dare say that. I think the world of you and you know it. But we all do stupid stuff when we're in love, and you can deny it all you want, but you are in *love* with that man, girl. Everybody can see it but you still don't want to admit it."

Tonette immediately wondered if Troy could sense her feelings for him. She thought she had done a pretty good job of maintaining her cool facade during his last visit, but now she wasn't so sure. She knew she had slipped up when they were at her door after their day of sightseeing; she had become captivated by him. Could his return have something to do with that? He certainly hadn't mentioned Toni during their call; he didn't say he was coming back looking for her, even though Tonette was convinced that was the case. But she had certainly noticed all the looks he had been giving her when he was here; could he possibly have feelings for her, as herself?

"Yeah, well," Tonette evaded, "Regardless, I am determined that by the time Troy goes back to Barbados this time, he will know everything he needs to know."

"I hope he does," Olarion replied. "So do you mind if Blue and I come over tomorrow? Or do you want to be alone with your man?"

"Whatever," Tonette scoffed, sucking her teeth. "I don't care if y'all come over. We're certainly not gonna be doing anything that you can't be witness to. And Troy is *not* my man."

"Uh-huh. Okay, then."

Troy's smile was immediate upon seeing Tonette the next day at the airport. He set his large duffel bag on the ground and pulled her in for a hug. Tonette couldn't help but notice how tightly he was holding her. There went that feeling washing over her again.

"Thank you again for coming," he said, his lips close to her ear. Tonette's eyes fluttered closed. "It is so good to see you again."

Gathering herself, Tonette plastered on a smile as their hug ended. It amazed her how he looked better and better every time she saw him. "It's good to see you, too, Troy. I'm glad you made it in safely. How was the flight?"

"It was pleasant enough. A friend of mine works for the airline and they got me an upgrade out of coach, so it was very nice."

"That sounds good; I've only ever flown coach, myself. Do you have all of your bags and everything?"

"Yes, it's just these two," Troy answered, indicating his duffel bag and rolling suitcase. "I am ready when you are."

"All right, well let's go," Tonette smiled, turning towards the exits. "You hungry?"

"Not really. Though I do look forward to you showing me more of the delicious southern cuisine."

"There's plenty of it," Tonette quipped as they stepped outside. The bright Atlanta sun washed over them as they headed to her car, making pleasant small talk. Tonette was trying her best to remain somewhat aloof, even though her insides were like jumping beans of excitement at being close to Troy again. With all the progress towards getting over him she had thought she had made over the past weeks since Troy left last time, she was surprised at how quickly all those feelings came rushing back as soon as she laid eyes on him. She had immediately wanted to run to him, jump into his arms, kiss those lips...it had taken all of her control to just stand there with her hands alternating between being clasped together and nervously rubbing her hips.

Once they made it back to her apartment, Troy threw her for another loop.

"I called the hotel I stayed at during my previous visit and was told that most of their rooms were unavailable due to some convention that had come to town," he said, pulling his phone from his pocket. "Can you recommend another place to stay?"

"You can stay with me," Tonette heard herself suggest. She didn't know where that suggestion came from, but she had blurted it out before she could even blink. *What the hell are you doing??* she scolded herself.

Troy's eyebrows shot up, clearly surprised himself. "Really? I don't want to be in the way. You were already kind enough to come get me from the airport...I should be able to get a rental car tomorrow or the next day, by the way."

"Don't even worry about it, Troy; about staying with me, I mean. There's no need in you spending money on a hotel when I have room." Tonette knew it was a bad idea, but she found herself wanting Troy to stay with her more than she cared about being sensible right then.

"Well, if you are sure..."

Just then, there was a knock on the door. Tonette jumped, temporarily jarred.

"Who is it?" she called out, stepping closer to the door.

"It's us, girl," Olarion replied.

Tonette had already forgotten that she had told Olarion that she and Blue could come over. She could just imagine their response when they found out about her offering for Troy to stay with her. With a nervous clearing of her throat, she opened the door.

"Kiss kiss, hug hug, now move...I've gotta pee!" Blue urged, rushing past them as soon as the door was opened.

Olarion shook her head as she closed the door behind her. She hugged Tonette, then turned to Troy with smile on her face. "Hey there Troy; it's good to see you again."

Troy returned her smile as she stepped over to her and took her hand, kissing it graciously. Tonette bit her lip at the sight; why was she feeling jealous over something as meaningless as that?

"A pleasure to see you again, as well," Troy informed Olarion, momentarily holding her hand in both of his before releasing it. "You are looking beautiful."

Olarion blushed; Tonette couldn't remember the last time she had seen her friend grin so hard. "You sweet-talker, you. Thank you, Troy."

"What are you and Blue going to do today?" Tonette quickly asked, wanting to break up this exchange for some reason. She regretted telling Olarion she could come over with Blue.

"I don't know; we might go to a movie later on. Y'all wanna go?"

"No thank you," Tonette responded quickly again. She glanced at Troy, who was looking at her curiously. "I mean...I figured you would be tired and everything from your flight and just want to get settled in."

"I could just do that when we get back home afterwards."

"What?" Olarion asked, her eyes turning to Tonette with a clear *I know you didn't do what I think you did* look in them. "You're going to be staying with Tonette during your visit?"

"Yes, Tonette was kind enough to offer that I stay here since the hotel—"

"You're staying with Tonette?" Blue asked, just having entered the room. He was rubbing lotion onto his hands. He looked at Tonette pointedly. "That's interesting."

"Would that be a problem for you?" Troy asked Blue, still thinking that Blue was Tonette's ex-husband. "I do not want to make things awkward..."

Blue scoffed, shrugging his broad shoulders. "Why should I care? It's not like I'm—"

"*Married* to me anymore," Tonette completed his sentence. She chuckled nervously at the look Troy was giving her. "Blue and I have been over for a while now. We're just very good friends; we can each do as we please."

"Oh, yeah," Blue confirmed, remembering the ruse. "Yeah, I have no ties on her like that anymore. Hell, sleep in her bed with her, if you want."

Tonette's face flamed with embarrassment; she couldn't *believe* Blue had just said that! Even Troy looked like he was blushing a little. Olarion had her head turned, trying to suppress a laugh.

"So, ahh..." she hedged, subtly hitting Blue in the arm, "We're going to go on ahead to this movie and let you all do your thing; Troy, maybe you can join us next time, if you're still here."

"Sure, that would be great," Troy replied.

"Awesomeness...Tonette, I need to borrow a shirt from you, if that's all right."

"What shirt?"

"I'm not sure...I might just need to see what you have. Come back here with me real quick."

Tonette knew Olarion just wanted to get her alone so she could get onto her about inviting Troy stay with her. "Yeah, okay. We'll be right back; make yourself comfortable," she said to Troy.

"Take your time," Troy replied.

"Come on, let's sit down, man...there's no telling how long those hens are gonna be," Blue said to Troy as he grabbed the remote and plopped down onto the couch.

"Hens?"

Olarion wasted no time getting on Tonette's case as soon as they were in her room and the door was closed.

"Um, do you just *look* for ways to make things more difficult, or..."

"I'm not making anything difficult. This does not have to be that big a deal. The hotel he stayed in last time wasn't available so I offered for him to stay with me. That's it."

"That's it? Are there not, like, a *thousand* other hotels or motels in Atlanta he could stay in?"

"What sense does that make? I have the room."

"That's not the point, T., and you know it."

"Well, enlighten me as to what your point is, then."

"You already know, but since you want to play clueless, I'll tell you anyway. You are setting yourself up for something I don't think you're ready for. You can't even acknowledge that you have feelings for the man, yet you keep doing this crazy stuff, acting like somebody else and pretending to be your own twin, saying you and Blue were *married*—"

"We don't need to itemize everything..."

"And now you're letting him stay in your place, knowing you're keeping all of this from him. Only people in love do stupid stuff like this."

"I'm gonna tell him, O."

"And what about Stanley? Have you even considered how you're going to explain another man staying with you?"

Tonette hadn't. She hadn't even thought about Stanley ever since Troy arrived. "That's not going to be a problem. Troy and I aren't dating or sleeping together or anything. He's not even interested in me, remember? The whole reason he came here in the first place was for Toni."

"And how have you explained Toni's absence this time? Is she still supposed to be out of the country looking for dinosaur bones?"

Tonette played with her fingers as she eased over to her closet, mindlessly starting to flip through it. "He actually hasn't asked about her yet."

Olarion gasped. "Did he ask about her yesterday when he called you?"

Tonette cleared her throat. "No."

"So either he knows the truth already, which I doubt, or he's here to see *you*," Olarion informed her pointedly.

"He's *not* here to see me."

"You don't know that. And I know you wouldn't have the guts to ask."

"Look," Tonette snapped, becoming exasperated, "You just need to chill out and let me handle this the way I want to handle it, all right? I know what I'm doing."

Olarion just looked at her friend sympathetically. "For your sake, girl, I really hope you do," she said sincerely. "Just remember that I'm on your side. And if I stay on you about all this, it's just because I don't want to see you end up getting hurt. Loving and losing is a bitch."

Nodding, Tonette grabbed the first blouse she saw out of her closet and tossed it to her friend. "I appreciate the concern, but the constant grilling can be a little much. Just be there for me when I need you, okay? That's all I ask."

Olarion crossed the room and gave Tonette a warm hug. "You know I'm here for you."

"Thank you. Now take this shirt so you can Blue can get on out of here. There's no telling what he's said to Troy by now."

Olarion and Blue left shortly after, and Tonette helped Troy get settled in, showing him how to fold out the sofa bed and where everything was.

"Just make yourself at home," she told him.

"Thank you, Tonette." He gave her one of his knee-weakening smiles.

Since Troy was feeling tired, Tonette suggested just ordering some Chinese food and hanging out, to which Troy readily agreed. They easily fell into conversation, telling each other more about their families, their goals and wishes, and other random things like what the best cereal was and which James Bond was the best one. Troy was giving her those random thoughtful looks again, sending Tonette's curiosity into overdrive. A couple of hours passed before Toni's name finally came up.

"You remind me so much of her," Troy commented, his eyes roaming over her face. "I know that seems like a silly thing to say, considering you two are twins. I just keep getting the feeling that I've known you longer than I have."

Becoming suddenly engrossed with her chopsticks, Tonette chuckled nervously. "Maybe I'm just one of those people that has a familiar face or something."

"No, no, it's more than that," Troy quickly insisted, turning fully towards her. "I really don't even know how to explain it myself, but I am just...I feel so at ease with you. Does that make any sense?"

Yeah, it makes sense, Tonette thought to herself glumly. *You feel comfortable with me like a buddy or a puppy or something. But there was this magnetic attraction drawing you to Toni that had you flying all the way from Barbados to Atlanta.*

"Kinda, yeah," she answered with a light shrug. "I've experienced something like that before."

Troy was gazing at her again. "I absolutely love your hair," he said softly. His hand moved towards her, hovering above her shoulder. "May I?"

Not being able to speak, Tonette just nodded. Troy gently eased his fingers into her thick, brown natural hair, his fingers sliding across her scalp in such a soothing way that Tonette couldn't help but close her eyes and sigh in contentment, leaning slightly into his hand. She absolutely loved for people to play in her hair; it was usually a good way to get her to relax. But this time, she was becoming more than relaxed; he was turning her on.

When she dared to open her eyes, Troy was looking at her with darkened eyes, his bottom lip pulled between his teeth. Tonette's breathing deepened as she became trapped in his gaze; she became very aware of everything around her. The low ticking of the clock on the wall, people walking by in the hallway outside her front door, and the rise and fall of her chest that had somehow synced with Troy's. The desire in his eyes was evident, and she was sure hers matched his because she was definitely feeling it.

Abort and escape, abort and escape, she warned herself.

"I should, um..." she croaked, surprised at how husky her voice sounded, "I should let you get your rest now. I didn't realize how late it was getting."

Troy continued to look at her for several moments before releasing his bottom lip, leaving a moistness behind that had Tonette wanting to dive across that sofa and taste it with her tongue. Slowly, Troy slid his hand out of her hair. He stood slowly before looking down at her and offering his hand. Placing her hand in his, she allowed Troy to help pull her up.

"Good night, then," Troy murmured, looking right into her eyes.

Tonette swallowed. "Good night."

Leaning in, Troy placed a soft, lingering kiss on her cheek. Her mind flashed back to the passionate kisses they had shared in Barbados. The scent of his cologne assailed her senses, and that along with the sensation of his moist lips on her face had her releasing a soft, involuntary moan that made her blush in embarrassment. With her body on fire, she made herself step around Troy and hurry the best she could to her room on her shaky legs.

Chapter 16

Tonette heard the faint knocking, but was sure she was dreaming it. She rolled over and buried her face in her pillow, but the knocking continued. Then she heard another knocking that was louder.

"Tonette," Troy's voice called out.

Throwing the covers off of her, Tonette scrambled out of bed and dashed over to open her bedroom door. Troy was standing there in pajama bottoms and a t-shirt, early morning stubble gracing his face, and Tonette tried hard to ignore just how frustratingly sexy he was.

"Someone is at your front door," he informed her.

"Oh?" Tonette noticed Troy's eyes wander downwards, and she suddenly remembered she was wearing a rather short nightshirt. Her cheeks flushed as she tried to ease behind her bedroom door. "Um, thanks for letting me know; I'll be right out."

"No problem."

Tonette closed the door and grabbed the first pair of shorts she saw in her drawer, yanking them on as she hurried down the hall towards the living room. Troy had made himself scarce, probably to the kitchen or the bathroom, but the sofa bed where he slept was still pulled out and adorned with rumpled sheets. Tonette had no idea who could be showing up at her door at nine o'clock in the morning.

She *certainly* wasn't expecting to see Stanley.

"Hey," she greeted, feeling suddenly nervous but trying not to show it. "What, um...I wasn't expecting you. Is everything okay?"

"Yeah, I just wanted to stop by and see you before I headed to work," Stanley replied, smiling down at her. "I tried to call you on the way but you never answered...figured you were knocked out. I haven't seen much of you these past few days."

"Oh, yeah. I've just had some things going on, that's all."

"Are you gonna let me in?" Stanley asked amusingly, noting how she was still peeking out at him through the slightly cracked-open door.

"Oh! I'm sorry, Stanley; of course...come on in," Tonette said, forcing a smile on her face as she stepped aside. *Just be cool*, she told herself. *If you don't act guilty, he won't get suspicious.*

As soon as he was inside the apartment, Stanley pulled her into a long, tight bear hug. He then leaned down to kiss her lips, and Tonette wondered exactly where Troy was right then. She gently pulled away.

"Morning breath," she explained, touching her fingers to her lips.

"I'm not worried about that," Stanley insisted, reaching for her again.

Tonette smiled sheepishly as she stepped out of his grasp, her fingers still over her mouth. "*I* am. You want some juice or something?"

"Nah, I can't stay long." It was then that Stanley noticed the pulled-out sofa bed. "You have company?"

Tonette knew it had been foolish to hope he wouldn't notice that. "Yeah, my...cousin is in town for a little while."

"Oh, okay," Stanley replied easily, seeming to believe her. "I guess that's why I haven't heard much from you, huh? How long will they be staying?"

"I'm not sure, actually," Tonette replied with a casual lift of her shoulder. "He hasn't been here that long."

Stanley's eyebrow arched curiously. "He?"

"Yeah." Tonette fought to keep her voice and expression even. "I haven't seen him in a while so we're just going to hang out, enjoy the city, get caught up...that kind of thing."

"Nice," Stanley eyed her, nodding slowly. Tonette wondered what he was thinking, but thankfully he quickly looked at his watch. "Well, I'd like to stick around and meet him but I need to get going; you know how rush hour traffic is. I'll give you a call later, okay?"

"Okay," Tonette replied, smiling and relieved that he was leaving.

He opened his arms for a hug and Tonette stepped into them, wrapping her arms around his waist and laying her head on his chest, keeping an ear out for Troy. He was obviously staying out of sight until Stanley left, and Tonette was extremely curious as to what he was thinking about this whole scene.

Stanley grabbed Tonette's chin and planted a quick kiss on her lips before stepping back and winking at her. "You see how much I must like you if I want to kiss you right after you get up."

Giggling, Tonette hit him lightly on the arm as he opened the front door to leave. "Have a good day, okay? And thanks for coming by." She figured she could throw that in to assuage any residual suspicion he might have about her male houseguest.

Stanley winked at her again before walking out.

After closing and locking the door behind him, Tonette turned around just in time to see Troy emerge from the hallway. He didn't look upset, but Tonette was still nervous as to what he might've been thinking. For some reason, she felt the need to explain herself.

"Troy, I don't know how much of that you heard..."

"I heard everything, Tonette."

"Oh." Her face flushed as she temporarily looked down at her hands. "Well, look, I'm sorry about that. Stanley is—"

"You don't have to explain anything to me," Troy interrupted with a wave of his hands. "I *did* just drop in on you rather unexpectedly. This is obviously the man you are in a relationship with, yes?"

Tonette shook her head emphatically. She didn't want Troy thinking she was off the market. "No, we are *not* in a relationship. I mean, we're dating but we're not...exclusive or anything."

"I see."

"And about me telling him you were my cousin...that just kind of came out," Tonette continued. "I just didn't want to have to answer a bunch of questions about who you were and why you're here. Does that make sense?"

"It does," Troy nodded slowly. "So I take it he would have a problem knowing the truth about me?"

Something about the way he said that made Tonette tingle. Stanley most definitely *would* have a problem knowing that Troy was the man that had a hold on her that she couldn't get out of, regardless of how hard she tried.

"I don't know, honestly," Tonette replied. "But I just didn't want to get into it."

"Understood. Would it be easier for you if I found another place to stay?"

"No," Tonette replied way too quickly. She blushed as Troy eyed her. "No, you don't have to do that. It's not necessary. Unless you just...want to go."

She held her breath without realizing it as she waited on his reply. Finally, he said, "No. I don't want to go."

Tonette had to bite her lip to at least somewhat contain the smile that automatically broke out. "Good."

Stanley called Tonette later that day to invite her out to a movie, but Tonette declined, saying she needed to entertain her cousin and didn't want to leave him alone in a strange city.

"Bring him with us, if you want. I'm not trying to leave the brother hanging."

"That's really sweet of you, Stanley, but he's very shy and I know he wouldn't be comfortable," Tonette evaded. The last thing she wanted was Stanley and Troy hanging out together. "You see how he stayed in the bathroom while you were there earlier. I certainly didn't tell him to do that."

"Oh. Well, all right then. But when am I gonna get to see you?"

"It'll be soon enough. I'm just kind of playing everything by ear right now; his visit was kind of unexpected."

"Where is he from?"

Tonette definitely didn't want to get into a round of twenty questions about Troy. "Boston. Hey, lemme go and get some stuff done...I'll call you before I go to bed tonight, okay?"

"Okay. And baby?"

For some reason that term of endearment made Tonette uncomfortable. "Yes?"

"I miss you."

Not being able to help it, Tonette smiled. Stanley was such a sweetheart towards her. "I miss you, too."

Do you really? She immediately thought to herself. She ignored it.

Tonette figured it would be a good idea for her and Troy to get out of the house after the little moment they had the previous night, so she took Stanley's suggestion about a movie and extended it to Troy.

"Yes, that sounds like fun," he said. "What are we seeing?"

"Whatever you want to see. We can check out what's playing; I admit I haven't been in a little while."

Eventually, they decided on a movie and went a couple of hours later. Troy was getting a lot of attention from the females, and Tonette felt herself getting upset. She didn't like the lustful looks the women were shooting at Troy, the flirtatious glances and even the comments she heard one or two of them make about how sexy he was. Tonette knew she had no right to feel jealous, but she couldn't help it. If Troy noticed any of this, he didn't comment or act on it; he was as gentlemanly and gracious as he always was. He didn't respond to any of the attention he was getting from the other women, nor did he try to act like he wasn't with Tonette. She appreciated that, but as soon as the movie was over, she was practically rushing him out of the theater.

"I'm hungry," she explained at his questioning eyes. "I'm surprised you couldn't hear my stomach growling in there."

Troy chuckled. "I am rather hungry myself, actually. Lead the way, pretty lady."

Blushing fiercely, Tonette slid inside of the car, turning on the AC to cool herself off.

They opted to just get something to go and eat it at Tonette's place. They sat on the floor in the living room as they ate, discussing the movie they just saw among various other things. Eventually, they turned on the television and watched a Kevin Hart comedy special, and they were both laughing so much they were falling over each other.

"I do not remember when I have laughed so much," Troy commented after the show was over. The smile was still on his lips and he released an occasional chuckle, apparently remembering parts of the show. "That was hilarious."

"It was! I love Kevin Hart; he has me cracking up every time." Tonette wiped the tears from her eyes, still smiling, herself. "I'm gonna go get some juice...you want anything?"

"I'm good, thank you."

Tonette wasn't able to wipe the smile off of her face as she padded into the kitchen and poured herself a big glass of apple juice. She took a long swallow as she headed back to the living room, and was surprised to see Troy standing and scrolling through his phone. He smiled when she entered the room, then returned his eyes to his phone as he slowly started walking closer to her.

"This is one of my favorite songs," he informed her, right before a smooth reggae song started to play from his phone. He closed his eyes as he started to slightly sway to the music.

Tonette became mesmerized while she looked at him, seemingly in his own little world. "Yeah, that *is* beautiful," she said softly.

Troy's eyes opened and he looked at her intently before setting his phone on the end table. He reached and gently removed the glass of juice from her hand and set it next to his phone, then took her hand in his.

"Dance with me?" he asked.

"Oh, um...I..." Tonette felt immediately flustered as Troy took her into his arms. "I'm not much of a dancer..."

"Just hold on to me," Troy said, his eyes on hers, "And let the music move you."

Biting her lip, Tonette didn't dare try to speak again. She did just as Troy said, her hands lightly gripping his shoulders, and let her inhibitions slowly melt away as she followed his lead, her body swaying in unison with his. Troy's arm slid tighter around her waist, and Tonette's arms crept around Troy's neck. Everything else ceased to exist. There was just something about that moment that just felt so right. Tonette felt warm, and safe, and...content.

Troy must have put the song on repeat because the dance lasted quite a while, not that Tonette minded. There was honestly no other place she would rather be right then, and no other person she would rather be with. Emotion swirled all through and around her body, and the feelings brought tears to her eyes that she fought hard to blink back. She might not have been willing to acknowledge what she was feeling to her friends, but she couldn't deny it to herself. She knew what it was.

Troy wasn't holding her like a friend or the sister of the woman he really wanted. He hadn't been looking at her like he had some other woman on his mind. Their bodies were closely pressed together, with Tonette's head resting on his shoulder, and his hands resting comfortably on her lower back. It didn't feel inappropriate, it felt *right*. Like this is how it was supposed to be.

And it wasn't lost on Tonette that Toni's name *still* hadn't come up again.

Chapter 17

"**A**re you out of your damn mind??"

"Come on, just do me this favor."

"This is not a favor, Tonette. Asking me to pick up your dry cleaning is a favor. Borrowing some of my clothes for a last minute date, *that's* a favor. Asking me to hit on the man you're in love with is *not* a favor."

"I am not in...look. I'm not saying to necessarily *hit* on him; I just want you to ask him out. See what he says."

"Why in the world do you want me to do this, T.?"

"Because I...I feel myself slipping a little bit and just want to see if I'm totally out of my mind for thinking that Troy might possibly maybe have feelings for me."

"You still don't think he does?"

"I mean, for all *he* knows, Toni and I are still two different people. He did all that stuff with me in Barbados when he thought I was Toni, and now he's looking like he's digging me here...maybe he's just a big flirt."

"I don't believe that and neither do you. Maybe he senses that you and Toni are the same person."

"Well, if that's the case, why hasn't he said something about it yet?"

"Maybe for the same reason you haven't, Tonette. Maybe he's scared of what will happen if he opens his mouth."

Tonette pondered her friend's words. She didn't think that there was a possibility that Troy had figured out that Toni was really her. He hadn't seen her birthmark or her tattoo or anything else incriminating. All those times when he looked at her with those intense eyes of his, like he was studying her or something...was that admiration or analyzing?

"I don't think he knows," Tonette finally said. "I can't imagine he wouldn't have said something by now. But regardless, I just want to see if what I'm feeling is crazy. I mean, the way he looks at me, and touches me..."

"Like he loves you?" Olarion finished for her.

Not wanting to acknowledge that statement, Tonette asked, "Can you just please do this for me?"

"Have you even considered all the ways this could possibly backfire? What if Troy *does* hit on me; how would you feel about that? Could you handle it? What if he declines my invitation because he doesn't want to upset you? Hell, I have a man myself...what if *he* found out? There are just *so* many reasons this is a bad idea."

"Olarion, please," Tonette begged. For some reason she really wanted to try this, even though she remembered how jealous she had gotten when Troy was getting so much attention at the movies. "I know it doesn't make much sense to you, but this is important to me. And you know I don't ask much of you. Please...just do this for me."

Olarion got quiet for a few moments and Tonette prepared herself to do some more begging. But finally, her friend heaved a heavy sigh and said, "Fine. I'll do it."

Tonette actually squealed. "Thank you so much! Okay, so just come over tonight and ask him out. Make sure you look good."

"When don't I?"

"Shut up."

"I just want to make sure that I'm still on the record for being strongly against this, but if it's that important to you, I'll go through with it," Olarion informed her. "I just want you to be prepared for it if it backfires."

So later that evening, Olarion knocked on Tonette's door at around seven o'clock. Tonette and Troy were playing cards on the couch and Troy looked at her curiously when he heard the knock.

"Are you expecting company?"

"No..." Tonette fibbed as she slid off the couch and headed for the door. She needlessly checked the peephole before swinging it open. "Hey girl! I didn't know you were coming by tonight!"

"Yeah, I'm sorry to just drop in on y'all like this," Olarion said as she stepped inside the apartment. She gave Tonette a hug and smiled at Troy, who was now standing.

"It is good to see you again, Olarion," he said, coming over to give her his usual kiss on the hand.

"You, too. You're actually the reason I stopped by."

Troy's brow arched curiously, his eyes quickly fleeting to Tonette and back again. "Oh?"

"Yeah, I wanted to see if you would join me for this art showing tonight; one of my friends has some paintings in it," Olarion said. She didn't look at Tonette. "I figured you could use a change of scenery after being cooped up in here most of the time."

Troy looked hesitant. "That sounds interesting but...just me? You are not extending the invitation to Tonette, also?"

"Oh, I already know my homegirl doesn't really care for this kind of thing," Olarion said with a wave of her hand. Tonette swallowed. "I took her with me one time and she just didn't enjoy it as much as I did. I just had the feeling *you* would, though."

Even though Tonette had been the one to practically beg Olarion to invite Troy out, she was already starting to regret that decision. She felt Olarion was dressed a little *too* sexy, with her low-cut shirt that showed so much cleavage even Tonette couldn't keep her eyes from straying to it, so she could only imagine Troy's reaction. He hadn't seemed to pay them much attention so far, but maybe he would act completely different once he and Olarion were alone.

Get it together, girl, she reprimanded herself. *This was all your idea. Remember, you're doing this for a reason.*

Troy turned to Tonette, his eyes still doubtful. "Would it be okay with you if I joined your friend?"

Internally thrilled that he was even asking her, Tonette kept her cool. "Sure, Troy, if you want to go, I have no problem with it at all," she insisted, smiling. "I'm sure you'll like that. Go on and enjoy yourself; Olarion will show you a good time."

Olarion glanced at her, but Tonette kept her eyes on Troy. She hadn't really meant anything by that statement but she wondered how Troy had taken it.

"Okay, well then yes, I would love to go with you, Olarion; thank you for thinking of me," Troy said. "I will go change very quickly and be right back."

"Okay, great," Olarion grinned, (a little too hard, in Tonette's opinion) as they both watched Troy grab some clothes and head off to the bathroom. As soon as he was gone, Olarion turned to Tonette. "You okay?"

"Yeah, girl, I'm fine," Tonette quickly insisted with a wave of her hand. "*I* asked *you* to do this, remember?"

"Yeah, I know," Olarion's eyes roamed her face. "I just want to make sure you're still cool with all this now that everything is in motion."

"Yep. I'm good."

"So what are you gonna do tonight?"

"Oh...I'm not sure. I'm sure there's a good movie on or something."

"Why don't you call Stanley, see if he's busy tonight?"

"Nah," Tonette replied quickly. "I'm sure he *is* busy. Besides, I need to be here when you guys get back to let Troy in, remember?"

"I have a key. Remember?"

Tonette pursed her lips. Thoughts and questions started filing through her mind like a family of ants at a picnic. *Is she just trying to get rid of me so she and Troy can be alone here? But that's ridiculous...she has her own place. But she might want to be with him here because there would be less chance of her man finding out; her man Aaron has a key to her place. She just seems a little too excited about all this considering I had to practically beg her to do it. And why are her boobs still out??*

"Oh yeah," Tonette mumbled, clearing her throat. "Umm, what time do you think y'all will be back?"

"Don't know," Olarion shrugged. "Not ridiculously late, I guess. We'll just kind of play it by ear."

Play it by ear, huh? "Oh."

"Why? Is there a certain time you *want* us to be back?"

"I'm not your mama," Tonette chuckled non-convincingly. "Stay out as late as you want."

Olarion was eying her curiously. "Are you sure you're okay, girl? I can make up an excuse and cancel, if you want me to."

"Nah, don't be silly. You're already here, he's back there getting dressed...it's fine," Tonette tried to assure her. She forced a smile onto her face. "I'm good. Really."

Olarion didn't look convinced, but she left it alone. Troy emerged a couple of minutes later, looking and smelling a little too good in Tonette's opinion, and in her mind smiling way too hard at her friend that he barely knew. But she had to again remind herself to get a grip. Nothing was going to happen between them, no matter how much cologne Troy wore or what kind of push-up bra Olarion had on.

After Olarion and Troy left, Tonette tried to keep herself busy. She pulled out a Toni Morrison novel that she hadn't read yet, but one look at the name on the cover had her shoving the book under her mattress. Then she tried watching the news, then a movie, neither of which could hold her attention. She even tried watching a reality show, which she almost never watched, and the ridiculousness of it managed to distract her a little bit, but as soon as it was over, she was checking her watch and wondering what was taking them so long.

Tonette flopped onto her back on the couch, groaning loudly. She knew she was losing it. Olarion had tried to tell her that it was a bad idea for her to go out with Troy, but Tonette had insisted. Now, she didn't know why she had felt the need to test Troy like that. He wasn't her man. Hell, he wasn't even Toni's man. Even if he *did* hit on Olarion, what could she really say about it? Tonette just remembered how she felt when all those women were ogling him at the movies, and a similar feeling had washed over her when Olarion showed up. Part of Tonette kind of thought (or even hoped) that Olarion would renege on her and back out, but she didn't. She came and asked Troy out just as Tonette had asked her to do, and she showed up looking way more enticing than Tonette had expected. But what *did* she expect? For Olarion to show up in a pair of sweats and some flip-flops?

She started to call Blue but figured that he would just get onto her for suggesting Olarion take Troy out in the first place, so she put her phone down. She thought about calling Stanley but realized she really didn't have much to say to him right then; plus she didn't want to have to field any questions about her supposed 'cousin.' So she scrolled through Netflix, selected the first action flick she could find (she certainly didn't want to see anything romantic), and forced herself to keep her eyes glued to it until she heard a key in her lock.

It was another couple of hours before that happened; Tonette was actually starting to doze off when she heard Olarion and Troy come in. She shot up off the couch, quickly rubbing her eyes and fluffing out her hair, trying to look nonchalant and unbothered.

Troy and Olarion were laughing amongst themselves when they came through the door, and Olarion's smile widened when she saw Tonette.

"Hey! You're still up," she greeted cheerfully.

Were you hoping I wouldn't be? "Yep, still up. So y'all finally made it back, huh?"

"Oh yeah, we had a great time at the gallery. Troy here seemed to know more about the art than I did," Olarion said, grinning over her shoulder at Troy, who returned her smile.

You're bragging on him now??

"Then we went and got something to eat," Olarion continued, running a hand through her hair. "We finally left when the staff started giving us those get-on-up-outta-here-so-we-can-go-home looks. I didn't even realize how late it had gotten."

"Shut the place down, huh?" Tonette clipped, folding her arms. She tried her best not to sound snippy but she almost didn't care if she did. She never once told Olarion to stay gone with Troy so long. What could they possibly have to talk about?

"Something like that."

"Yes, we had a great time," Troy chimed in, the smile still on his lips. It was the one time it made Tonette sick to her stomach to see it, because it was caused by another woman. "I appreciate you allowing me to accompany you, Olarion."

"No, thank *you* for going! You were such good company...and you can *really* hold your liquor!"

They both burst out laughing as if it was some kind of inside joke between them, and Tonette wanted to roll her eyes so bad they itched. This little love fest they had going on was starting to make her stomach hurt. So they were out drinking together, too? *And why are they still smiling so much??*

"Yeah, well..." Tonette hedged loudly, since they seemed to temporarily forget she was there, "Thank you for getting Troy home safe and sound, Olarion, even though drinking and driving is kind of reckless. Were you having so much *fun* that you forgot that?"

Olarion and Troy looked at her, and Tonette tried to keep her expression even.

"I'm just saying," she added with a fake smile and a light shrug of her shoulder.

"It wasn't anything like that, T.," Olarion responded, frowning slightly. "All we did was—"

"Hey, it's none of *my* business!" Tonette interrupted with her hands up, still forcing her smile. "As long as y'all had a good time together, that's all that matters, right?"

An uncomfortable moment passed before Troy stepped towards Tonette, who subtly stepped back. "Are you all right?"

"Just peachy!"

Olarion sighed. She had been afraid this would happen. "Tonette—"

"Well, now that I know you're both in one piece, I'm gonna go," Tonette announced, sliding her feet into her flats that were by the couch and snatching up her purse from the end table.

"Where are you going??" Olarion asked her, trying to get her to make eye contact. But Tonette wouldn't look at her or at Troy, who was eying her with obvious confusion and concern.

"I think I'm going to go see Stanley, after all. I mean, y'all shouldn't be the only ones to enjoy yourselves tonight, right?"

"But I thought you were—"

"You two crazy kids can stay here and hang out, if you want...*enjoy* each other some more," Tonette cut her off again, slinging her purse over her shoulder and becoming very engrossed in re-adjusting her watch. "I'd hate for the party to stop. Just don't drink all my wine, and try to keep it in the living room, 'kay? The couch should have more than enough room."

Olarion's jaw dropped. "Tonette!"

"What? I meant for you both to lounge around on, that's all," Tonette replied innocently. She skirted around them, still keeping her eyes everywhere but on them. She knew she was acting like an idiot, but she couldn't seem to help it. "See you later!"

Both Olarion and Troy called out to her as she snatched the door open and hastily retreated out into the hallway, but she ignored them both. She just hoped neither of them followed her as she sped-walked down the hall, trying her best to keep the tears stinging her eyes at bay. When she reached the lobby, then her car, she allowed the tears to fall, realizing that neither of them had in fact followed her.

Tonette never made it to Stanley's. She ended up just driving around for a while before finally going to Blue's, having called him on the way. Olarion had been calling her nonstop, but Tonette hadn't been ready to talk to her yet. Remorse about how she had behaved was slowly starting to creep in, but her stubbornness was still overpowering it enough to where she still felt justified for tripping out like she did. She was sure Olarion had filled Blue in on everything, and when she got to his house, she just shook her head as he stood in the door, looking at her with his arms folded across his broad chest.

"Don't say anything," she pleaded in a soft voice. "I already know. And I feel bad enough. Can you please not say anything?"

Blue looked at her red eyes and tear-stained face and sighed, dropping his arms. He knew Tonette needed a friend more than she needed a lecture, so he just reached out and took her hand, pulling her inside. As soon as he closed the door behind them, he wrapped her up in his arms just as the floodgates opened again, and he just stood there holding her as she cried against his chest.

"Just let it out, boo," he whispered, resting his cheek on top of her head. "I got you."

Tonette didn't finally take one of Olarion's calls until the next day.

"Are you still at Blue's?" Olarion asked immediately.

"Yes," Tonette replied in a low voice.

"I'm on my way."

Tonette was still nervous about this conversation she knew they needed to have, but she also knew she couldn't avoid her friend forever. Shame over her actions had overtaken the stubbornness and she knew she needed to apologize. "Okay."

Olarion showed up about twenty minutes later, and wasted no time getting down to business.

"Do you see why I told you that me asking Troy out wasn't a good idea?" she asked, joining Tonette on the couch as she handed her a bottle of orange juice. Blue had left them alone, having gone to do a hair appointment. "I knew this was gonna happen."

"I'm sorry, O.," Tonette said, turning the bottle around in her hands. "I didn't think I would react that way."

"Girl, whether or not you admit it to me out loud, I know how you feel about Troy," Olarion informed her, placing a hand on her arm. "I would never hit on Troy or let anything happen between me and him, even if I wasn't already in a relationship myself. I would *never* do that to you."

"I know. I know you wouldn't."

"Hopefully you know this already, too, but I still want it to be said that absolutely *nothing* happened between me and Troy last night," Olarion continued. "We went to the exhibit, we got something to eat, and we came home. Yes, we had a good time, but that was it. He was an absolute gentleman and the only time we even touched at all was when he helped me out of the car."

Tonette wasn't surprised to hear that; Troy was always a gentleman. And even though she always knew in the back of her mind where her common sense had apparently been duct taped the night before that nothing had happened, she was still a little relieved to actually hear that confirmed.

"Nothing happened between Troy and I that I wouldn't have been comfortable with Aaron seeing," Olarion said, looking right at her. "And I told him all about it, by the way."

Tonette sighed. The more Olarion talked, the more ridiculous she felt. "I am so sorry," she said again, turning to face her friend. "You didn't deserve me flipping out on you like that, and I can only image what Troy must be thinking of me..."

"Yeah, he had no idea *what* was going on," Olarion confirmed, leaning against the back of the couch. "He was really worried about you."

Tonette's hopeful eyes snapped to her friend. "Really?"

"Yes, really. Even he knew something wasn't right, and asked if you were upset that the two of us had gone out without you."

"And what did you say??"

"I didn't call you out, even though I wanted to. I just said you were going through something. He actually started to come after you, but I told him to let you go; I figured you needed to get your head together."

"That's putting it mildly."

"That man cares about you, T.," Olarion dished. "A lot of our evening consisted of him talking or asking about you. Truth be told, I think he was a little disappointed that you didn't come with us. He even brought you something back to eat."

"He did??" Tonette hadn't even noticed that. She had been too busy creating that stupid scene, which now made her cringe when she thought about it. It was almost embarrassing to look at Olarion now, remembering how she acted. "I feel like an absolute idiot."

"You certainly acted like one," Olarion teased, playfully nudging her shoulder.

Tonette covered her flushed face with her hands. "Oh my god..."

"Tonette..."

"How am I even gonna be able to look at him after this?" Tonette asked, referring to Troy. "You were right; this was a stupid, *stupid* idea."

"I never said it was stupid, T.; I just said it wasn't a *good* idea," Olarion corrected. "On some level, I can see where you were coming from, even though I didn't really agree with your logic. It's like what they say about not asking questions you don't really want to know the answer to; you don't suggest the man you're in love with go out with another woman if you can't handle seeing it when he does."

Pursing her lips, Tonette just nodded silently.

Olarion eyed her. After a few moments, she softly said, "You know this is the first time you didn't automatically deny being in love with Troy after one of us said you were?"

Tonette just looked at her before her eyes floated down to her hands. She couldn't bring herself to say anything.

"That's progress," Olarion observed. "Now you just need to actually admit it."

Just as Tonette didn't have the energy to deny her friend's words, she didn't have the energy to confirm them, either. And Olarion didn't press her about it, thankfully. They both knew what the truth was, anyway.

Stanley called to invite Tonette out to a movie, and even though she still wasn't quite ready to be around him yet, she accepted the invitation. She had sent Troy a text letting him know she'd be back later and headed to meet up with Stanley.

They saw some movie with Channing Tatum in it, but she couldn't recall the plot or anything else about it if you paid her. Her mind was on what she was going to say to Troy whenever she finally worked up the nerve to face him. She knew she had to go home and do it soon; she couldn't keep leaving him there in her apartment by himself. Not only was it cowardly but it was rude, knowing that he was there as her guest. When she had texted him earlier, he just said that he hoped she was okay and that he would be waiting on her when she got there.

Tonette couldn't get her mind off of what Olarion had said about Troy talking about her so much while they were out. She hadn't anticipated that at all. She figured he and Olarion had hit it off so well that they weren't even thinking about her. But unless Olarion had just been lying to make her feel better, and she knew her friend wouldn't do that, she had been wrong. It did something to her to know that Troy had been out with Olarion, who was beautiful with a smile that could light up a room (not to mention her pushed-up boobs), and he still seemed to have his mind on her. The thought made her smile, and filled her with a giddiness that made her anxious to get home to him. But it also made her feel even sillier for how she acted and not *quite* ready to face him yet, so when Stanley invited her back to his place after the movie, she accepted.

It didn't take long at all for things to get intimate. Stanley had obviously missed her, and he wasted no time showing her how much. He kissed her eagerly and hungrily, and his hands groped her body with an urgency that Tonette recognized all too well. But she didn't stop him or ease back like she usually did; she let him touch her as he pleased, kiss her as he pleased. She replied to his moans with moans of her own, but she didn't utter any whispered words of how much she missed him or how glad she was to be there like he was doing. It was almost like she was on autopilot; her body was with Stanley, but her mind was on Troy.

"You okay, baby?" Stanley breathlessly asked, looking up at her from where he had been kissing her stomach.

"Yeah; yeah I'm fine," Tonette quickly answered. The last thing she wanted was another confrontation with Stanley; she was hoping that eventually she would get more into what Stanley was doing the longer she let him do it, and have at least a temporary reprieve from thinking about what she was going to say to Troy when she saw him.

Seemingly satisfied with her answer, Stanley resumed what he was doing. His hands moved to unbutton her jeans, and Tonette let him. She could tell his movements were somewhat cautious, as if he was waiting on her to pump the brakes at any second, but she never did. She let him pull her jeans down, and licked her lips when he licked her inner thigh. Her body was slowly starting to respond, and when his lips brushed against her womanhood through her panties, she gasped. And when she thought of the many times Troy had gone below her waist...she came.

"Damn," Stanley whispered, looking up at her in surprise. "Did you really..."

Too embarrassed to look at him, she just covered her flushed face and nodded.

"Wow. Glad to know you enjoyed it, baby, but I'm just barely getting started."

Tonette wasn't about to burst his bubble. She could let him think that had been about him even though it hadn't. "Right."

Standing, Stanley quickly removed his shirt and tossed it aside. Tonette's shirt was already off, having been discarded by Stanley not too long after they got through the door. He kicked his shoes off then climbed on top of her, his intensity doubled and confidence soaring after thinking he had already brought her to one quick orgasm. Tonette again returned his kisses and reciprocated his moans, and her body was now on fire, but Stanley had very little to do with it.

Eventually they were both down to nothing but their underwear, and Tonette could feel Stanley's straining hardness pressing against her. Her eyes were squeezed shut, and in her mind, it was Troy that was on top of her. She recalled those few moments in Barbados when Troy was inside of her, and she shuddered at the memory. She again thought that those few moments were better than all the times any other man had been inside of her combined, and that was no hyperbole. Everything in her ached to have that again.

"Can I have you this time, baby?" Stanley panted, leaning back slightly to look down at her. "If you want to stop, you need to tell me now."

"Keep going," Tonette quickly responded in a whisper, her eyes still squeezed shut. She tried to pull Stanley down on top of her, but he resisted.

"You okay?"

"Yes! Don't stop..."

"Tonette." Stanley had stopped moving. "Tonette, look at me."

"Stanley, please, I don't want to talk or have some deep discussion right now...let's just *do* this." Tonette's eyes were still closed. She jutted her breasts towards him. "This is what you wanted, right? I'm telling you that you can have it."

She heard him grunt, and a moment later she felt his hand slide up to her heaving breasts. Biting her lip, she whispered for him to keep going. She told him to put his mouth where his hands were, and he did. She told him to grind on her, and he did. She was trying everything she could to just get lost in the moment, and hang on to the fantasy that was playing in her mind.

Things got really intense, and eventually Tonette hastily pushed her underwear down and Stanley followed suit. She couldn't see how he was looking at her and how she was probably throwing him for a loop; they had never gone this far before and she had certainly never been as into things as she was then.

"Please tell me you have condoms," she panted, winding her hips against his. Her movements had become more urgent than his; her hands clawed at his back. "Do you have condoms??"

"Yeah," Stanley replied in a throaty grunt. "Yeah, I do..."

"Put it on. Now."

She ignored the slight hesitation as he raised off of her to do as she requested. Tonette hadn't even noticed that his intensity had decreased at the same rate hers had increased.

He slid inside of her, and Tonette emitted a grunt in a voice even she didn't recognize. In her mind, that was Troy on top of her, Troy slowly pumping between her legs, Troy softly kissing her lips. She was totally into it, having managed to fool herself into thinking she was with the man her heart wanted, but she wasn't fooling Stanley.

"Tonette," he said after a few moments, his movements slowing.

"Don't stop!" she shrieked, almost in a panic.

"No, look at me." Stanley's voice was strong.

Tonette didn't want to look at him. But she eventually eased her eyes open. "What's wrong?"

"You tell me." Stanley was looking down at her strangely, a slight frown marring his sweaty brow.

"What do you mean?"

"I think you know what I mean. You're not all here; I can tell. You don't even seem like yourself."

Her face burning, Tonette tried to wave off his eerily accurate observation. "I don't know what you're talking about. Why are we stopping?? Doesn't it feel good?" She asked seductively as she squeezed herself around him.

Stanley's breath caught in his throat and his eyes momentarily fluttered closed. "It absolutely does," he said after a moment, his voice low. "But it would be better if your mind wasn't somewhere else."

Tonette's breath caught in her throat and she blinked rapidly. Her mouth opened to respond, but nothing came out at first. "Stanley, I'm here with you. I'm *with* you. I thought you would be happy...what's the problem?"

"Tonette," Stanley sighed, easing out of her and sitting up on his knees. He ran both hands down his face wearily and looked at her, as if he was trying to gather his words. "This is our first time together and you're not all the way here. It's obvious, baby."

Tonette chewed her lip for a few moments before sitting up on her elbows. "I don't know what you want me to say, Stanley."

"I want you to say I'm trippin' and there's no reason at all you can't even keep your eyes open and look at me while I'm inside of you," Stanley replied emphatically. "I want you to tell me you want me as much as I want you; as much as I've *been* wanting you. I want you to tell me you're ready to be my woman, 'cause I definitely want to be your man. But you can't tell me any of that, can you?"

Tonette's heart burned at the pained expression on his face. She hated the thought of hurting Stanley; she sincerely cared about him and she knew he cared about her. If she had never met Troy, Stanley would be so right for her. But she had, and regardless of how she tried, she couldn't get him out of her head or her heart.

"Stanley," She didn't even know how to explain herself, "I'm sorry. I...I just..."

After hanging his head for a few moments, Stanley eased off the bed and reached for his clothes on the floor. He blew through his teeth as he shook his head, as if he couldn't believe this was happening. Tonette just watched him, feeling like the scum of the earth.

"I can't keep doing this, Tonette," Stanley finally said, yanking his shirt over his head. He pulled on his pants but didn't button them; he just stood and looked at her. "I want you; I've never made a secret of that. And I thought that you were at least on your way to getting on the same page I'm on. I want a relationship with you; I wanna be your man. But I'm finally getting that that's not really what you want."

"I never said that," Tonette protested softly, even though he was right.

"You didn't have to say it," Stanley replied sadly. "Your actions have been saying it for months, but I was hoping I was just being paranoid. But I'm not. Am I?"

Tonette just looked down, not having the heart to tell him he was right but also not wanting to insult him by trying to deny it.

Cursing under his breath, Stanley turned his back to her, a hand clamped on the back of his neck. "Please go home, Tonette," he said softly, his voice pained. "Call me when and if you decide I'm what you want. Until then, I just can't look at you."

With embarrassed tears stinging her eyes, Tonette eased off the bed, calling out an apology to Stanley's back as he left the room.

Chapter 18

Tonette felt horrible for hurting Stanley. They hadn't spoken since he asked her to leave his house that night, and she wanted to reach out to him to at least try to explain herself. But she couldn't bring herself to do that because for one, he said he didn't want to hear from her until she could tell him she was ready to be with him, and two, she really just didn't know what to say. He hadn't been wrong; she *wasn't* all the way with him, especially since Troy came back. He had thrown her all off kilter, and reignited all the feelings that she sincerely thought she had gotten over. The look on Stanley's face haunted her; she never, ever meant to hurt him like she did.

When she had gotten back to her place that night, Troy had been asleep, thankfully; she had been in no mindset to talk to him right then. But the next morning, she apologized for her behavior the night he went out with Olarion. He had graciously accepted her apology, and asked her if she was all right, but he seemed to be glad that she was better and back to her old self. Tonette could tell he had been concerned, and that made her heart swell. With every day that passed, Troy was just digging his way deeper and deeper into her heart.

The following day, Tonette laid in bed for a while after waking up, thinking about the situation she was in. Hugging her pillow, she still wanted to pinch herself that it was all even happening; Troy was still here, and he seemed to really care about her, and not just the general concern you might have for your fellow man. With the way he had looked at her that night he massaged her scalp, and the night they danced, and what Olarion had said about him constantly talking about her the night they had gone out, that all had to mean something. Not to mention the fact that Troy still wasn't really talking or asking about Toni much at all; he didn't seem concerned about her or when she was coming back. If Tonette didn't know any better, she would think he had come back to Atlanta just for her.

Eventually, she threw the covers off herself and rolled out of bed. She quickly did her morning ablutions as she wondered what she and Troy could do that day; she was just glad that there wasn't any awkwardness between them after the recent happenings and they were back to the rapport they had shared before.

To her surprise, though, Troy was already dressed when she went into the living room.

"Good morning," he greeted her with a smile. He was finishing folding up the sofa bed.

"Good morning," Tonette replied, smiling at him curiously. "What's up? I'm surprised to see you dressed already. I was gonna ask what you wanted to do today."

"Oh yes; well, your friend Blue contacted me and asked if I wanted to hang out with him today."

Tonette's eyebrows shot up. "He did?"

"Yes. He said he figured I needed some man time after being around you and Olarion so much. Not that I was ever complaining about that," Troy winked.

Chuckling nervously, Tonette stepped forward to help him fold the blanket he had just picked up. "I didn't know you and Blue were in touch like that."

"He got my information from Olarion, he said."

"I see." Tonette hadn't known Troy and Olarion had exchanged numbers, but she told herself not to start tripping about that. "I hope you don't feel like you have to hang out with Blue if you don't really want to, Troy. Blue can be very...in-your-face and persuasive sometimes."

Troy released his own chuckle as he moved closer to Tonette so they could bring their ends of the blanket together. "Not at all. I look forward to it." His eyes met hers. "Though I wouldn't mind spending today with you."

Their eyes were locked as they brought their blanket corners together, their fingertips brushing against each other and lightly intertwining. Sparks shot down Tonette's arm and she wondered if Troy noticed how she shivered slightly. They continued to stand there and gaze at each other, the blanket between them, their breathing deepening. It wasn't until the doorbell rang that they each snapped out of it.

"Um...I'll get it," Tonette said softly.

Troy just nodded, his eyes following her as she went to the door.

Tonette tried to compose herself as she quickly checked the peephole and opened the door for Blue, hoping he wouldn't he able to tell that she and Troy had just shared another moment.

"Hey, hey," Blue greeted loudly as he entered the apartment, clapping his hands loudly. "What's up, people?"

"Stop yelling," Tonette admonished with a smile, accepting his kiss on the cheek.

"Good morning, Blue," Troy said as Blue came over to give him some pound.

"Morning, man. You ready to get out from under this woman for a while and come hang with the boys?"

"Blue, please don't traumatize Troy with any of your foolishness," Tonette said. "I want him to be in one piece when he comes back."

"What exactly is it we will be doing today?" Troy asked, looking a little worried. Tonette and Blue laughed.

"Don't listen to her, bro. You're in nothing but good hands when you're hanging with me. I just think she doesn't want you to go," Blue replied, waving his hand dismissively at Tonette.

Troy looked at her, and Tonette felt her face flame. Why did Blue say that??

"You ready?" Blue asked Troy.

"Yes, I just need to run to the restroom first, if that's all right."

"Sure thing, bro. Take your time." He pulled his phone out of his pocket.

Troy headed down the hallway, and Tonette immediately hit Blue on his shoulder.

"Why did you just tell him that?" she hissed.

Blue looked at her, confused. "What?"

"That little line about me not wanting him to go?"

"Was I lying?" Blue asked her with a cocked brow.

"That doesn't mean you need to say it!"

"Whatever. He probably doesn't want to go without you, either. Olarion told me how he couldn't stop talking about you when he went out with her."

"So what made you invite him out with you today? What are you gonna do?"

"You don't need to be worried about all that. Man stuff."

"What the hell is *man stuff*?"

"Like I said, don't worry about it. He needs some testosterone, for a change. I'm sure you can entertain yourself until we get back. Call Stanley or something."

Tonette looked down at the floor, shaking her head. "That's really not an option right now."

"What do you mean?"

"I'll have to get into all that later, but just know I probably won't be seeing much of Stanley any time soon. It's...it's a long story."

Blue eyed her intently. "You okay?"

"Yeah...it was probably for the best."

Blue started to say something else but Troy then came back into the room.

"All set," he said to Blue.

"Cool." Blue turned to Tonette. "We'll see you later."

"How long are y'all gonna be gone?"

"We'll be back when we get back, woman!" Blue responded as he moved to the door and opened it. "And don't be blowing our phones up, either!"

"Shut up, Blue!"

Troy chuckled at their exchange before his eyes rested on Tonette. "I will see you later," he said to her, pulling her into a hug before following Blue out the door. Blue raised his eyebrows pointedly at her before closing the door behind him and Troy, leaving her standing there tingling and missing Troy already.

While the guys were gone, Tonette busied herself by going to the gym, treating herself to lunch, and grocery shopping, among some other errands. Several times she had been tempted to text Blue or Troy to see what they were doing and how things were going, but she made herself refrain from doing so. But she couldn't help but be curious, because she couldn't imagine Blue and Troy having that much in common.

They still weren't back when Tonette made it back home in the late afternoon. As she put away her groceries and things, she thought about everything that had been going on. Troy had been here for a while, and she still hadn't told him the truth about Toni. Truth be told, she hadn't really thought much about it recently, probably because Troy wasn't mentioning her like he used to. It was foolish to think he might have forgotten about her, but Tonette did flatter herself to think that he simply wasn't as concerned about Toni as he used to be; he was enjoying the time with Tonette so much that he didn't need Toni. But Tonette knew that didn't mean that she was off the hook about telling him the truth. Only thing was, she still didn't know if she would have the guts to do it.

Blue and Troy came back a couple of hours later. Tonette was cooking dinner when they arrived, and moving around the kitchen to some reggae music. Troy smiled upon seeing her.

"Hey! Y'all have a good time?" she asked, resisting to rush over to Troy and give him a hug like she really wanted to.

"Oh yeah, it was a blast and a half," Blue replied. "Your boy is actually a lot of fun."

"I really enjoyed myself," Troy chimed in. "I appreciate it, Blue."

"Not a problem; anytime." Blue peeked over Tonette's shoulder. "What you cookin' in here?"

"Just grilling some salmon, and I have green beans and some baked sweet potatoes. You want some?"

"Sounds good, baby, but I need to head on out," Blue replied as he checked his watch. He leaned down and kissed her cheek before turning to Troy with his hand extended. "We'll need to link up again sometime, man. Feel free to give me a call any time."

"Absolutely, thank you," Troy confirmed with a nod as he grasped Blue's hand in his and they bumped shoulders. "Get home safe."

"Y'all have fun," Blue winked at Tonette before letting himself out, motioning that he'd call her later.

Suddenly simultaneously nervous and anxious about being alone with Troy, Tonette turned back to the food on the stove. "You hungry?"

"A little, yes; that smells really good, Tonette," Troy commented, coming up behind her.

Tonette's breathing quickened, noting how close he was to her. She inhaled the scent of his cologne, and resisted the urge to turn around and bury her face in his neck. "Thank you. Um...it'll be ready in just a few minutes."

"Can I help you with anything?"

"Nope, I'm good. You can just go relax in the living room or something, if you want."

But Troy didn't want; he stayed in the kitchen with Tonette as she put the finishing touches on dinner. They didn't say too much to each other; just moved around in a comfortable and familiar silence.

When they finally sat down to eat, they told each other about their days as they shared a bottle of wine. Then, when they finished that one, they cracked open another. After a while, they were sprawled on the floor in the living room, lounging against each other and laughing at every little thing. Needless to say, they were both a little drunk.

"Let's dance, Troy!" Tonette exclaimed, pushing off the couch to stand, giggling as she stumbled a little.

"Really?" Troy asked, surprised, as he looked up at her.

"Yes! Come on, put on some of that good music you have in your phone and let's boogie!"

Chuckling, Troy pushed himself off the floor. He caught Tonette by the waist when she swayed into him. "I would love to dance with you," he said to her, still holding her.

"Well, let's do it!"

His smile widening, Troy grabbed his phone and put on some music. This time, though, instead of slow dancing, they moved to a more upbeat song. Or at least, they tried to; they both kept losing their footing. Each time one of them stumbled or swayed a little too much, they each laughed uncontrollably.

"Do you think maybe we have had too much to drink?" Troy chuckled.

"Maybe, but who cares?" Tonette replied with a wave of her hand, smiling as she wrapped her arms around his neck. "We just have to hold on to each other...you don't mind catching me if I start to fall, right?"

"Not at all."

"Good. You can hold me tighter if you want to. My legs are a little wobbly."

Troy found this incredibly funny and released a loud laugh, but his arms tightened around her waist as he did so. The smiles never left either of their faces as they talked about things that probably would make no sense to anyone else, but they each seemed to understand each other perfectly. They danced, they flirted, they stumbled, they held each other up...they were both having a ball. Tonette hadn't felt this uninhibited since she was in Barbados parading around as Toni.

Eventually, they both gave up on trying to stay upright and fell to the floor, still giggling at nothing. Leaning against each other, they fell into a comfortable silence, goofy smiles still adorning both of their faces.

"Tonette, I hope you do not get mad at me when I say this...I mean no disrespect," Troy said after several moments.

"What?"

"I think your friend Blue might be gay."

Tonette burst out laughing.

"Is that the reason you two divorced?"

Tonette laughed harder. Troy just looked at her in confusion before not being able to resist joining in the laughter, and it only intensified when Tonette fell onto her side, holding her stomach.

"Oh my god," she gasped, trying to catch her breath. Tears were rolling down her face from laughing so hard. She rolled onto her back, her chest heaving, her hand resting on her belly. "That was *too* funny."

"Was I wrong for saying that?" Troy asked, leaning on his elbow next to her as he tried to regain his own composure.

"Nah, you might actually be on to something with that," Tonette chuckled, wiping her eyes. "I'm not even gonna ask what happened today to make you think that, though."

Chuckling, Troy reached down and wiped a stray tear from Tonette's cheek, letting his fingers linger on her face. They gazed at each other, both still smiling, each of them as happy in that one moment as they had ever been.

"I must admit something," Troy said softly.

Tonette swallowed. "What's that?"

"I have not really thought much about Toni since I have returned this visit," Troy informed her, his finger languidly tracing her hairline with the tip of his finger. It trailed around her ear and Tonette's eyes drifted closed momentarily, a slow burn starting to form in her body. "I am kind of surprised by this; she is supposed to be the reason I am here. But I must say, Tonette...and please forgive me for this...I have been enjoying my time with you so much I haven't even missed her." His eyes bore into hers. "Is that bad?"

Momentarily transfixed by his stare, Tonette swallowed again. She wondered if this was a good time to go ahead and tell him the truth about everything; the wine would help fuel her courage and hopefully dull his anger at hearing that Toni didn't exist. She opened her mouth to speak and Troy's eyes immediately drifted down to her lips, and she felt her throat dry up like a sponge in the sun.

"No," she finally whispered with a slow shake of her head. Her gaze was still held captive by his. "That's not bad at all."

"Do you think ill of me? To come here for one sister and become so ensconced in the other?"

Arousal jolted through Tonette's body, and she squirmed slightly beneath him. Her thighs rubbed together, and her breasts started to ache. Finally tearing her eyes away, she focused on his arm that was mere inches from her face.

"I don't think I could ever think ill of you, Troy," she responded wistfully. She turned her eyes back to his. "I love having you here. I love our time together. I love..." *You*, she mentally finished the sentence, not quite having the nerve to say it out loud, even with all the wine bolstering her.

Troy looked at her, and she wondered by his expression if he knew what she had been about to say. His hand began caressing her face. "Me, too," he replied simply.

"Troy..." Tonette whispered, licking her lips.

"Yes?" He slid his hand into her hair.

Not being able to resist her eyes closing and a quick intake of breath at the action, Tonette tried hard to control the rapidly-rising desire that was taking over her body. Her heart felt like it was about to beat out of her chest. "I...I hope you don't think badly of me, either. I don't...I would never try to take another woman's man—"

"I was never Toni's man," Troy interjected. His hand continued to slowly massage Tonette's scalp, his eyes roaming her face thoughtfully and lustfully. "I thought I wanted to be, but...the connection I share with you has me rethinking things. I have been thinking about this a lot, Tonette...there has to be a reason Toni has barely crossed my mind recently. Everything in me had been sure that she was who and what I wanted. But even she and I did not share the rapport and the connection that you and I have. I feel like I have friend in you; with Toni, it was more of an almost volatile, intense physical connection. And that was great. But with you, it feels like..." His face inched closer to hers. "...everything."

Tonette felt her heart and emotions burst at his words. He felt about her the way she felt about him. He no longer cared about Toni; he wanted her. And she had no doubt she wanted him; she wanted this man more than she had ever wanted anything. And not just physically; she wanted him every way she could possibly have him.

"I feel the same way," she whispered, her fingertips tentatively coming up and grazing his jawline.

"Good," Troy whispered, his lips right above hers. His eyes went from her eyes to her lips and back again, silently requesting permission to do what they both wanted.

Tonette licked her lips, every inch of her body on fire. "What about Olarion?"

"I was never interested in Olarion, nor she in me." His hand drifted down to her waist, his fingers lightly playing with her exposed skin under her shirt. "What about Stanley?"

"Who?"

In the next second, Troy's lips were on hers. He kissed her gently, but deeply. They both released sighs and groans of contentment as their tongues met, the kiss continuing slowly, languidly, yet with an increasing intensity. Tonette's hand slid up to caress the back of Troy's head, holding him to her.

Troy lowered his body onto hers, and Tonette's legs automatically widened to accommodate him. His arousal was obvious and bore down into her, and Tonette felt the wetness flood her panties as every cell in her body exploded like pop rocks.

Troy whispered her name as they slowly began winding against each other, on cue and in rhythm. He gripped a handful of her hair as leaned down and sucked her neck, gently pulling her head to the side as he did so. The action only turned Tonette on more; no man had ever pulled her hair like that. Her hips repeatedly met his in an erotic, sensual dance that made her feel like she was melting into her carpet.

Their hands met and slid above their heads, their hips still winding to the beat of the music neither of them had realized was still playing. The kiss continued, unrushed, unhurried, but still deep and intense. Time stood still for both of them. Emotion radiated from their bodies with a heat that would burn anything that tried to stop them; it was an unspoken cementing of what had been building between them since Troy initially showed up at her door from Barbados.

A while passed before either of them began removing any articles of clothing. Troy pulled his t-shirt over his head, and Tonette tossed it away from them. The buttons on her short-sleeved shirt were slowly undone one by one, and the clasp on her front-closure bra was released. Troy's hands slid down her outstretched arms and massaged her aching breasts, taking their time, kneading and appreciating and exploring them, before his lips began to partake in the assault on Tonette's deteriorating composure. His tongue slowly swirled around her nipple, closing his warm mouth over it before teasing and flicking with the tip, and Tonette didn't even try to contain her scream. His other hand steadily worked the other breast, his fingertips teasing and pinching, knowingly driving her crazy and enjoying the ride as he did so.

Eventually Troy turned his oral attention to her other breast, and Tonette's eyes rolled to the back of her head. She wanted this man inside of her, more and more with every passing second. Her body was screaming from every pore. Her hands held his head to her chest, her back arched, as she continuously whimpered and murmured some indecipherable language. Troy slid down her body, kissing down the length of her toned stomach, and his hands gripped the waistband of her jeans. It wasn't until his fingers had deftly undone the button that Tonette remembered the sun-shaped birthmark on her hip, and the tattoo on her lower back. Troy would surely remember both of them, especially the birthmark; he had been so fascinated by it when he saw it in Barbados. She might be able to explain the tattoo, but she knew her having the exact birthmark in the exact same place as he knew Toni to have it would raise a glaring red flag.

"Oh my god!" she gasped in a mild panic, scooting away from him as she yanked her shirt closed. The burning arousal she had been experiencing just moments before was now replaced with a freezing wave of fear. This couldn't be the way Troy found out the truth, despite what he had said earlier.

Clearly surprised, Troy looked up at her.

"I'm sorry," she mumbled, running a hand down her face as the other clutched her shirt together. "I'm...its just—"

"No, *I* apologize," Troy quickly interjected. He sat up onto his knees. "I, um, I lost control. I should not have—"

"No, Troy, please...you didn't do anything wrong. I enjoyed every second of what we were doing. Please don't apologize. It's not you at all, I'm just..."

"You don't have to explain," Troy waved off her words before running both hands down his face. His face showed clear anguish as he looked at her. "Clearly, I crossed a line."

"No!" Tonette protested, her voice desperate. She didn't want him thinking he couldn't ever touch her again. The previous half hour or so had been a slice of heaven that she had savored with every fiber of her being. She sat up on her own knees, facing him. Her eyes pleaded with him to understand something she knew he never would, because he didn't know the truth. "You didn't!"

"Then why did you freak out so suddenly like you did?"

Tonette wanted to tell him she was on her period or that she hadn't gotten a bikini wax or some other excuse as to why she had slammed on the brakes when he started to take her pants off, but she didn't want to lie to him anymore. She had been doing enough of that, and she found she still didn't have the nerve to right that wrong to his face. Sitting there across from him, she so wanted to just come clean about her

Toni alter ego and hope to high heaven he understood, but when she opened her mouth to do so, she couldn't make any words come out.

After a few moments, Troy just nodded as he held up his hands. "It's all right," he said, his voice low. "I get it."

"No, Troy, you don't..."

Standing, Troy clamped his hands onto the back of his neck as he paced in a short circle in front of her. He eventually dropped his hands as he looked down at her, his erection not fully gone, his face a gut-wrenching mixture of remorse and pain.

"Please forgive me," he said softly. Before Tonette could respond, he turned and walked down the hall. Tonette heard the door to the bathroom close softly behind him, and she felt the tears roll down her face as she held the sides of her shirt together with both hands, wishing he would come back. But he didn't.

Chapter 19

Tonette prayed Olarion was still up as she gripped her steering wheel.

"Hello?" Olarion finally answered. She didn't sound sleepy but Tonette could hear music in the background.

"Hey," Tonette hiccupped, wiping the tears that were blurring her eyes only for them to be replaced with more. She hadn't been able to stop crying since she left her apartment thirty minutes before.

"Tonette?" Olarion's voice immediately sounded concerned. "Are you crying? What's wrong?"

"Can I come over there? Please?"

"Of course," Olarion quickly replied. "Aaron is here but he'll understand."

"I'm sorry; I didn't mean to interrupt you two." Tonette stopped her car at a red light and wiped her eyes with the sleeve of her sweater. She tried her best to compose herself, even if it would just be only temporary. "Don't worry about it."

"Tonette! You know you can come over here! What in the world is the matter? Where are you?"

"I'm in my car. I just...needed to get away for a minute to clear my head. But I don't want to come over there and interrupt your time with Aaron. I'll be fine."

"Well can you at least tell me what happened to have you so upset?"

Taking a deep breath, Tonette leaned her head back against the headrest. "I messed up with Troy. Things had been going so well; perfect, even. And I ruined it."

"What do you mean?"

Feeling suddenly drained, Tonette shook her head. "I'm sorry, girl, I just don't have the energy to get into the details of it right now. I'll...I promise I'll tell you everything later."

"Okay," Olarion replied cautiously. "But can you promise me you'll be careful, wherever you are? You shouldn't be out driving at night when you're this upset. Where is Troy?"

"He's still at my place."

"Does he know you're gone?"

"He might, by now."

"You just left without telling him?"

"I couldn't face him, O. I just scribbled a note saying I'd be back in a while and left while he was in the bathroom."

"Oh my gosh," Olarion marveled. "Did you tell him the truth about all the Toni stuff?"

"No. But I should have. But I punked out yet again and now he thinks..." Tonette sighed as fresh tears fell from her eyes. "I am such an idiot!"

"Tonette, girl, please come over here. You don't need to be out and about right now."

"I'm okay," Tonette insisted, trying her best to sound like she meant it. "I'm, um...I'm about to go somewhere and get my head together. I just need to get my head together."

"You going to Blue's?"

"No; he said something about going out and he probably isn't home. I'll be all right."

Olarion wasn't convinced. "Well, can you promise me that you will call me if you need anything? Even if it's just to cry or talk or scream or whatever else. Just let me know you're okay whenever you get where you're going. Can you do that?"

"Yeah, I can do that. I'm so sorry for messing up your evening with Aaron."

"Girl, shut up. He knows what it is; you're like a sister to me and if he had a problem with me seeing about you when you needed someone then he obviously wouldn't be the man for me. Don't even worry about that."

Despite herself, Tonette smiled. She counted herself blessed to have a friend like Olarion. "I love you, O."

"Love you, too, girl."

Ending the call, Tonette bit her lip as she tried to gather herself. She took several deep breaths, and glanced at her surroundings. She didn't even know how she had ended up where she was; she had just gotten in her car and mindlessly started driving. Still not quite ready to go home and face Troy, she bit her lip and turned her car in the direction of Stanley's house, not even knowing what she would possibly say to him once she got there.

"Tonette?"

Looking up, Tonette saw Stanley standing outside her driver's side window, frowning slightly. She had been parked in his driveway for a while, not having the nerve to get out and knock on his door or even call or text him to let him know she was outside. Eventually he had noticed her sitting out there and came to see what was up.

She looked up at him shyly, lifting her hand in a half-wave.

Peering at her, Stanley opened her car door and leaned his arm on the hood of the car. His expression was both curious and concerned; it was clear she had been crying. Despite everything that had happened, he still cared about her.

"You all right?" he asked, his eyes roaming over her.

Tonette glanced up at him and then down into her lap, where her fingers were fumbling against each other. "I'm sorry for just showing up at your house like this."

"What's up?"

Shaking her head, Tonette knew she had made a mistake going there. What was she supposed to say? That the man she loved still didn't know she was really the same woman he had met in Barbados and she had freaked out when he was about to find that out as they were about to get busy on the floor? Stanley didn't want to hear that, and she didn't want to insult him by telling him.

"I'm sorry," she said again. She couldn't look at him as she reached for the door, intending to close it. "I shouldn't have come. I'll leave."

"Tonette, hold up a second," Stanley said, blocking the door with his hand. "Talk to me; you're clearly upset."

"It's nothing for you to worry about. I'll deal with it." Her head was still turned away from him.

There were several moments that passed before Stanley reached down and gently took her hand. "Come on in the house," he said.

"Stanley—"

"Please," he cut her off. The sincerity in his voice both warmed Tonette and made her feel silly all at the same time. "I don't like the idea of you driving when you're this upset. We don't have to talk if you don't want to; just come in and get yourself together. Okay? Please?"

Not having the energy to protest anymore, Tonette just nodded and let him gently pull her out of the car.

Once they were inside the house, she immediately burrowed herself in the corner of his sectional in the living room, still too embarrassed to make eye contact with him. Stanley came and sat next to her, turning on the television and waiting patiently. He stretched his arm along the back of the couch behind her.

"You want some water or something?" he asked her after a while.

"No, thanks."

Stanley continued watching the news program he had turned it on, and eventually Tonette turned her eyes towards the television. Trying to get her to relax a little, he changed the channel to an old episode of *Martin*, hoping to make her laugh. She didn't, but she did visibly relax, eventually leaning her head against his arm. Stanley was glad to see a smile tugging at the corners of her mouth at some of the crazy scenes playing in front of her.

He was glad when she let him pull her closer to him, resting her head on his chest. She didn't seem like herself, and he was sincerely worried about her. He couldn't deny being glad to see her, even if it wasn't under the circumstances he would have liked. Since the night he had asked her to leave after they started to make love and she was clearly thinking about something else, he had thought about her more than he had been able to help. More than a few times he had started to call her, just to hear her voice, but he never did.

His hand gently and comfortingly rubbed up and down her arm as they continued to watch television. Tonette felt marginally better than she had when she had arrived at his house, grateful that he wasn't trying to pull an explanation out of her. She needed his patience and understanding right then; even when she couldn't resist giggling at Martin and Gina, she still didn't feel ready to explain why she was there. For the time being, she just wanted to forget the past couple of hours.

"You okay?" he asked softly.

Not wanting to say she was when she wasn't, Tonette just slightly shrugged a shoulder, her eyes still on the TV. When she dared to glance up at him, she was surprised to see him already looking down at her, his caring eyes roaming hers. Before she could stop herself, she impulsively leaned up and brushed her lips against his. When he didn't protest, she leaned up and pressed her lips to his, letting them linger this time. When she felt his hand hesitantly cup the back of her head, she gripped the front of his shirt as her lips parted against his. Her mind was screaming at her how stupid this was, what a bad idea this was; she had no business kissing Stanley like this when she really wanted to be back at her apartment still up under Troy. But she just wanted to forget about everything for a little while, and she didn't want to think about how she would feel whenever she and Stanley stopped kissing and she would be left to explain herself or apologize or both.

Stanley knew what they were doing was probably a bad idea. But he couldn't resist her. There were many times he had wished she was right there doing exactly what she was doing now, and now that she was, he couldn't make himself stop her. Even though he knew that at the end of it, she would probably just go home to whatever she was running from and he would be right where he was before she showed up in his driveway.

Their kiss intensified steadily, with Tonette eventually ending up on Stanley's lap. Neither of them missed the desperation in the kiss, from both sides, but they were both too caught up in it for their own respective reasons to care. Stanley's arms tightened around her, and when Tonette started to grind against him, he moved with her. Before too long, they were tearing each other's clothes off.

"Do you think we should be doing this?" Stanley asked breathlessly. He yanked her bra straps down her arms.

"I don't care," Tonette replied dismissively, flinging her bra to the floor and wrapping her arms around his neck. He stood, lifting her up with him, and she set her feet on the floor long enough for them each to get their pants off. Once they were both naked and Stanley covered himself with the condom he hastily retrieved from his wallet, they fell back onto the couch, kissing each other wildly. Tonette climbed back onto his lap, immediately lowering herself down onto him, biting her lip as she did so. They both sighed, wasting no time increasing the pace. Both of them knew this wasn't making love; they were screwing each other, each using the other and each willing to be used.

I just wanna forget...I just wanna forget, Tonette repeatedly thought to herself as she bounced on Stanley's lap. He held on to her hips as he roughly sucked her breasts, and when he abruptly slapped her bare bottom with his hand, Tonette threw her head back, appreciating the pain. Stanley repeatedly spanked her, wanting to punish her for not being his. He threw her onto her back and pounded into her, gritting his teeth and burying his face in the crook of her neck. Tonette grunted as she took it, encouraging him to give it to her as hard as he could, and he did his best to oblige her, throwing her leg over his shoulder and banging her so hard that her back ended up halfway off of the couch.

They both rolled to the floor, never stopping. Each had a lot of built-up frustration to release, and they were more than willing to help each other release it. Tonette happened to glance at the clock on the wall and note that it was almost midnight, and she automatically wondered what Troy was doing and what he thought about her being gone. Part of her wanted to check her phone to see if he had called or texted her, but instead of doing that, she just grabbed Stanley's behind and pulled him into her deeper, throwing her hips back at him and begging him to go harder. And he did.

Eventually, they slowed down, both becoming tired and spent. Tonette had managed to push her emotions to the back closet of her mind while she and Stanley were sexing, but as soon as he slowed down, she started to remember what had made her come over there in the first place, and she felt the tears coming back to her eyes. She didn't want to cry about Troy in front of Stanley, but she knew she wouldn't be able to help it. Stanley felt good inside of her, but he wasn't who she wanted. Remembering how close she had been to being in this position with the man she did want just released the hold on the floodgates, and the tears started pouring from her eyes.

Stanley looked down at her and felt his chest tighten. He hated to see her cry, and he had a feeling as to why she was doing it right after they had just finished having sex. And why she had probably showed up at his house in the first place.

"You have feelings for someone else, don't you?" he asked, his voice low.

Not having the energy to deny it, Tonette just nodded, covering her face with her hands.

"You love him?"

She nodded again.

Sighing, Stanley swiped a hand over his sweaty face and just gathered her into his arms. He had suspected this had been the case for a while, and that it was the real reason why Tonette had never been able to fully give herself to him. Part of him wanted to be upset, but the other part couldn't fault her for it; you couldn't help who you fell for. Just like he hadn't been able to help falling for her.

"I'm so sorry, Stanley," she sobbed against his chest. "I sincerely never meant to—"

"I know," Stanley softly cut her off, smoothing down her wild hair. He buried his face in it, his own emotions starting to creep up on him. "I know you didn't."

Tonette sniffled as she looked up at him, taking his face in her hands. "I really do care about you. *So* much."

"I know," Stanley said again. He wiped her tears with the pad of his thumb. "And I care about you. As cliché as it may sound, I'm always here for you if you need me, Tonette. And I mean that. Okay?"

"Okay," she replied softly.

Realizing he was still inside of her, Stanley started to retract, but Tonette tightened her legs around him.

"Not yet," she said when he looked down at her questioningly. "I'm not quite ready yet."

Knowing exactly what she meant, Stanley just nodded and held her tighter. She wasn't ready to go face what she had been running from no more than he was ready to let her go.

About an hour or so later, Tonette took a deep breath as she headed back to her apartment. She surprisingly felt a lot better after leaving Stanley's, still a little surprised at her behavior but feeling way more renewed than she had been when she had gone. She knew she had to tell Troy the truth, and she vowed to herself that she would do exactly that as soon as she got back home. He deserved to know, and he deserved to be told to his face. As hard as it was going to be to do it, she had to woman up and just tell him everything.

But when she opened the door to her apartment, she was surprised to find Troy gone, and there were no traces of him being there. She rushed towards the hallway, thinking he might be in the bathroom or the office or even in her room, but he wasn't. He wasn't in the kitchen. And his duffel bag and suitcase were gone.

Feeling herself start to freak out, she grabbed her phone and called him, but it went straight to voicemail. She tried again and again as she searched the apartment for a note or something explaining where he was, but there was none. He hadn't left her any messages; he had just left. The thought of him being gone and them leaving things as they had left them made her start to cry uncontrollably.

"Stupid stupid stupid!" she admonished herself, banging her palm against her forehead. She paced around the living room, wondering what she could do, if anything. She had no idea where Troy was, and he apparently didn't want to talk to her. She had managed to make an even *bigger* mess of things.

Not caring about the time, she called Olarion as she shifted her weight from one foot to the other, chewing on her lip impatiently.

"He's gone!" she exclaimed as soon as Olarion groggily answered.

"Who?"

"Troy! He left!"

"What do you mean, he left? Where did he go?"

"I don't know!" Tonette shrieked, plopping down onto the couch and burying a hand in her disheveled hair. "I just got back and he wasn't here! Even his bags are gone!"

"Hold up; you're *just* getting back? You called me at least three hours ago. Where have you been all this time??"

Hesitating only slightly, Tonette responded, "I was at Stanley's."

"At Stanley's??" Olarion was fully awake now.

"Yes."

"What the hell were you doing at Stanley's?"

"Well, to be blunt, screwing him."

"*Excuse me?!?*"

"You heard me. I hadn't been ready to come home and face Troy and I just went over there on an impulse. I hadn't been planning on having sex with him when I went but that's where it ended up going."

"So..." Olarion was clearly thrown for a loop and Tonette prepared herself for the lecture she was sure she was about to get. "You...umph. How 'bout you just tell me everything that happened from the beginning." Tonette heard a door close, as if Olarion had gone to another room. Aaron must have still been there.

"Fine." Tonette proceeded to tell her friend everything that happened from the time Blue dropped Troy off after their day out until Tonette left Stanley's house a little while ago. She didn't leave out a single detail, and Olarion almost couldn't even find her words when she had finally finished.

"I don't even know what to say right now," Olarion marveled when Tonette finished talking. "I am certifiably speechless."

"Yeah, well. That's what happened."

"I still can't believe you and Stanley went there. You just boned each other 'til you couldn't move anymore, huh?"

"Pretty much. Surprisingly, I'm kind of glad we did 'cause I felt better once I left, if for no other reason than it gave Stanley and I having some semblance of closure. He thankfully understood that I have feelings for another man and didn't try to hold that against me."

"And you all had to have rough sex on the floor to get that closure?"

"I didn't say it made any sense. But we're on good terms now; I needed comfort and a reprieve and that's what he gave me. And I had some clarity when I left. I had every intention of telling Troy everything when I got home, but," Tonette's voice cracked. "He wasn't here. And he's not answering his phone and I have no idea where he is..."

"Oh, I didn't realize I had a text..."

"For all I know he could be on a plane back to Barbados, thinking the worst of me. I need to make this right."

"Hold on a second, Tonette."

"Troy and I had been *so* close to making love; girl, it was absolutely amazing. I couldn't even begin to tell you how good it felt if I tried. But then I thought about him seeing my birthmark and I freaked. Now he's gone wherever he is, thinking he's done something wrong when he didn't. I have to make this right, girl. I *have* to."

"Tonette..."

"I wish I knew where he was! How could he just leave like that? At least when I left, I left a note! He didn't leave *anything*!"

"He's at Blue's."

"He's not even *from* here; I hope he's not out roaming around," Tonette rambled on, not hearing her. "He could wander into some bad neighborhood or something. I don't even know where to start looking for him! Hell, now I'm worried..."

"Tonette!" Olarion called out. "Did you hear me?"

"What?" Tonette replied distractedly.

"I *said*, Troy is at Blue's. Blue texted me a while ago but I'm just now seeing it."

"Oh my god," Tonette sank against the back of the couch. She had never been more relieved in her life. She grabbed her keys and bolted upright. "I'm going over there."

"No! Do not go over there!" Olarion exclaimed. "Just...leave him alone for right now, T."

"What?" Tonette's hand flew to her chest. "Did Blue say that's what Troy said he wanted?"

"Blue said that's what Troy needs right now; he apparently was pretty upset when he called him earlier."

"Damn it!" Tonette muttered, throwing her keys to the ground. She pressed her hand to her forehead. "I cannot believe all this is happening right now..."

"Yeah, girl, it's pretty crazy. But Blue said he'll bring Troy back in the morning."

Sighing, Tonette dropped back onto the couch, emotionally drained. It was probably good that she had a while to herself before facing Troy again. "Okay. Okay, that's good."

"Are you okay? Do you need me to come over there?"

"No, I'm fine. I just...I can't believe I screwed all this up. Toni wouldn't have let all this happen; she would've had the confidence to just be honest from the beginning and count it his loss if he couldn't deal with it."

Olarion was quiet for a moment, as if she was trying to find the best way to say what she needed to say. "Tonette...do you realize how much you do that?"

"Do what?"

"Refer to Toni as if she's a real woman. You do that a lot."

"Really?" Tonette knew she referenced Toni mentally a lot, but she didn't realize she did it out loud *that* much.

"Yes, really. Why do you do that?"

"I guess...Toni is more like the woman I wish I could be." Tonette was glad she was alone because she was a little embarrassed to admit that.

"Are you serious?"

"Yes, O. I mean, I've always been fine with myself as I am, or, at least I thought I was. But when I was in Barbados, I felt so free...the things I always say in my head, I just said out loud. I didn't spend time analyzing things before I did them; I just acted. I threw caution to the wind. I know that's not always a good thing, but it felt so good to do it. I just don't think Troy and I would have gotten as far as we did if I was acting like my regular self."

"Obviously that's not true, given how taken he is with you now," Olarion disputed. "You said yourself that he said he hadn't even thought about Toni since he came back this time; it's been all about you. So you should really quit thinking you need to be like Toni to get Troy's attention, or that you need to be anything other than who you are."

"Yeah," Tonette admitted. "But it just...it felt so *good* to be Toni. I can't really explain it..."

"But who says you're not? It wasn't necessarily a 'Tonette' move to go to Stanley's house and ride him 'til the wheels fell off. That sounds like a *Toni* thing, to me. Girl, Toni is *you*...you just know when to bring her out and when not to."

Tonette had never thought about it like that. Now it seemed silly to have been so intimidated by Toni...she was more like Toni than she realized. Or at least, Toni became more evident since she came back from Barbados.

"Girl, it's kind of fun having an alter ego you can bring out when you want to," Olarion continued. "I know Aaron loves it when I let Keisha out of her cage."

Tonette couldn't resist laughing out loud. "Keisha?"

"Yes, Keisha! Girl, I throw on that red wig and my stilettos and feel like a whole new person."

"Oh my gosh..."

"Don't knock it, Ms. *Toni*," Olarion chided. "It's all about when you bring it out. Save Toni for when you need her but keep in mind that you've gotten along all these years just fine as *Tonette*. And that's more than good enough."

Tonette knew she was right. She didn't have to be Toni all the time; she could channel her when she needed to, or wanted to. And she knew she would need to when it came time to tell Troy the truth about everything.

So the next day, when Blue called to let her know he and Troy were on their way back, Tonette told herself to think positively; that she was finally doing something that she should have done weeks ago. She hated the thought of Troy hating her, or telling her that he never wanted to see her again. She didn't want him to think this had been part of some sick game, or that everything she had ever said to him, either as Toni or as herself, had been a lie.

Olarion came over for moral support, and once Troy and Blue arrived, Tonette didn't want to waste any time.

"Troy, I'm *so* glad to see you're all right," she said as she hugged him tightly, then held onto his hand as she sat on the couch with her feet tucked underneath her. "I was worried sick when I came home and realized you had left."

"I am sorry for not letting you know where I was," Troy said, sitting down next to her. "I should have left a note for you, like you did for me. But I was upset..."

"I *totally* understand..."

"And I know I need to apologize to you for...what happened before that," Troy said, glancing at Blue and Olarion curiously. Tonette imagined he was probably wondering what they were still doing there for what probably should have been a private conversation. But Tonette needed her friends there, otherwise she might chicken out again when Troy looked at her with those eyes of his.

"No, Troy you don't owe me any apology for that. *I* should be apologizing to *you*."

"Tonette—"

"Troy, please," Tonette interjected, briefly covering her face with her hands. "Please, just...let me say what I have to say before I lose my nerve *again*. I *have* to tell you this now...I should've told you a long time ago, really..."

"Okay," Troy looked at her intently. He turned to face her, giving her his full attention. "What's wrong?"

Tonette took a deep breath, channeling some of that Toni confidence. With an encouraging nod from her friends, she forged ahead.

"It's about Toni," she began. "She doesn't...she doesn't exist."

Troy frowned in confusion. "What do you mean? I spent time with her in Barbados."

"No, Troy...you spent time with *me* in Barbados. She is me...*I'm* Toni."

Rearing back, Troy's frown deepened. "I am not sure I understand."

"Troy...when I went to Barbados, I had planned to completely just let my hair down and be the total opposite of the person I usually am, complete with some new hair and sexier clothes. I wanted to *really* have fun. Then I met you on my first night there, and when you asked me my name, *Toni* just came out. I hadn't planned on doing that, but I also didn't plan on...us spending so much time together and getting so close. And over time, I didn't know how to tell you the truth. Then I came home and figured I'd never see you again, but you showed up, and I still couldn't bring myself to tell you. So I made up that stuff about me being Toni's twin. It was stupid and I should have been woman enough to be honest with you, but Troy..." Tonette's hands flew to her chest as tears began to sting her eyes. "I didn't expect to fall for you like I did. Truth be told, I fell for you in Barbados. And I am *so* sorry for all of this; it was never, ever my intent to deceive you or anyone else."

Troy just sat and looked at her, as if he was processing everything he just heard. Tonette was just beginning to hope that he might possibly be understanding and forgive her for everything when he angrily shot off the couch.

"So you are telling me that all of this between us," he waved his hand back and forth between them, "has been a lie?"

"No!" Tonette exclaimed, the tears streaming down her cheeks. "Troy, please..."

"You have been lying to me all this time??"

"No! I mean, not about everything! Not about anything that *really* matters!"

"And you two were in on this too, huh?" Troy accused, turning to Blue and Olarion. "Is this what you do, play games on unsuspecting foreigners? Make a fool out of me? This is some cruel joke to you all, right?"

"It wasn't anything like that—"

"I don't want to hear it!" Troy yelled, cutting Blue off. Tonette cried harder; she had never heard Troy raise his voice like that. "I thought you were my friend and now I find out all this time, you were lying to me, too?"

"Hey man, I didn't lie to you about anything!" Blue retorted, standing.

"That's not what it sounds like to me! Were you and Tonette really previously married?"

Blue pursed his lips, shooting an *I told you to leave me out of this* glance at Tonette. "No."

"Why am I not surprised?" Troy sneered, shaking his head.

"Look, how 'bout you just calm down and let's all sit and discuss this," Blue suggested, trying to diffuse the rapidly-growing tension. "Let's not make this bigger than it has to be."

"Don't you *dare* say that to me right now!" Troy yelled, stepping closer to Blue with his fists balled.

"Troy!" Tonette shrieked, jumping up to hold him back.

"Y'all, please, let's not do this!" Olarion exclaimed, jumping from her own seat to restrain Blue, who was about to charge back at Troy. She braced her hands against his chest, warning him with her eyes to calm down. "This isn't going to help anything!"

"You will *not* tell me to calm down when I am the one that has been made a *fool* of by *all* of you!" Troy hollered, pushing Tonette's hands off of him. Her eyes pleaded with him as sheets of tears cascaded down her face.

"Please..." she cried.

"I just cannot believe this," Troy marveled, turning his eyes towards Tonette. The hurt in them was just as evident as the anger, and it tore Tonette's heart to shreds to know she had caused that look. She hung her head.

"Troy, I know all of this looks bad but Tonette's feelings for you are real," Olarion jumped in, trying to plead her friend's case. Her own eyes were tearing up, watching her friend in so much pain. She was still holding Blue behind her back, preventing him from moving towards Troy again. "None of us wanted to—"

"But you *did*," Troy interrupted bitingly. "*All* of you were in on this lie. And here I am thinking I was coming here for one woman, and it turns out that woman wasn't who I thought she was." He looked at Tonette, the hurt in his eyes glaring. "I feel like such a fool."

"I am *so sorry*," Tonette pleaded, stepping closer to Troy. She stretched her hands out, and her heart wrenched when he moved away from her. "I didn't mean for...Troy, *everything* I've ever said about what I felt for you is true. I was just too scared to tell you the truth because I was in love with you and didn't want to lose you."

Troy glared at her.

"I might have lied about my name and my occupation and some other insignificant things," Tonette continued, her eyes pleading with him to understand, "But my feelings for you are as real as they can get. Every moment we shared together, both here *and* in Barbados, was sincere. I need for you to believe that because when I tell you I love you, I mean that more than I've ever meant anything."

Troy continued to look at her, his eyes starting to glisten. Tearing his eyes away, he shook his head vehemently and stalked out, slamming the door behind him. Tonette keeled over, crying uncontrollably. Her friends immediately came over to support her, with Blue's strong arms encircling her waist, and she fell against him, seemingly too weak to stand on her own.

"It's gonna be okay, baby," Blue tried to assure her, holding her against his chest. Her hands clutched his shirt. "He just needs some time to cool off."

"But what if he doesn't?" Tonette whined. "What if he doesn't forgive me for this??"

"Girl, I know it might not seem like it right now, but you absolutely did the right thing," Olarion replied, deftly avoiding the question. She wiped her eyes and wrapped her arms around her friends. "I *know* that was hard for you; I hate seeing you hurting like this. But I am *so* proud of you for finally telling him, 'cause he needed to know. Like Blue said, he just needs some time to process all this...I'm sure once he's thinking rationally again, he'll be ready to talk about everything."

"Did you see how he looked at me? How he didn't want me to touch him? Oh god...I think I'm gonna be sick,"

Tonette groaned, clutching her stomach. "What did I do?!??"

"Baby, you did what you needed to do," Blue insisted. "You know that. Come on, come sit down."

Tonette let him ease her down onto the couch before burying her face in her hands. She rocked side to side, already replaying the look Troy had in his eyes when she told him everything. If he ended up not forgiving her, she already knew that look was going to haunt her. Her chest ached at the thought. Yes, she needed to tell him. Yes, he had deserved to know. But that didn't change the fact that she had hurt him, all because she didn't have enough confidence in herself to *be* herself. And now she might have lost the only man she ever really loved.

Chapter 20

It wasn't until a few hours later that Troy came back. Olarion and Blue had left, and Tonette was just curled up on the couch, biting her nails and constantly checking the time on her phone. She had tried to call Troy several times, as well as sending him a few texts, but outside of acknowledging he was okay, he didn't respond to her. She was relieved to see him come back safely, but she was nervous about what he would say to her.

She sat up upon him entering the living room. Her eyes were still puffy and red and she knew she looked terrible, but she couldn't care about that right then.

"Are you okay?" she asked softly.

"Yes, I'm fine." Troy peered at her.

Tonette wanted to let him make the first move, but she was itching to talk about everything and see where they stood. She just hated everything being so up in the air.

Eventually, Troy sighed and sat down in the armchair next to the couch. Resting his elbows on his knees and clasping his hands together, he hung his head for a few moments before lifting his eyes to her, studying her as if he was meeting her for the first time.

"Please just tell me why, Tonette," he finally said in a low voice. "Why did you lie to me like this?"

Mentally telling herself to keep it together, Tonette nervously wrung the handkerchief she was holding in her hands. "It all sounds so silly now, when I think about it; to let it get this far was ridiculous. But at the time, Troy, I just...all that was on my mind was being a totally different person and enjoying my vacation. But like I said before, I didn't go there intending to give out a fake name or deceive anyone. And I certainly didn't think I would fall in..." her voice trailed off as she looked down into her lap. Troy looked at her intently.

"Did you not think that I would be interested in you if I knew you as you really are?"

"Honestly, at first, no; I didn't," Tonette admitted. "The hair and the sexy clothes I wore over there had me acting way more confident than I've ever been here. And the thing is, I've always been comfortable with myself; I don't have low self-esteem. Or at least, I didn't think I did. But when you seemed so interested in me and getting to know me and us spending so much time together, I guess I felt like that's the kind of woman you went for."

"I don't like just *one* kind of woman, Tonette," Troy informed her. "It is not all about the physical with me. I am more interested in how she is on the inside than I am with her hair or her clothing."

"Yeah, I realize that now," Tonette replied softly. "There were so many times I wanted to tell you the truth, Troy, but I guess I felt I was in too deep by then and would just ride it out. Once I got back home, I couldn't get you off my mind...but I didn't want to tell you something like that over the phone. You deserved better than that."

"So...why did you send me that birthday card?"

Shaking her head, Tonette said, "Honestly, that was a mistake. I had bought the card and addressed it, but had changed my mind about actually mailing it. Olarion is the one who sent it off, thinking she was doing me a favor."

Running a weary hand down his face, Troy just shook his head and looked away.

"What are you thinking?" Tonette asked shyly after a few quiet moments.

"All this time, since I came back for this visit, I have felt this closeness with you that I couldn't explain," he began, playing with his watch as he looked at the floor. "There was something familiar about you, and not just because you were supposedly Toni's twin. I felt it during the first visit, but once I returned home, I found myself thinking about you more than I was thinking about Toni. And I could not bring myself to leave things like that, so I requested time off work and came back. I hadn't really planned on staying this long, but I did not want to leave you; I really felt at home here. I looked forward to seeing you every day and spending time with you; I often imagined that we were a couple and we lived here together."

Tonette felt her chest cave in upon hearing this. She had had those same fantasies many times since Troy had been staying with her, and when she had stayed with him in Barbados.

"You said that you had fallen for me," Troy continued, finally turning to look at her. "Is that true?"

"It's absolutely true."

"The feeling is definitely mutual," Troy informed her, his voice low. His eyes looked right into hers. "You've had me since that first night I took you home in Barbados."

Excitement surged through Tonette. She dared to think there was hope for them.

"But I detest dishonesty," Troy continued. "And while I get your reasoning and don't think you really meant any harm, that doesn't excuse you letting this go as far as it has. I just...I cannot help but feel foolish for falling for someone that isn't real."

Tonette started to protest that she *was* real, but knew it wouldn't make any difference. All this time he had thought he was in love with Toni, and now he learned that it was nothing more than Tonette playing a part...she could definitely see how he would feel foolish upon hearing that. She probably would, too.

"I'm so sorry," she expressed. "I know there's no excuse, Troy, and I'm not going to try to make any. I just hope and pray that you can forgive me."

"I'm sure that I can," Troy replied, to Tonette's relief. "But...I am going to return home in the morning."

Tonette's eyes snapped to him, panic ripping through her. "What? Why??"

"Because I need to get back to my own life," Troy said, leaning back in the chair. "I have become too wrapped up in you and everything here...and to find out that things were not as I thought they were is a little daunting. I need to go back to my own house, my work, my friends, my environment, and just get my head together." He looked at her. "I am not angry anymore, Tonette; I am just disappointed. And I just think it is best if I leave."

"But what about..." Tonette felt the tears coming, but she tried her best to keep them at bay. "What about us?"

"I cannot be around you right now," Troy replied gently. "Please understand."

He might as well have punched her in the gut, 'cause that's how much his statement had hurt her. The tears streamed down her cheeks unchecked. She almost didn't even know how to respond to that...part of her wanted to beg him to stay, but the other part could understand why he felt he had to leave.

"Can I at least take you to the airport?" she asked softly, looking down into her lap.

"I will take a taxi."

He didn't even want to take a car ride with her. Tonette knew she had blown it, and the realization made her skin burn. She wanted to ask if they could at least keep in touch; if she would ever see him again, but she didn't have the nerve. If he said no, to either question, she just didn't know how she would handle it.

They just sat there in a somewhat-awkward silence, neither really knowing what else to say, before Tonette finally made herself get up and go to her room. As she passed by Troy, he reached out and took her hand, bringing it to his lips. He pressed his face her to wrist, inhaling her skin for several moments, before gently releasing it. Not being able to resist, Tonette leaned down and wrapped her arms around his neck from behind, and felt mildly comforted when his hand rubbed her arm. Placing a hasty kiss to his temple,

Tonette quickly retreated to her room before she totally lost it.

The next morning, Tonette woke up early. She just laid there for a while, recalling all of the events of the last forty-eight hours. It was crazy to her, thinking of everything that happened; finally becoming intimate with Troy again, impulsively dropping in on Stanley and sexing him like she did, telling the truth to Troy finally, them clearing the air and him informing her he was leaving. She didn't know what she expected to happen when she finally told him the truth; part of her had hoped that he would say it didn't matter and that they could be together the way they both seemed to want to be. But that's not what happened; Troy was leaving, and she didn't know when or if he would be coming back.

The thought had her hurriedly tossing back the covers and rolling out of bed, rushing to her adjoining bathroom to brush her teeth and splash some water on her face. She adjusted the silk scarf on her head, wanting to rip it off and undo the twists that it was covering, but she didn't want to take the time to do all that; she wanted to take advantage of the little time with Troy she had left and didn't want to waste any of it worrying about her hair.

When she emerged from her bedroom, though, intending to maybe make Troy some breakfast and make another plea for taking him to the airport herself, she found the living room empty. The sofa bed was put away, the sheets he had used folded neatly on top of it, and all of his bags were gone. Her chest began to heave as she started towards the kitchen, and then she noticed the note on the end table. She snatched it up, her eyes widening as she read it:

Tonette,

I thought that it would be best to go ahead and leave, even though it was very hard for me to do so. Nothing about this is easy for me; I do not want to leave you. But for now, it is best that I return home, and I know I would not be able to say goodbye to you.

I love you,
Troy

Her eyes re-read the note over and over until the tears blurred her vision so much she couldn't see it anymore. She hated that she didn't get a chance to tell him goodbye, or hug him one more time. Sadness overtook her, and she sunk down onto the arm of the couch, clutching the note in her hand. She allowed herself a few minutes to cry before wiping her eyes, telling herself to get it together. Maybe Troy had a point; maybe it was best he left like he had. She knew she would be much more of a mess if she had taken him to the airport and watched him walk off with his bags, and she didn't put it past herself to beg him again to reconsider leaving.

As if in a daze, she made herself get up and get her day started. She was kind of on autopilot at first; it was still a little hard for her to process that Troy was actually gone, and for all she knew, for good this time. She had become used to him being there, and found herself preparing breakfast for two like she had been doing. When she realized she would be eating alone, fresh tears came to her eyes again.

She missed Troy already, and she knew that wouldn't be changing any time soon.

Thank goodness school would be starting back soon and she would have something else to focus on. In the few days after Troy left, Tonette moped around her apartment, praying and wishing that he would just show up at her door again or call her and let her know he was on his way back because he missed her so much. But that didn't happen; Troy had let her know he had arrived back in Barbados safely, but other than that, they hadn't communicated much at all. Tonette wanted to video call him on several occasions, but she stopped herself. If he wanted or needed space from her, then she needed to respect that. If and when he wanted to talk to her, he knew where to find her.

A couple of months went by, and Tonette hadn't heard a word from Troy. She couldn't help but be hurt by this, but she knew she couldn't wallow in self pity over it; she had to keep it moving. The school year had started back and she was back into the swing of her regular schedule, and she was glad to have something to keep her occupied. She hung out with her friends, but made them promise to stop asking her about Troy; she couldn't keep talking about him because it would just make her miss him more. And she certainly missed him enough already as it was.

One night when she was at home in her office paying some bills, she came across the paper with Troy's contact information on it in her desk drawer. Biting her lip, she impulsively opened her laptop and began typing an email to him; she told him how much she missed him, how things were going with school so far, and again how sorry she was for everything. She just poured her heart out, and unlike the birthday card she had bought months ago, she went ahead and sent the email. She usually would have written an actual letter, but she didn't have the patience to wait for that; she wanted Troy to see this as soon as possible. Part of her didn't even expect to get a response back, but she felt a little better having sent it, sure that he would be responding within a day or two.

But when a couple of weeks passed without a word, Tonette had to come to the sad realization that it might really be over. He hadn't called, texted, and now he had ignored her email, too; that had to mean something. He had said he could forgive her, but maybe he had reconsidered. Or maybe it was an out-of-sight-out-of-mind thing. Or maybe, and she hated considering this possibility, he had met someone else. The thought of Troy with another woman made Tonette cringe, and she hoped there was a viable reason why she hadn't heard from him by now.

Tonette put on the best face she could every day, but when she was in bed at night, the tears came almost automatically. She missed Troy no less now than she had when he first left, and she wondered when it would stop hurting so much, him not being there. Her body literally ached for him; she just missed being in his presence, laughing, dancing, and of course, kissing him and feeling those hands of his on her body. Everything in her wished he was there with her, that she could at least talk to him, but the few times she dared to try to call him, she never got an answer. It hurt that he was shutting her out like he was, and at times it even angered her, but she figured she deserved it. If she had just been honest, none of this would be happening. She had to remember that she had brought this all on herself, and if nothing else, she learned a lesson or two from it.

She didn't see herself getting over Troy any time soon, but he was clearly moving on; she had to find a way to do the same.

Chapter 21

Tonette checked herself in the mirror, turning to check out the rear before fluffing out her hair. She adjusted the short brown leather jacket over her cream bodysuit, and put on her gold hoop earrings as she glanced down at her brown ankle boots. She had to admit, she felt cute and sexy, which had been what she was going for.

It had been seven months since Troy had left, and still next to no word from him. He had sent a couple of very short, very terse responses when she would reach out to him, but that was it. It was like all the time they had shared since they met almost a year ago hadn't even happened, or mattered. Tonette had spent more than her share of time crying and yearning for this man, and Olarion was constantly in her ear telling her she needed to get back out there and meet someone else. Tonette hadn't wanted to be bothered, but she finally figured Olarion had a point; maybe what she needed was to throw her proverbial fishing line back and try to catch one of those other fish in the sea.

Truth be told, Tonette had actually been on a few dates in the last couple of months, but nothing ever really panned out from them. She liked to think she was giving these men a fair shot and tried her best not to compare everything about them to Troy, which she had to admit wasn't always easy to do. Whether she liked it or not, Troy was still her epitome;

her dream man. She still loved him. But she couldn't put her life on hold waiting around for him to talk to her.

Olarion managed to convince Tonette to go to a club, even though that really wasn't Tonette's scene. She told herself to think positively as she and Olarion approached the building.

"Girl, you are *killin'* it in that oufit," Olarion observed, giving her another once-over. "I'm almost jealous of you."

"Stop it," Tonette dismissed with a smile, grateful for the compliment. "I was worried about it being a little too form-fitting..."

"It's not."

"But I actually feel a little overdressed," Tonette admitted, observing the more revealing outfits some of the women who were also headed inside were wearing.

"You shouldn't. This is an over-thirty spot. And you don't have to show everything to be sexy."

"True enough."

"The men in here are gonna be *all* over you, trust."

"If you say so."

"Watch what I tell you."

Once they were inside and had had a couple of drinks, Tonette felt herself loosening up and actually enjoying herself. She joined Olarion on the dance floor, thankful that the DJ was playing music that she actually recognized, and just went with the flow when men came and started dancing with her. That wasn't something she would have done before but she was trying to come out of her shell a little bit, and be a little more uninhibited and a little less reserved.

After a while, Tonette took a break from dancing and went to get another drink from the bar. She was still sipping on it when Olarion made her way over to her.

"Whew! You've got the right idea, girl...I need some refreshing after all of that dancing. Can I get a chardonnay, please?" she asked the bartender.

"It's a pretty good crowd in here," Tonette observed, resting her elbow on the bar and peering out at all of the people on the dance floor.

"Yeah...it's thick but it's not overly crowded, thankfully. I hate being in clubs where you can't move an inch without bumping into somebody."

"I'm glad I let you talk me into coming; I'm actually enjoying myself."

"Yeah, I see...who is that fine hunk of masculinity that you danced through three straight songs with?"

Tonette blushed, knowing exactly who she was talking about. A tall, caramel-skinned cutie with a bald head and chiseled features had started dancing with her a while back, and didn't seem to want to stop. And once Tonette had gotten a good look at him, she didn't mind it at all. The middle of the dance floor wasn't exactly conducive to getting to know each other so she didn't even know his name, but she couldn't deny enjoying him grinding against her to the music. And he smelled like an orgasm in a bottle.

"I don't know what his name is," Tonette replied, trying to suppress her smile as she took a sip of her drink.

"You two certainly seemed familiar on the dance floor. I hadn't seen that much grinding since the last time Aaron and I watched something from our porn stash."

Tonette's mouth fell open and she playfully hit her friend in the arm. "Olarion!"

"What? You know you were working it out there on him."

"We were just dancing," Tonette tried to say casually, still trying not to smile.

"Uh-huh. What are you blushing for, then?"

"I'm not blushing!"

"The hell you aren't. You should see your face right now."

"I have no idea what you're talking about. And it's not like you weren't out there dancing, yourself."

"Yeah, I was dancing...I wasn't simulating sexual acts while I was doing it, though."

"Olarion!"

"Play innocent if you want to," Olarion winked at her as she took a long swig of her wine. "It's not like there's anything wrong with it. I'm thrilled that you're enjoying yourself so much."

"I really am."

"You know Blue is gonna be mad we didn't bring him."

"I thought he had a date tonight."

"There's no telling, girl. Last time I talked to him, he did."

"Well, he'll be all right. It's not like he takes us everywhere with him."

"Girl, I don't even *wanna* go to some of the places he goes to."

Tonette giggled. "I'm about to go to the bathroom," she said, finishing her drink and placing her glass on the bar.

"Cool. I'll probably be back out there shaking my ass when you get back."

Chuckling, Tonette just shook her head as she headed in the direction of the restrooms. Once inside, she relieved herself then checked out her appearance in the mirror as she washed her hands. She had removed her jacket a while ago, after Olarion had gotten the bartender to agree to keep it behind the bar until they got ready to leave. Her face was a little flushed but she still looked good, she thought. Giving her outfit one last check in the full-length mirror by the door, she exited the bathroom, ready to get back to the dance floor, hopefully with the great-smelling gentleman she had been grooving with before.

She certainly didn't expect to see him hanging out in the hallway, though. He was leaning against the wall, checking his phone. When she approached, he looked up at her and smiled, revealing a set of teeth that should have been on somebody's toothpaste commercial. Was he waiting on her?

"Hey," he greeted when she got closer to him.

"Hi," Tonette replied. She looked up at him cautiously.

"I saw you head back here and I figured it would be a good chance to formally introduce myself," he said with a smile. He held out his hand. "I'm Will."

Smiling, Tonette put her hand in his. "Tonette. It's nice to meet you."

"Nice to meet you, also. Are you having a good time?"

"I am...this is my first time coming here."

"Yeah, I was thinking that I've never seen you in here before; I don't come here often but I've been a few times."

"My friend suggested I come with her; she loves it."

"I'm glad she did," Will grinned, revealing a dimple in his right cheek. Tonette couldn't help smiling back and blush.

"I like your outfit, there," Will complimented, his eyes roaming over her. "I see it criss-crosses in the back...that's nice."

"Oh...thank you," Tonette replied, blushing harder. "I appreciate that."

They stood there talking for a little while longer before returning to the dance floor, where they proceeded to dance pretty much exclusively with each other for the remainder of the night. Tonette hadn't had so much fun in a while, and she was surprised at just how attracted she was to Will. She actually didn't *want* to dance with anybody else, and when he asked for her number at the end of the night, she gladly gave it to him, already looking forward to talking to him again.

She and Olarion had retrieved their jackets from behind the bar and were headed out to Olarion's car, talking about their evening when Tonette heard her name being called. She turned to see Will trotting towards her.

"Well, hello again," she smiled when he got closer to them.

Will smiled and Tonette felt her stomach clench; he was even sexier outside than he had been inside. "I hope you don't think I'm crazy since you *just* gave me your number not twenty minutes ago, but I just realized I'm not quite ready to let you go yet...what do you think about maybe going to get something to eat or some coffee or something?"

Clearly surprised, Tonette glanced at Olarion, who was just looking at her with a mischievous smirk. "Tonight?"

"Yeah. If you can't or don't feel comfortable with it, I totally understand, but I didn't want it to be said that I didn't ask."

Tonette wanted to look at Olarion again for some hint as to what to do, as this wasn't necessarily a situation she was used to. But she just asked herself something that she had grown accustomed to asking when she was unsure about something: what would Toni do?

Truth be told, Tonette *wanted* to go with Will, even though she hadn't even known him a full three hours. But she had trusted her gut with Troy the first night she met him in Barbados, and she would trust her gut again. At least this time she would be going to a public place.

"If you want, your beautiful friend can come, too," Will continued, glancing over at Olarion. "But if not, I don't mind giving you a ride home, since it appears the two of you rode together."

Tonette and Olarion shared a glance, and Tonette just gave her a slight nod before saying to Will, "I'd love to."

"And I don't have to go," Olarion chimed in. "But I *am* gonna need to see your I.D." When Will chuckled, Olarion just looked at him with an arched brow. "You think I'm playing." She held her hand out.

Realizing she wasn't kidding, Will glanced at Tonette before reaching into his pocket for his wallet. Tonette watched as Olarion snapped a picture of his license and of his face, then pointed a finger up at him. "I know a lot of people I can get to find you and beat your ass if you do anything to my homegirl."

Even though Tonette knew Olarion was serious, she thought it was amusing watching her threaten someone who was twice her size and towered over her by at least six inches. But to his credit, Will totally took her seriously, any trace of a smile gone from his face.

"I got you," he told her, nodding. "You have my word; your girl is in good hands, aight?"

"Yeah, okay. She better be." Olarion stepped over to Tonette and gave her a hug, telling her to call her if she needed to. Then with one last warning glare at Will, she got into her car and drove off.

Tonette tried to keep her surging nerves at bay at the realization that it was now just her and Will, and she didn't have anyone else to rely on to keep him entertained. But that nervousness didn't take long to melt away, though, when she and Will got to the closest IHOP and spent the next couple of hours talking. She felt rather comfortable with Will, telling him more than she usually shared with a man on the first night. She shared stories about her upbringing, her family, her job, her friends, hobbies; and everything she told him was the truth. Will told her that he was the oldest of five, owned a moving company, practiced martial arts, and was divorced with a five-year-old daughter. The fact that he had a child only endeared Tonette to Will more than it did repel her, especially when it was clear he was a proud father, the way he showed off the pictures of his daughter and bragged on her. Tonette actually thought it was cute; she had never dealt with a man with children before and felt better about seeing him again after that night when he assured her that there was no baby-mama-drama to worry about.

It was pretty late when Will finally dropped Tonette off; she declined his offer to walk her to her door, but shared a rather lengthy hug with him and an agreement that they would be seeing each other again soon. The smile was still on her face as she headed to her apartment, glad that her evening had turned out so well. She knew Olarion would be expecting a full report, and told herself to text her when she got inside.

She could see the letter taped to her door from a little ways off, and a slight frown marred her face, her steps quickening a little so she could see what it was. There was nothing on the front of it other than her name, and she glanced up and down the hall before removing it from her door and quickly going inside her apartment, dropping her purse and keys on the couch. Before she forgot, she sent a quick text to Olarion letting her know she was home safely, then she reached for the letter, sliding her nail under the taped flap to open it. When she pulled out what looked to be a handwritten letter and scanned it, she gasped when she realized it was from Troy. It fell from her hands as if it was suddenly too hot to touch, and she reared back on the couch with her fingertips at her lips. She felt her heart racing; this had been the *last* thing she had been expecting. The good feelings she had been experiencing just moments before were now replaced with a trembling trepidation.

After several moments of preparing herself for anything, she reached down and retrieved the letter from the floor, biting her lip as she began to read:

Tonette,

I know it's been a long time since you have really heard from me, and I must apologize to you about that. There have been a few things going on here that contributed to that, but mainly I was just trying to process everything that has happened between you and I, and figure out what I wanted to come of it.

I have not been able to stop thinking about you, Tonette. Every moment that you and I have shared together has replayed in my mind a million times, and there is no denying that I miss you terribly. I did get your email, and I appreciate you sending it. As upset as I was upon learning about your deception, I could not make that outweigh my love and desire for you. Even with everything that has happened, you are still the woman my heart calls for.

At the end of the day, Tonette, I want us to be together, or at least try to be. I know it has been many months since I left Atlanta, and I have not kept in contact with you, so you may have very well moved on by now. If that is the case, I can do nothing but respect that. I will always consider you my Lovely, regardless.

Troy

Tonette's jaw was on the floor, and her hand had started clutching the letter in a vice grip without realizing it. Her breath quickening, she read the letter two more times, not believing what was in front of her own eyes in black and white. Troy wanted to be with her? After all this time...Tonette honestly thought she had fallen into some deep sleep at some point and this was all some kind of dream. All of her past feelings for Troy came rushing back with the force of an angry wave, as if the past seven months of almost no contact had never happened.

Realizing she had the letter practically balled up in her hand, she quickly smoothed it out, not being able to resist reading it again. A smile spread across her face and warmth cascaded down her entire body like lava down a volcano. Her heart was actually beating out of her chest, and out of nowhere she found herself collapsing onto her back on the couch, kicking her feet and squealing with happiness. She really wanted to scream and jump up and down until every picture fell from her walls. Was this really happening?? Just when she had given up, Troy had finally come around?

Tonette stopped suddenly in realization, something suddenly occurring to her. The envelope had been taped to her door, not mailed; there was no return address; and it had today's date on it. That meant Troy had to be in Atlanta. But where was he? She started to grab her phone when she noticed that there was more writing on the back of the letter that she hadn't noticed:

If you still feel for me what you used to, and you
share my desire to see where a relationship between
you and I could go, I will be staying at the
Wyndham hotel downtown, room 313. I will only
be here for the weekend. If I do not hear from you
by Sunday, I will assume that you have made your
decision, and will not bother you again.

Tonette had snatched up her purse and keys before the letter made it back to the couch.

When she threw open her front door, she screamed upon seeing Troy standing there, his hands in his pockets, looking as achingly delicious as ever. She actually had to reach out and touch him, because part of her didn't even believe he was real. She *had* to be hallucinating. But she wasn't; when she touched his arm, then his chest, then his face, he was as real as he ever was.

"Oh my god..." she whimpered, tears springing to her eyes. "Troy..."

"Tonette, baby," Troy whispered, grabbing her by her waist as he stepped into the apartment. Kicking the door closed with his foot, he brought her face to his and laid a kiss on her that showed her exactly how much he had been missing her over the past seven months. Tonette eagerly returned his kiss, her hands clutching his shirt. She couldn't get close enough to him. They each moaned and sighed continuously as the kiss went on and on, their hands all over each other. Neither of them seemed to realize that they were both crying.

After what seemed like a long while, their kiss finally tapered off, but they never let go of each other. They each held the other's face in their hands, their foreheads pressed together.

"I'm so sorry for everything," Tonette said to him, sniffling.

"I am sorry, too," Troy quickly replied, his fingertips gripping the back of her neck and his thumbs repeatedly stroking her cheeks. "I have missed you *so* much..."

"I've missed you, too!"

"Tonette..."

"I was starting to think I was never going to see you again," Tonette rambled, her hands sliding down his shoulders, up his chest and through his hair. Part of her still couldn't believe he was there, and in her arms, holding her right then. Tears continued to stream down her cheeks, but they were grateful, happy tears. She had never been as happy as she was feeling in that very moment. "Troy, you have *no* idea how glad I am to see you..."

"So I am not too late?" Troy asked, looking into her eyes. Tonette felt him grip her tighter. "Are you still available for me?"

"Yes!" Tonette exclaimed. She forgot all about Will or any other man she had dated in the past seven months, just like that. If she had a choice between Troy and any other man, she would always choose Troy. "You are all I ever wanted, Troy."

Grinning, Troy leaned in and kissed her again, wrapping his arms around her so tight Tonette actually gasped, but she didn't care. She just let him squeeze her as long as he wanted to, because she was squeezing him right back.

Eventually, they moved over to the couch so they could talk. Even though she had done so already, many times, Tonette apologized yet again for lying to him and hurting him like she had, and Troy told her that he had (eventually) been able to understand her reasoning for why she had run with the whole Toni thing. And he admitted that when he thought about it, there were certainly worse things she could have done; he didn't want to let his pride keep him from the woman that he knew in his heart was made for him. When Tonette heard him say this, she grinned so hard her face cramped up.

"So..." she hedged, grazing her fingertips up and down his forearm. Her legs were draped across his lap. "What happens now?"

"Now," Troy began with a deep sigh, "I ask you how you feel about me possibly moving to the states."

Tonette's eyes widened excitedly. "Are you serious??"

"Yes..." Troy eyed her, the smile playing on his moist lips. "What would you say to that?"

"I'd say *hell* yeah!!"

Troy laughed, throwing his head back. For a split second Tonette wondered if he had been messing with her about moving, but he assuaged those fears by clamping a hand on her thigh and saying, "There it is, then...it looks like I will be moving to Georgia."

Tonette couldn't believe her ears; Troy was actually going to be near her full time? Permanently? She remembered those times in Barbados when she fantasized about Troy being with her all the time, but she never thought it would actually happen. Then when he came to visit and started staying with her, she had gotten used to them being there, and again allowed herself to fantasize about them in a relationship. One thing she had been worried about in the back of her mind was the prospect of a super-long distance relationship if she and Troy *had* managed to work things out. She had told herself that she would be willing to do it, even though she knew it would suck only getting to see Troy primarily through video chats. But to know that he had already thought beyond that, and that he was serious enough about them that he was willing to make such a move without her even having to ask, warmed everything inside of her. And she vowed right then that she would be the absolute best girlfriend (and hopefully eventually more) to him she could be; she wanted to be sure to make it worth it for him.

Even though the last thing she wanted to do was discourage him or put doubt in his mind, she still felt compelled to ask, "Troy, are you sure? I'm thrilled about the thought of you being close to me all the time, but this is a *huge* step...I just don't want you to get here and then regret it."

"You don't have to worry about that, Lovely," Troy assured her, tweaking her chin. "In the letter when I mentioned there were other things going on that contributed to me not reaching out to you, this is what I was referencing. I was preparing to come here and be with you."

Tonette's jaw dropped again. *This is straight out of one of those romance novels back there in my room*, she thought to herself. "Seriously??"

"Seriously. Selling my house, putting in my resignation at the school, searching for another position here, getting everything else in order...all so I can come here to you. To stay. This is where I want to be, Tonette."

Practically diving on him, Tonette threw her arms around Troy's neck, squealing with happiness. She grabbed his face and smothered it with kisses, straddling him as she did so.

"I love you so much, Troy," she gushed, looking at him dreamily. She caressed his face as she gazed into his eyes; those eyes that had her from the very first night on the dance floor in Barbados. "You just have no idea."

Licking his lips and simultaneously making Tonette's insides clench, Troy grabbed her hips and pulled her into him, smiling when she groaned in response. "I think I do," he said in a low voice. "I meant it when I said you've had me since the beginning, Lovely. And I do not want us to waste any more time."

"So...we're together now? We're a couple?" Tonette asked with a smile. When Troy chuckled and shook his head, she shrugged, grinning. "Hey, sometimes a girl just needs to hear the words."

"Yes, baby," Troy confirmed. "We are absolutely together. And if I have anything to say about it, that is how we will remain."

"So where are you gonna stay? You can stay *here*!" Tonette suggested, not even caring how eager she sounded. Now that they were finally together, she didn't want him to leave.

"As tempting as that is, I think I should get my own place, at least initially," Troy replied, chuckling again when Tonette pouted at his response. "I would like the opportunity to court you properly, date you, and for us to continue getting to know each other. I want us to last, Lovely. And I don't want to mar that by moving too fast."

Tonette scoffed playfully. "Oh, *now* you're worried about moving too fast when your head was between my legs mere hours after first meeting me?"

Laughing loudly, Troy threw his head back again as he pulled her to his chest. "I have no defense to that," he admitted, reaching up to grab her face. He kissed her gently before he slowly began easing her onto her back, biting his lip as he looked at her seductively. "Truth be told, I wouldn't mind being between them again."

Releasing a shaky breath when Troy grazed his fingers against her womanhood, she wished the tight bodysuit she was wearing could vanish into thin air. Arousal was now taking over every other emotion in her body, and she had every intention of satisfying it to the fullest this time.

"Well if you go ahead and get me undressed," she teased, rubbing her leg against his shoulder, "I'll show you my birthmark again."

"Say no more."

Fun fact: I got the idea for this story when I was in the back of the car on the way to my aunt's house for Thanksgiving several years ago. Crazy how it happens, huh?

Thanks so much for reading! I appreciate every reader and supporter who has shown me love over the years. Hope it brought you at least a little enjoyment, which is my main goal, especially now.

If you liked this story, please consider leaving a review. And if you want to show *extra* love, share that you read it on social media! ☺

You can find me on Instagram and TikTok at @authorjessicaterry and on Twitter at @ItsJessicaTerry.

Also by Jessica Terry

Some Like 'em *Thick*
It's All Right...Now
Not By a Long Shot
Get Right
Decisions and Consequences
Take One For the Team
When You Share Too Much
Backtalk
Emasculated
Restless
The Beginning of Again
Always and Nevers
Split By the Bell
The Karma Call
Forehead Kiss

The Introvert Series
An Introvert's Christmas
Wooing the Introvert
The Introvert Roast
I, Take Thee Introvert

About the Author

Jessica Terry caught the writing bug at a young age and loves little more than holing up at home in Douglasville, GA, cranking out contemporary novels. And eating.

Another thing she loves is interacting with her readers. Sign up for her email list and keep up to date with new releases at www.jessicaterry.com.

Read more at https://www.jessicaterry.com/.